THE
FORBIDDEN
KING

For more information, address:

stfernandezwrites@gmail.com.

Published by Azalea Press, LLC

First ebook, paperback, and hardcover editions December 2024

Book cover design by Krafigs Design

Map by Samantha Gase

Taíno Language Citation: The Modern Taíno Dictionary from Jatibonicu Taino Tribal Nation | Higuayahua: Taíno of the Caribbean

Edited by Sarah Wentworth

ISBN 979-8-9886397-7-0 (paperback)

ISBN 979-8-9886397-6-3 (ebook)

ISBN 979-8-9886397-8-7 (hardcover)

www.stfernandez.com

FOR THOSE WHO ARE BUSY CHASING
THEIR DREAMS.

KEEP THAT SHIT UP...

TRIGGER/CONTENT WARNINGS

(THIS BOOK IS INTENDED FOR READERS 18 AND OLDER)

Death

Depression

Grief (Parent, Spouse)

Human Exploitation by Fae

Murder

Profanity

Sexually Explicit Scenes

PLEASE READ WITH CARE

PRONUNCIATION GUIDE

Airelandia: eye-reh-LAHN-dee-uh
Akani: Ah-KAH-nee
Anacaona: Ah-nah-cah-OH-nah
Atlantis: at-LAN-tis
Baba: bah-BAH
Bibi: bee-BEE
Borike'n: Boh-REE-keh-en
Calichi: kah-LEE-chee
Cibao: SEE-bow
Cobo: KOH-boh
Corenathia: Kor-reh-NAH-thee-uh
Earthos: ER-thohs
Fotuto: Foh-TOO-toh
Guake'te: gooah-KEH-teh:
Guali: GOOAH-lee
Guaraguao: gooah-rah-gooah-OW
Hekiti: heh-KEE-tee
Lomeage: low-meh-AUJ
Maboya: mah-BOY-yah
Sabana: Sah-BAH-nah
Shingu: Sheen-goo
Wylemei: WHEYE-leh-may

CHARACTER NAME PRONUNCIATION GUIDE

Asherah Delmar: ah-SHER-uh   del-MAR

Atabey: ah-tah-BAY

Aurelio   Martenos   Anthysius: Ahoo-REH-lee-oh MAR-teh-nohs an-THEE-see-uhs

Braeliah Morvyn: bray-LEE-uh MOR-vin

Cathan Rosahan Delmar: KAY-thuhn   ROH-sah-hahn del-MAR

Dax Lumeya: daks loo-MAY-uh

Draevyn Eliron: DRAY-vin el-er-RON

Gina: GEE-nuh

Jaelyn Diaz: JAY-lin DEE-ahz

Jimani: Gee-MAH-nee

Kane Ruema: kayn roo-EH-muh

Kristos Morales: KRIS-tohs Mohr-RAH-les

Mayana Yaralyn: mah-YAH-nuh YAH-rah-lin

Melysah Velafyn: meh-LIS-uh VEH-luh-fin

Millie: MIL-lee

Myles Anthysius: Mahyels an-THEE-see-uhs

Neleah Delmar: neh-LEH-uh del-MAR

Reneah Diaz: reh-NEH-uh DEE-ahz

Samani Eliron: sah-MAH-nee el-er-RON

Tobias Diaz: TOH-bee-ahs DEE-ahz

Zoriato Eliron: zoh-ree-AH-toh el-er-RON

ATLANTIS
BORI
JIMAGUA
SOLITARY COLONY
SABANA

ICHI
CIBOA
UNIVERSITY
PALACE
PALACE
GARDENS
MPLE PARK
GUARDIAN
TRAINING
FACILITY
GATES
OF ATLANTIS
PLE OF ATABEY
FOTUTO
DRAEVYN'S
CAVERN

CATHAN

PROLOGUE

A SOFT WIND BLEW the long, silky black strands of Neleah's hair away from her heart-shaped face, the fire lit in the bowl above our heads from where we stood at the top of the temple steps flickering in her crystal blue eyes. The Bohiti patiently waited for us to overcome the incredible sensations of the ceremony and take each other's hands, the mortar and pestle gently resting in her hands at her middle. I slid my left palm next to Neleah's, forming a cup between us, my heart brimming with hope.

Neleah, my best friend, who'd captured my heart with her wit and charm, agreed to present herself with me before the Bohiti. The overwhelming pull between us was so strong that to deny its call was to dishonor the goddess, despite us both puzzled by it. Our friendship spanned over centuries. How had we not been called to each other sooner? But the goddess... She always had her ways. Who were we to deny her request? So, with the cool marble floor holding up my shaky legs, I began my declaration, my heart hammering in my bare chest. "My goddess-blessed name is Cathan Rosahan, and I present Neleah Delmar before the goddess and ask her to honor our union with a sacred bond so that we may honor each other in body, mind, and spirit as long as our souls walk the realms."

Neleah glanced toward the Bohiti, the latter giving her a delicate nod of encouragement. Neleah blew out a breath. "My goddess-blessed name is Neleah Delmar, and I present Cathan Rosahan before the goddess and ask her to honor our union with a sacred bond so that we may honor each other in body, mind, and spirit as long as our souls walk the realms."

The Bohiti stepped forward and poured her sacred oil into our joined palms, the herbs and broken leaf petals drifting on the surface as they landed within. "Should the goddess bless this union, we ask that she reveal the bond to the realms so others may know of the honor bestowed upon them," the Bohiti said in a rehearsed tongue. "With your right hand, gather the sacred oil and place it upon the divine skin of the other. If goddess-blessed, your bondmark shall appear."

My fingers shook as they grazed Neleah's within our palms. With the oil gathered, my gaze locked on hers. I brought my fingers to the left side of her chest, slipping underneath her ceremonial garments. She did the same to me, my bare skin pebbling with her touch just as much as hers did for mine. A burning sensation bled across my skin, causing my mouth to twitch in both pain and satisfaction. I witnessed the ink spreading across Neleah's ample breast, and I flashed her a grin. But my hopeful smile dropped when her breath hitched and her eyes went wide with alarm.

I felt it then.

Something odd.

Something... different.

With both of us frozen in place, we waited for the bonding wave from our union to crest over the park and tear through the town. We waited. And we waited.

Neleah's panicked gaze swung to the Bohiti, asking a silent question I couldn't understand.

The Bohiti's lips pursed momentarily before her attention went beyond us. She gave a very minor flick of the wrist. A wave crested then and nearly brought me to my knees. "What—"

But my question was silenced when Neleah crushed her mouth against mine. Her salty tears slipped between our lips, and my brow furrowed. She drew away with haste.

"Go," the Bohiti commanded.

Neleah gripped my hand and pulled me into the darkness of the temple. Instead of heading for the bonding sanctuary where we would consummate our bond, she aimed for the closest pillar, hiding us in the shadows. Neleah's chest rose and fell with quick breaths, her mouth opening and closing.

I took her shaky hands in mine. "What is it, Nellie? Tell me."

Her throat worked on a swallow. "*Tanama* bond."

And with those two simple words, my life changed...

Forever.

RENEAH

CHAPTER 1

MY LIGHT, BLACK LEATHER work shoes whispered against the stone floors of the palace, my heart hammering in my chest as I processed the news my mentor and boss, Kristos Morales, had informed the palace staff. The Queen was in peril in the Above World. King Cathan was on his way to Atlantis… with their daughter.

They had a daughter.

An *heir*.

The Heir of Atlantis.

And they'd kept her secret from everyone, save the Council. How someone on the Council hadn't divulged that particular secret would remain a mystery, but hearing their reasoning for the secrecy… Well, that brought me immense comfort. "They did it so that she may know the way of the humans, so that she would empathize with humankind," Kristos told his most trusted palace leaders. Never in the history of Atlantis had the humans taken priority over the needs and interests of the Fae. We fit into the Fae's world, not the other way around. So, to hear that our Queen and King had decided to raise their heir amongst the humans in the Above World so that she may better know their ways? My already high level of respect for them soared through the palace roof.

With the Queen's quarters on my direct route to the princess's floor, I made it my first stop to ensure everything was in order. As the slight creak of the front door ground to an open, the low hum of music hit my ears, and the crisp lemon scent assaulted my senses. I couldn't help but smile at the pristine living area, the beautiful deep crimson Persian rug, with intricate black accents that made the brightly lit room pop. The drapes of a similar color had been pulled back, with the dust long removed. Fresh lilies sat in an ancient vase on the table by the tall arched window that likely cost more than our townhouse in Borike'n—the pastel pink petals fading into deep fuchsia at its core. With one final glance around the kitchen, that had been cleaned within an inch of perfection, I followed my way to the bedroom, where the sound of my fellow chambermaids' voices carried.

"Oy! Millie! Throw me that pillow, will ya?"

"Oh, sure! Let me just stop cleaning the sacred porcelain throne and get that for you!" Millie bellowed, her voice echoing across the bathing chamber. I pressed a hand to my mouth to stifle my laugh as I leaned against the doorjamb.

"Hush up! I didn't realize you were busy!" Gina bellowed from underneath the bed, likely checking for a stray dust bunny.

"We're all busy, you nitwit. The Heir is coming to Atlantis."

"The Heir." There was a long pause before Gina continued. "Imagine that. Raised in the Above World with the humans."

"Ay."

There was a hint of wonder in Millie's tone. I daresay all the humans in Atlantis would hold the same wonder in their tones as they went about their day today. I strolled across the room and grabbed the pillow Gina had been looking for, giving it a pat or two to rid it of any dust. "I believe you were looking for this?"

Gina jolted and hit her head against the bottom of the bed. "Ow!"

"Careful, Gina."

She shimmied her plump derrière from underneath the bed and turned to sit on the ground facing me, her chestnut eyes casting me an incredulous look that had a giggle leaving my lips. "Aren't you supposed to be preparing the Heir's quarters, Leader Diaz?"

"Oh, we're busting out the formalities, are we?"

Gina rose from the floor and took the pillow I held out for her, her perfect, crinkly, light brown hair wisping around her face on an exhale. "When you sneak up on me like that and send my heart out of my asshole, yes. The formality is due."

"Well, I'll make sure not to make a habit of it."

"Yes, please do."

"Oy! What are you two fussing about out there?" Millie emerged from the bathing chamber, sweat glistening across the golden skin of her forehead as she held a toilet brush like a trident. "Greetings, Rennie. What brings you to our assigned quarters?"

I lifted my shoulder in a casual shrug. "Just wanted to check in on things," I replied, smoothing out the bright white duvet.

Gina placed her hands on her ample hips. "And? What is your assessment?"

"The same as always."

Millie's full lips spread into a satisfied smile, and her cloud-gray eyes lit like a faelight. "We're perfect status?"

"No one is ever perfect status, Millie. You know that," I told her.

"But close to it, right?"

The corner of my lips twitched. "You're close."

Gina and Millie squealed like little faelings. I let loose a laugh I couldn't suppress as I made my exit. "I'll catch up with you all later."

"At Sinkers?"

"Maybe," I called to them as I opened the door.

Truth be told, I wasn't entirely sure I'd have time for an ale at Sinkers, our beloved pub in Borike'n. As a leader of the royal faction of the palace staff, I had to ensure everything was perfect for Queen Neleah, King Cathan, and Princess Asherah's arrival.

Assuming that Queen Neleah was okay. I prayed to the goddess that she was.

I sighed as I ascended the stairs to the third floor, where Princess Asherah would reside, trying to remember the last time the King and Queen were at the palace. Their visits had been sporadic at best, a problem the Council adored remarking on. One would think they would understand that her time would be limited with an entire queendom to run. And while Queen Neleah's time was limited, the King's time was an entirely different matter. To think he'd been in the Above World caring for their daughter the whole time. That would explain his mysterious absence.

I opened the door to the third-floor quarters, the dust assailing my nostrils as it flew up in the air. "Oh, no. That won't do," I muttered to myself, dashing my hand in the air.

A trip to the hallway broom closet to collect all my necessities was in order. As I entered the tiny closet, I paused momentarily, my lips pursing. *Desperate times did call for desperate measures.* I'd have to put my favorite furniture polish to use for the occasion. The stuff was like gold amongst the palace staff, which was why I didn't mind squirreling some away to use on my assigned quarters, team be damned. I reached behind the canister of bath salts on the third shelf from the floor, my hand wrapping around the cool canister. "Perfect status," I murmured. As I brought it out from its hiding place, my hand accidentally brushed against my black leather notebook, causing it to fall against the floor with a thwack. I crouched to pick it up but let myself linger amongst the open pages for a moment—my clothing designs staring back at me like a tempting invitation into a life I'd never live.

Sometimes, I'd come into the tiny broom closet just to jot down a design that wouldn't let me go on if I didn't get it on paper. The first half of the notebook was already worn with use, the latter half patiently waiting for me to draw all the fashion I'd held hostage in my head. With a blissful sigh, I flipped to some of my favorites. I'd never get over the longing to do something with it. *Get your head out of the clouds, Ren!* I reluctantly rose and gave my notebook a quick pat to dust it off, returning my dreams behind the bath salts to keep them hidden.

As I returned to the room and began polishing the coffee table to a spectacular gleam, my thoughts drifted to our King. He'd been here with General Lumeya several times in the past few years, but besides those few visits, he'd been gone for nearly twenty years. If the rumors from the staff, who caught a glimpse of the Heir in the bailey upon their arrival, were true, she must be in her early twenties—a fact that thrilled me, seeing as how I was due to celebrate my tenth annual twenty-first birthday come the new year. So, you see, we're both in our early twenties. Isn't that exciting?

Yes, yes. I know. I'm not *really* in my twenties.

Don't judge me.

If Princess Asherah was in her early twenties, the Queen must've had her attend university in the Above World. Queen Neleah's love for education was well-known. The halls of Cibao University were her greatest pride and joy. She spared no expense when it came to having the most up-to-date texts and professors teaching their classes, with no shortage of students from the other realms. If I were a betting woman—I'm not, just in case you're wondering—I'd say she'd also value education in the Above World for her daughter.

This means King Cathan's more frequent visits to Atlantis in recent years would make sense, since the Heir was likely away at university. To study what? I was curious to find out.

As I exchanged my polish rag for a fresh one, in order to clean the granite kitchen countertops, the front door swung open with a bang against the wall, causing me to nearly jump out of my skin. I brought my hand to my collarbone, setting my gaze on Millie and Gina in the doorway—a panicked expression held firmly across each of their faces. Instant dread consumed me. "What's the matter?"

Millie's lower lip trembled and gray eyes welled with tears. "The Queen. She's dead."

RENEAH

CHAPTER 2

ANCIENT HINGES CREAKED LOUDLY as I entered our town-house, the savory scent of my mother's potato soup washing over me as I strolled to the back of the home. I'd have to remember to oil them again, a pastime handed down from Diaz to Diaz for centuries. The sound of my mother's hum reached my ears as I stood before the kitchen. I took a moment to enjoy the calm, to enjoy my mother in her happy space, before the stovetop she often cooked the most fabulous meals on. Our home held so many memories, laughter, and surprises. And the news I carried with me would dash all that happiness away. So, I slid into the kitchen nook as quietly as possible, watching as she chopped fresh tarragon with unparalleled skill, the steam from her beloved stock pot drifting in the air and coating the rustic brown cabinetry with condensation. A pile of metal mixing bowls and wooden spoons of every size peeked from the top of the shiny copper farm sink. I'd have to help her with the cleanup. I doubted very highly she'd even feel like eating, much less cleaning, after I told her of the Queen.

Neleah.

My heart still ached with the news. Never in the history of all the realms had there been a Queen so generous, so caring—especially to the humans. She ruled this realm with a steel hand, but she cared fiercely for all her people, even the ones who opposed her mission to welcome the humans during the upcoming ice age and to take care of those still left from the last.

I still remember the first time I met Queen Neleah...

"Make sure your shirt is tucked in at all times, Rennie," Mother had told me as we ventured down the first-floor hallway of the royal quarters. "She fired one of my staff for refusing to do so. She has no patience for backtalk or willful disregard for the rules. Remember that." She reached out and pressed down on the black metal handle, the sleeve of her chambermaid periwinkle long-sleeve shirt riding up her wrist as she'd carefully opened the door. I remember my heart hammering in my chest that day as I entered the room. I'd never met the Queen before. There were balls held in honor of the palace staff that she would appear at, but to be in the Queen's quarters? That had been a first for me. I can still hear the slurp of the drain echoing in the walls of the bathing chamber beyond the bedroom door as my mother showed me around the living quarters. The Queen had been bathing, and there I was, taking a tour of her living space. It was surreal, to say the least.

"Our Queen enjoys her sweets," Mother said, motioning to the crystal candy bowl on the granite kitchen countertop. "It's imperative to keep this filled at all times. In the hallway storage closet, you'll find a large tub of it sealed away. Make sure it stays airtight."

"Or perhaps not, Jaelyn. It would be nice not to work so hard to burn off all that delicious sugar."

I'd wheeled around at the sound of the Queen's voice from the bedroom doorway, immediately dropping into a curtsy at the sight of her. I'd taken the opportunity to glance down at my shirt to ensure it was tucked in. Thankfully, it was.

When I rose, Queen Neleah appraised me with amusement as she fastened an earring to the lobe of her tipped ear. They complimented the navy blue silk blouse and deep black pencil skirt she donned over her exposed skin. It had been clear she was headed for the Above World and doing so in fashion.

"Your Majesty, may I present my daughter and apprentice, Reneah Diaz."

Neleah had placed her hands on her hips and given me the warmest smile. I remember feeling slightly at ease. "Well, you have an apprentice. I can't believe how much she's grown."

"I can hardly believe it myself, Your Majesty," Mother replied with pride.

"Well, Reneah. It's a pleasure to meet you."

"The pleasure is all mine, Your Majesty. And may I say, you look lovely. The color compliments you."

Neleah smoothed out her shirt with a smile. "Why, thank you. Someone near and dear bought it for me. She'll be pleased to hear she picked well."

It dawned on me that my first time meeting the Queen had been shortly after Mother's Day. I wondered whether the blouse was a gift from her daughter. I'd like to think it was.

A lid clanking against the pot drew me from my reminiscing and back into our kitchen—the painful news waiting on the tip of my tongue. Mother pivoted from the stovetop, reaching for the silverware drawer on the island behind her. She started when she finally saw me in the kitchen nook. "Reneah Diaz. You will kill me, sneaking up on me like that."

Did I mention I'm great at sneaking up on people?

"Well, perhaps you shouldn't have taught me to be light as a feather on my feet," I told her as I shot her an amused grin.

She pointed at me with her weathered wooden ladle. "Too well, apparently." She turned back to her pot, lifting the lid and stirring the contents within. "What news from the palace?"

The smile dropped from my face in the blink of an eye. Breaking bad news was never easy, especially knowing how much Mother cared for Neleah. She even fashioned my name after the Queen's so that they were similar, after all. "I'm afraid the news isn't good."

The click of the stove turning off echoed like a pin dropping. Mother dried her hands with a bright red cotton kitchen towel as concern spread across her face. "Whatever is it?"

I swallowed past the lump in my throat. "Queen Neleah... She's..."

I've never seen Mother freeze up the way she did, her natural golden skin paling and her russet eyes filling with unshed tears. "No. No, no, no." She shook her head violently, the bun of her dirty blonde hair loosening.

My lips trembled, and I fought hard to get the words out. "Queen Neleah is dead."

Water dripped from the faucet into the empty pot where it sat in the kitchen sink, the contents of which had been carefully placed in metal storage containers and stacked in neat rows in the fridge. I had to force Mother to eat her fill. A part of me felt guilty for doing so, knowing that I had as little desire to eat as she did.

The steam rose from Mother's teacup as she stared blankly into it. A few graying ash blonde strands of hair had fallen forward, and she did little to push them behind her ear. My heart ached for her. Neleah Delmar had been so much to many at the palace, but to Jaelyn? They'd had their share of conspiracies together—thick as thieves, the two of them.

Jaelyn Diaz had long retired from the palace—the mandatory retirement age for humans in Atlantis being fifty-two—but even after she did, she'd kept in touch with Neleah, always making sure the Palace Leader was behaving.

That's me.

I'm the Palace Leader.

Not only did Jaelyn ensure I was behaving, but she'd also given Neleah the scoop on the palace staff drama. One day, during my apprenticeship, I'd been tidying up the bedroom when I heard my mother and Neleah chatting it up in the living room.

"You mean to tell me she went into the broom closet with that scoundrel who relies on corny one-liners?" Neleah had asked, aghast.

"Hard to believe, isn't it?"

"I'll say. He's been shacking up with half the palace staff. I thought she was smarter than that."

"Perhaps she had an itch to scratch."

Neleah's laughter filled the entire room. "Perhaps she did. And what of the kitchen lead? Did she have her baby yet?"

And so they went, on and on, for hours at a time, whenever Neleah was at the palace, which had been less and less often for reasons we couldn't discern.

But now we knew.

She had a secret Heir to tend to in the Above World.

I placed my hand over Mother's. "What can I do?"

Jaelyn shook her head, her expression filled with deep, deep sorrow. "There's not much to be done but grieve, my dear." Her gaze snapped up. "But you must take care of that poor male and his daughter. They'll need help adjusting, especially the Heir."

"Yes. I can't even imagine how she's feeling right now." I blew out a steady breath, shaking my head. "To lose her mother and then arrive in a whole new world. I'd be spiraling if I were her."

"Of course," Jaelyn agreed, taking a long sip of her chamomile and mint Earthos tea.

My mind drifted to more memories of Neleah, her kindness, and her generosity. "Do you remember when she housed little Tobias in the palace for a week?"

"How could I forget? I daresay the story will be the cornerstone of every family gathering until his ashes are cast beyond the dome," Jaelyn said as she huffed a weary laugh. "What Neleah did was incredibly gracious. There's no way I could've cared for him during his recovery *and* tended to the staff."

My finger chased a stray tea droplet on the rim of my mug. "Her heart was always very giving like that."

Jaelyn's bottom lip trembled. "She was the best of us."

Tobias had been in a bad, bad way. His week in the palace left quite the impression on him, and he'd recant his childhood tale to anyone who'd give him a second of their time. Despite being impaled with ice daggers by Akani members and barely living to tell his tale, all he remembers is being treated like a little Prince. Neleah read him bedtime stories every evening as he recovered. Her nurturing comfort came from knowing that his parents—my Uncle Jack and Aunt Marie—hadn't been so lucky. They'd fallen victim to the rebel

Akani, who sought to rid Atlantis of humans. Tobias came to live with us after that.

Tobias was sprouting into his late teens, quite literally. He nearly towered a whole foot above me. Although, in truth, most people did—something I'd become used to over my lifetime. With Tobias partaking in my apprenticeship program, he'd be the most skilled valet in all the realms. I'd see to it.

"I'm serious, though, Rennie," Mother said, bringing me back to the present.

My brow dipped. "About what?"

"King Cathan. Princess Asherah. I want you to spend a considerable amount of time at the palace for the next few months."

"Aren't you retired?" I asked, sipping my lukewarm tea to hide my amused smile.

Mother straightened her spine, a superior expression replacing the heavy grief on her face. "I may be retired, but I'll never stop teaching you—not as long as I draw breath, anyway."

"I daresay you'll continue even after you cross the veil."

Jaelyn clicked her tongue. "You'll miss me, my little smartass."

The corners of my lips lifted. "How could I not?" I mused as a vision of King Cathan came to mind. "He must be devastated."

"To lose one's bondmate?" She blew out a long breath. "They say the disconnection is like your heart hollowing out."

I shook my head. "That poor male."

"You must take care of them."

"I believe you said that already, Mother."

She leaned back, her wooden chair protesting. "Yes, well, let this serve as your reminder."

"What would you have me do? Move in with the poor, grieving male?"

"If that's what it takes."

"Shall I climb into bed with him, too?" I asked, as the corner of my mouth twitched.

Mother's russet-colored eyes went wide. "Reneah Ana Diaz. Don't even joke about something like that."

A chuckle burst past my lips. "Your face was worth it."

"You know what happens to palace staff who tumble in the sheets with the royals. You mustn't joke about that."

I *did* know what happened to the palace staff who dared to have a tryst with a royal. They went down in scandalous chambermaid history, as the palace staff called it. Take, for example, the infamous Scarlett May, who was said to be the best chambermaid in all four realms—that is, until my family came along. Her affair with the Prince was one of great scandal, and she paid the price. One morning, her leader found her naked as the day she was born, tied and spread-eagled over the bed. She'd been left there by her lover like an afterthought, the Prince long gone, having been summoned for his wedding to the Princess of Airelandia the next day.

The Diaz family didn't joke about having affairs with royalty.

In truth, if Scarlett were alive today, I'd thank her for her indiscretions. Our family wouldn't have been granted the prestigious lead title had it not been for her actions, which was why my mother's look of shock was totally valid. The consequences for crossing the line with royalty would be grave: banishment from the palace, and because the housing was part of the gig, we'd be without a place to live.

I shuddered at the thought and placed my hand over hers. "You have nothing to worry about. I'm sorry for the joke."

"You've been living in those romance books of yours for too long," she huffed.

My shoulders lifted in a shrug. "Nothing wrong with that."

She rose from her chair and gathered our now empty teacups. "Best you get up to bed."

I sighed dramatically. "Yes, boss."

"And Reneah?" Mother called before I exited the kitchen. I pivoted to her with a questioning brow. "You're doing a fine job. Neleah said as much," she said, her voice cracking on the last.

The image of Mother standing in the kitchen doorway blurred as I swallowed past the lump in my throat. "Thanks." I ascended the stairs to the second floor of our townhouse, filled with renewed determination. I'd make sure King Cathan and Princess Asherah wanted for nothing. That's what Neleah would want, and I'd see to it.

RENEAH

CHAPTER 3

N^o MATTER HOW STEALTHY my steps were, the coffee cup rattled on the saucer sitting on the wooden tray, laden with whole wheat toast and piping hot chicken soup. It might have been because my hands trembled endlessly. During my entire career, I'd traveled to the infirmary a million times, bringing food to royal guests or injured Guardians housed for recovery in the palace.

But never to the King.

Don't mess it up, Rennie.

The door to Dax's infirmary room was propped open, the light from the tall window spilling into the darkened hallway. I slowed as I crossed the threshold on quiet feet, and my breath instantly caught in my throat.

What was it about this man that had my pulse beating wildly every time I was around him? The first time I met King Cathan, I'd been just as nervous. I still remember the way he sat in his reading chair, sipping on his coffee so gracefully that you'd think his element was anything other than a fearsome Guardian. I'd been mesmerized by the way his long, masculine finger paged through whatever correspondence he had been reading that day.

"Your Majesty," Mother had softly greeted him. I wanted to introduce my apprentice, my daughter, Reneah Diaz."

I still remember the way King Cathan's cafe noir eyes had swung to where we stood in the doorway to the Queen's quarters and the handsome smile that had spread on his face. "Hello, Reneah," he'd said to me in the smoothest tone, reaching deep into my eighteen-year-old soul. Even at that age, I'd already been taken with him.

And now, some fifteen years after the first time I'd laid eyes on him, he remained just as breathtaking. The only difference now was that I'd aged while he hadn't. The beautiful panes of his face still resembled someone in his late twenties. It's a funny thing that I appeared older than King Cathan, when he was centuries older than me. The dark circles under his eyes were a bit of a concern, but it was to be expected given everything the poor King had been through in the past twenty-four hours. Hopefully, a little chicken soup would help.

I cleared my throat to announce my arrival, and my heart absolutely shattered when he glanced my way. The olive skin around his eyes was blotched with red, causing the tiny flecks of gold to stand out amongst the sea of deep, rich brown around his irises. His clear look of despair would likely be there for the days and weeks to come. "Hello, Reneah," he said to me, just as the first time I'd met him, only this time, that wondrous voice cracked with the lack of use.

The damn coffee cup rattled again as I dipped into a curtsy. "Your Majesty." I rose and made my way to the bistro table. "I've brought you a little something to eat."

King Cathan cleared his throat. "Thank you, Reneah. Although, I don't have much of an appetite at the moment."

I placed my hands on my hips. "When was the last time you ate, Your Majesty?"

His dark brow furrowed. "In truth, I can't remember."

"Perhaps you should try to eat a little something. You'll be no good to General Lumeya or Princess Asherah if you're not at your best," I insisted on the tail end of a wince. "Sorry, that was probably untoward."

King Cathan fluttered a hand. "Not at all. You're absolutely right, of course." He rose from his chair and approached the bistro table on long, scaled legs. When he carefully settled on the tall, high-backed bistro chair and reached for the large handle of his soup bowl, I shook out the burgundy cloth napkin, placing it across his lap. It was then I noticed his shoulders shaking with laughter. "Just like your mother," he mused.

My lips lifted into a smile. "I'll take that as a compliment."

"As you should." He motioned to the chair across from him. "Have a seat. You might as well keep me company for a while."

My limbs froze. The King had just asked for my company, something Kristos would surely frown upon. But Queen Neleah and Mother had formed a friendship, so it must be acceptable.

Right?

I slid into the chair across from him, my fingers fidgeting in my lap as my gaze traveled over him in concern.

"So, Reneah, how is your mother? Is she enjoying retirement?" he asked in between mouthfuls of soup.

"Mother's just as spirited as she's always been, retirement be damned. I don't think she'll ever fully leave the palace life behind. She seems determined to keep her toe in it."

His eyes gleamed. "Seems about right."

I glanced down at my lap. "She sends her deepest condolences."

"That is very kind of her. Be sure to send her my gratitude." His full lips curved up in a solemn smile, and I had to suppress the urge to examine them.

"Of course, Your Majesty."

"Cathan."

I blinked in astonishment. "I'm sorry?"

"Cathan. Please call me Cathan. I've never really liked 'Your Majesty'. The formality is even more foreign now that it's been decades since I've heard it repeatedly."

I blew out a breath. "Well, then. I certainly wouldn't want to irritate you. Cathan it is," I assured him. I could feel the telltale heat rising on my neck as he blew on his soup to cool it, his eyes never leaving mine. I shifted my attention to Dax, providing him a moment of silence to consume the last remnants of his soup.

Not hungry, indeed.

Dax was terribly burned all over his body, a body so massive it took up the entirety of the bed. The side of his scalp was severely red from the Fae fire that had been used against him. I tried to suppress a grimace at the state of him, but failed. "Is he going to be alright?"

Cathan heaved a sigh, setting his now empty soup bowl on the tray. "He'll be devastated when he learns of Neleah's passing. They were best friends, the two of them. They'd been friends since he arrived in Atlantis for his Guardianship." He shook his head, the wavy strands of his dark brown hair falling forward across his brow. "I... I still can't believe she's gone."

My gaze returned to him just as a blanket of grief swept over his features and caused my heart to pang. "Queen Neleah was the best of us."

"That she was. I…" He huffed out an indignant laugh. "Never mind."

I tilted my head. "Please. You can tell me whatever you'd like," I implored.

"It's silly."

"I'm sure it's not."

Cathan ran his fingers through his hair. "I just wish I had more time, and that's silly, considering that I'm speaking to a human whose life is but a fragment of mine."

My shoulders lifted in a shrug. "You're allowed your feelings, despite your present company."

"But am I? How privileged am I? I had thousands of years with my mate. We created such a beautiful life with countless memories I'll cherish for the rest of my days. I should be satisfied."

"But you're not," I said as a matter of fact.

"No, I'm not," he admitted, his Adam's apple bobbing as he swallowed his emotions. "I don't know how I'll navigate this world without her. And it's selfish of me, but I want her back. I want her here. I want my daughter not to have to go through all of this. *I* don't want to go through all of this."

I don't know what compelled me to be so bold. I reached across the table and placed my hand on his arm, giving it an encouraging squeeze. "You may be without Neleah, and how I wish she could be here as well. She was a phenomenal Queen, and I'm almost certain she was a great mother."

Tears welled in his eyes. "She loved Asherah deeply."

"I'm sure she did with all her heart. But you're not alone. And Asherah isn't, either. It is my honor and privilege to help you both through this. If you need to vent, you'll find no judgment from me. I'm an ear to listen. If you're hungry, I'm a damn good cook."

A genuine laugh shook his broad shoulders as he rubbed his eyes. "Modest, aren't you?"

"I'm just stating the truth."

I stopped breathing when he placed his warm hand over mine, which, for some unknown reason, hadn't moved from his arm despite being widely inappropriate. But his warm smile had me returning his with ease. "Thank you, Reneah."

"Anytime, Cathan."

His beautiful smile spread even wider. "Asherah's going to adore you."

My shoulder lifted in a shrug. "What's not to adore?"

Cathan's chuckle was a delightful sound after such a heavy moment. I removed my hand from his arm and immediately missed its warmth as I gathered the tray. "I best get back to it, then. I wouldn't want to face Kristos' ire if he found me relaxing on the job."

"Tell Kristos if he has a problem with it, he can come to me."

My mouth dropped open in fake surprise. "Oh! I love that. I'll be sure to let him know."

And as his low laugh followed me out of the room, I felt like I'd done something right and brought a little light into the dark.

RENEAH

CHAPTER 4

M Y SHEER, PASTEL PINK Atlantian garments fluttered on an errant wind as we stood before the Temple of Atabey with the palace staff at the head of the crowd. I held my gaze on Asherah and Cathan at the base of the temple steps. Neleah's body had been perfectly wrapped in her Wylemei cloth and now lay on the pyre at the Temple entrance. My heart ached for both the remarkable Queen who had been so kind to my family and for the grieving family she left behind.

The remnants of grief from my own experience with death had peaked, as I was all too familiar with losing a parent. I can still recall the deep despair that had overwhelmed me, accompanied by the deep sense of gratitude I had for the additional time we had with him. Little did anyone know, if it hadn't been for our Queen and her healers, Father would've never lived as long as he did. Goddess, she was so generous that way. But eventually, having fought as hard as he could against the cancer that had overtaken his body, he transitioned beyond the Veil.

I still remember how Neleah had been there for Mother at Father's Wylemei as Mother wept before his body. I can still see Neleah in my mind's eye, with her slender arms wrapped around Mother's shoulders, her chin resting on Mother's head, and her eyes brimming with tears. The Queen had shown up at Father's Wylemei to mourn with the palace staff. Her actions had been whispered across the town, admired even.

And now... Now we mourned her.

When Cathan's shoulders shook with an obvious sob, I couldn't hold back my own tears—the flames on the pyre now overtaking Neleah's body. "I'll take care of them. I promise you, I will," I whispered to Neleah's spirit beyond the Veil. "They'll not be alone."

Suddenly, something shone bright as the morning sun in my periphery. I could have sworn it was Neleah's apparition, but the expression of pure evil I beheld at the top of the steps told me otherwise. Fear immediately seized my entire body; my wide gaze held on the Akani member as he threw a fireball in Asherah and Cathan's direction. Before I could bellow a scream in warning, a dome of water appeared over them, and the Fire Fae was tackled to the ground. Mother's fingers dug into my arm, shaking me out of my trance. "Come, Rennie! We have to get out of here!"

My heart leapt out of my mouth as we ran through the crowd, the screams cutting through the air around us. Atlantians pushed and shoved their way through the grassy park, all heading toward Borike'n for safety.

"Don't stop!" Mother warned in between heavy breaths. "We don't know how many of them are here."

My arm came around her back to help her. "You're breathing heavily. We can sneak into an alley for a break."

"No," she said as she huffed. "I won't risk it. We're nearly at the human quarter, anyway."

We hurried down the cobblestone streets. The crowd thinned as they entered their homes for safety. With lungs purchasing for air, we arrived at our doorstep, throwing the door open with a bang against the wall. "Tobias!"

Footsteps thundered down the stairwell, and a moment later, Tobias stared at us wide-eyed over the banister. "What the hell happened?"

I ushered Mother into the living room and locked the door behind me. "Fucking Akani. They attacked at Queen Neleah's Wylemei."

Tobias' expression grew turbulent. "They didn't."

"They did," Mother croaked.

"Sit down, Auntie. Your face is as red as a tomato."

Mother fluttered a hand as she dropped onto the pearl-white sofa. "I'll be alright."

"I'll get you some water." I rushed into the kitchen, filling a glass of water to the brim, and returned to Mother, whose breathing was beginning to even out. "Here. Drink this."

Mother gulped down the water with an expression of pure relief.

"They're getting bolder," Tobias seethed.

He wasn't wrong. While some of the Fae frowned upon the Atlantian humans, the Akani—an extremist rebel group determined to rid the realms of humans—took it one step further. Random human murders and outright assaults were becoming a more common thing. And as humans, we were mostly powerless against them if they chose to come for us. It sent a desperate chill down my spine. "That they are," I fumed.

A crease formed on his brow. "Who were they trying to attack?"

"Who do you think?"

"Not the Princess?"

My brow lifted to my hairline.

Tobias's baby-blue eyes went wide. "Holy shit. They tried to kill the Princess."

"And nearly had," Mother said as she settled back a little further. "If it weren't for the Commander, she'd be dead."

I shook my head. "I can't believe they did that. Poor Asherah. Coming to a whole new world, finding out she's a Princess, and nearly getting killed while grieving her mother. I bet she's frightened half to death."

"By the looks of it, she is," Tobias remarked with his gaze fixed on something beyond the bay window at the front of the house. We rushed to it to get a better look.

Sure enough, a tight group of Guardians protected Asherah and Cathan, with Commander Eliron hovering close at their side. Their gazes scanned their surroundings as they hurried down a dark alleyway in the direction of the palace.

I let loose a long sigh. "And there's no doubt Melysah's calling a Council meeting at this very moment."

"Wretched witch," Tobias murmured.

"Yes, she is that," I agreed.

We returned to the living room where Mother rested, finishing the last of her water. "Well?"

"It was them," I confirmed, taking the empty glass from her hands.

She shook her head. "That poor girl. The Council's going to be pure chaos." Her brown eyes snapped up to meet my gaze. "You need to get to the palace."

I sighed. "Yes, I've already gathered that. Are you okay, though?"

"I've got Auntie," Tobias said, sinking onto the sofa next to Mother.

"You need to go, as well, Tobias," Mother instructed.

"We're not leaving you here alone," I insisted.

Her ash-blonde eyebrow rose in an arch. "Your mother hen-ing skills are not as good as mine, daughter."

"Well, they'll have to do because Tobias is staying here. That's an order."

If the situation weren't dire, I'd laugh at the look of defeat on Mother's face. Retirement hadn't rid her of her stubbornness.

With a final look of gratitude to Tobias, I climbed up the stairs to gather my things and face whatever chaos awaited me at the palace.

"You want me to handle the Princess?"

"Yes. Please, Millie," I told her. "I want to check on the King myself."

Her head dipped in a determined nod. "Consider it done."

"Thank you," I said, breathing a sigh of relief. "Gina, if you could accompany her, that would be great. Just a simple knock and an inquiry will do. If she doesn't want to be bothered, let her be. Both of them have been through enough."

"No worries, Rennie, " Gina assured, my own worry over the Princess and King reflected back at me with the expression flitting across her face. "Go check on our King. We've got this."

We filed out of the staff common area and headed for the royal wing. My hands wrung as I climbed the stairs to Cathan's quarters. As most gossip does, word of the Council meeting that followed Neleah's Wylemei had traveled far and wide throughout the palace within minutes. I fumed with the news I'd heard. One had to wonder what Melysah was playing at, inserting herself in the goddess' will. What was she trying to achieve? Wiggle her way to the throne like she had any right to be there? Her elemental mark was for leadership, not a Queen.

And now, after caring for Asherah in the Above World for so long, Cathan is Regent. His calling is Guardianship, for the goddess' sake. It was apparent to those of us in his vicinity that he had no idea how to lead a queendom. It wasn't his calling. Cathan had to be beside himself. Worry and dread seeped into every fiber of my being as I climbed the final steps leading to the Queen's quarters. I took a long, deep breath before I knocked on the door. When I heard nothing, I quietly called, "My King? I don't mean to disturb you. I—"

"Come in, Reneah," he called from the other side of the door.

I slowly opened the door and found Cathan on the sofa, with his head resting on the back as he stared blankly at the ceiling. I let out a compassionate sigh. "I've heard the news."

"Wonderful. Now everyone in the palace knows I've failed my dead mate," he said in a tone of despair.

I gently closed the door behind me. "You didn't fail her."

Cathan tipped his head in my direction. "But haven't I?"

"No," I said firmly, straightening my spine. "You haven't. Melysah's a wicked wench trying to make a power grab."

Cathan dragged his hands down his face. "We haven't even had time to grieve."

"That's something I'm sure she's counting on. Coffee?"

He let loose a heavy sigh. "Yes, please."

I approached the kitchen and scrounged for the coffee press, finding it tucked away in the cabinet. "Cream? Sugar?"

"Both, and lots of it," he called.

"My kind of guy," I playfully responded, wincing when I realized what I'd said. Thank the goddess, I had my back to him as I poured the dark roast grains into the press.

But my anxiety washed away when he said, "Well, then. You might as well make enough for two and join me."

And so I did.

With two full-to-the-brim cups of coffee, made with the Atlantian farmland's signature cream and Earthos' gourmet sugar, I handed him his light blue ceramic cup before sliding into the plush sitting chair across from him. As I drank my first sip, my eyes closed, and a light moan escaped my lips.

When I opened them, Cathan was peering at me in amusement, with a smirk on his handsome face. "Good, isn't it?"

"Some of the best. I might prefer Sabana's grains over Earthos'. I don't know what it is about our Atlantian soil that tops the other realms, but I much prefer it."

"I couldn't agree more." He took a long sip from his cup and looked at it approvingly. "And you make the perfect cup of coffee."

I lifted a shoulder in a shrug. "One of my many talents."

Cathan chuckled lightly, and seeing something other than sadness on his face warmed my heart. As if my thoughts had summoned the existence of the world around us, his slight smile slowly fell away. "I don't know what to do."

"You do what she would have done," I said firmly.

Cathan shook his head, the act making him appear youthful. "I wouldn't know a thing about what she would have done. Before Asherah, my time was spent with the Guardians and far away from Council politics. This was always Neleah's arena. Not mine."

I set my nearly empty cup on the coffee table. "What exactly did they say needed to be done for Asherah to take the throne?"

He ran a hand through the dark waves of his hair, my gaze lingering on his bicep a little longer than appropriate. "She needs to learn our customs and ways and those of the other realms. She has six months."

"Well, Asherah doesn't strike me as someone who doesn't take their studies seriously."

Cathan huffed. "To say the least. When she was growing up, Neleah wouldn't have anything less than an A-minus in her studies. Even when I asked her not to put so much pressure on an eight-year-old, the notion flew over her head. Neleah insisted on it, but Asherah always met the challenge. She never once complained. She truly was the greatest child...faeling, rather." He shook his head. "I don't know if we did the right thing."

My head gave a tilt. "The right thing?"

"Raising her in the Above World," he said as he placed his empty cup on the coffee table.

My fingers fidgeted in my lap. "I can tell you from a human's perspective that what you did is strongly admired by those of us in Atlantis. No one..."

Cathan's inquiring gaze fixed on me, his brown eyes imploring. "Whatever it is, you can say it. I hope you've determined I'm not a harsh King by now. You're safe with me."

Something about how he said that last part gave me a rather... odd feeling.

I shook my head to dash those feelings aside. "Very few Fae have cared about the Atlantian humans. Sometimes, I feel like we're an afterthought because our lives are so fleeting."

He leaned forward on his elbows. "But your life isn't fleeting, Reneah. Not to me, and it certainly wasn't to Neleah. She cared about so many of you like you were her own family. That's something she and I felt in our souls. Despite your longevity, humans have so much to contribute to this world. You deserve to be heard."

My lips lifted in an appreciative smirk. "I believe you have your answer, then."

"About what?"

"About whether or not you did the right thing. If you aimed to raise your daughter with compassion for humans, you've achieved that aim."

He returned my smile. "I believe you're right."

"They may not see it now, Cathan. But eventually, the Fae will come to appreciate the sacrifice you and Neleah made."

Cathan appraised me as if seeing me for the first time. "I like it when you call me Cathan."

I stiffened. "I'm so sorry."

"Please, don't be. It's nice not to be called Your Majesty. I feel..."

"Normal?" I provided.

His head dipped in a single nod. "Yes, normal."

We held each other's gazes momentarily before I rose from my chair and gathered the empty coffee cups. "Is there anything else you need?"

"No, you've been helpful enough just sitting here talking with a grieving male."

I busied myself cleaning the first coffee cup—the hot water heating my cool hands. "I doubt Kristos would consider my chatting abilities to be helpful."

Cathan snorted as he turned on the sofa to face me. "Kristos has a lot of opinions."

I set the last clean coffee cup on the drying rack next to the sink. "He's the best, or else he wouldn't be where he is."

"Do you want to replace Kristos when he retires?"

I tilted my head in thought as I dried my hands with a dark, burgundy dish towel and set it on the stove handle to dry. "I've thought about it," I admitted.

"And?"

I rested my hands on my hips. "I think I'd prefer to take care of you all for as long as I can. I enjoy the coffee breaks and chats."

Cathan bellowed with laughter, a delightful sound that immediately made me smile. "Then I'm happy you won't take over his position. I think I like the idea of you taking care of us. Neleah…" His smile dropped like an anchor in the open ocean, and his eyes widened.

I rushed to the sofa when I noticed fresh tears gathering in his eyes. "Whatever is it?" I asked as I sank onto the couch next to him.

My heart absolutely shattered as he brought his gaze to mine—the unimaginable grief was heavy and palpable. "I can't believe what I was just about to say."

"I'm sure you're being harder on yourself than you need to," I said, rubbing circles on his back.

He buried his face in his hands. "It's an awful thing to say."

"Why don't you say it and let me be the judge of that? Not that I will, mind you. This is a judgment-free zone."

"You'll think the worst of me," he muffled through his hands.

I clicked my tongue. "That's nonsense. Tell me."

His hands dropped in his lap as he hung his head. "I was... I was going to say... that Neleah never took care of us. Not like you have, anyway." I gave him the most unladylike snort, causing an incredulous look to spread across his face. "You're laughing at me."

"I assure you, I'm not laughing at you."

"You are, though. You're trying to hold back your smile."

"Of course I am."

He blinked a few times, his grief morphing to shock. "But why?"

"She was raised a Princess and crowned a Queen, Cathan. She had chambermaids dusting the ground she walked on her whole life. Of course, she didn't know how to do the things I do, or any of the other chambermaids in Atlantis, or any of the other mothers in all the realms." I grimaced. "I'm guessing you were the one to take care of the household chores in the Above World?"

"Yes. I didn't mind it. I'd do anything for my daughter. And my mate." Cathan leaned back, nearly pinning my hand at his back. Somehow, it ended up casually resting on his shoulder, but he didn't seem to mind or notice. "I love... loved Neleah. I suppose I'll love her till I take my last breath. But being the bondmate to a Queen is..."

"Challenging?"

He nodded solemnly. "Yes, and I have no right to complain about it."

"You're allowed your feelings, too, you know."

The corner of his full lips tipped up in a smirk. "She was amazing in all the ways she knew how to be. I'll miss her smile and her laughter. Goddess, she had the courage of a pride of lions. And the stubbornness of a mule." His chin began to tremble. "Why? Why didn't she let us stay and help her that day? She could be alive right now!"

My own eyes began to well with tears as Cathan's entire body wracked with sobs. I could do nothing but hold him to me, placing his head on my shoulder as I caressed his back. Deep down, I understood that, when someone was in pain, it was best just to offer an ear to listen and nothing more. Sometimes, they just needed someone to be with them as they moved through their pain and grief.

And so, I held him.

I held him for a long time, until his sobs abated and his sniffling subsided. I reached for a tissue on the coffee table and handed it to him.

"I'm so sorry," he whispered.

"Do not apologize, not to me."

Cathan gave me a solemn half-smile. "Thanks."

"There's no need to thank me, either," I said, rising from the sofa. "Why don't you try to get some rest? It will do you some good."

"Will the grief ever go away?" he murmured above a whisper.

I rested my hands on my hips. "You may not feel like it now, but as the days pass, the memories... They won't seem to hurt anymore. I promise there's peace on the other side of your grief."

Cathan dipped his head in a nod. "You're an angel."

I feigned excitement. "Oh! An angel, am I? I'll have to tell my mother that one."

He laughed through his tears as I headed for the door. I glanced at him over my shoulder, his features appearing a little lighter and warming my soul. "Rest now, my King. Tomorrow is a new day."

CATHAN

CHAPTER 5

A FEW DAYS AGO, a knock sounded at the door. Forcing myself to momentarily pull my mind out of my grief, I rose from the couch to answer. Dax stood in the hallway—a rueful smirk on his rugged face and his hair barely growing back in patches. The dark circles on his eyes were the only remaining tell that he wasn't one-hundred percent back to normal. "Hello, friend. Mind if I come in?"

"I don't have the energy to refuse you."

He grimaced. "I'll be quick."

I ushered him inside with a furrowed brow. "What's going on?"

Dax folded his arms with his lips pressed in a line as he glanced away.

"Well, this can't be good."

He blew out a breath. "It's bittersweet," he confessed, returning his gaze to me. "I need Neleah's trident."

My entire body locked up, and my face fell—the breath in my lungs seemingly left the space it occupied. As was typical of the magic surrounding a Queen's trident, Neleah's had been lying in our bedroom the day she passed away, as if her spirit put it there for safe-keeping. I'd propped it up in the corner of the room, where, during the long, lonely nights without my mate—nights where her absence became permanent and not due to some duty to her queendom—I could stare at it. Embarrassed to admit, there were many times when I'd talked to it, like Neleah could hear me somehow. Her unending presence when I did so told me she was listening somewhere beyond the Veil. "No."

Dax rubbed a hand down his face. "It's customary, Cathan."

"No."

"Don't be stubborn. You know, as General, I have to take possession of it until your daughter is ready to learn the art of the trident. I've given you more time than usual."

Call me selfish, but I'd been avoiding this moment for as long as possible. Dax had mentioned it shortly after Neleah's death, and I swiftly declined to hand it over. My mate... She was everything to me, and her trident was the last remaining piece of her. It was as if she was still accompanying me through my daily life. If I let her trident go, it would be like letting her go, regardless if it went to my one and only daughter. I shook my head vehemently. "I'm not ready."

His bushy blond eyebrow rose to his hairline. "Will you ever be ready? I can tell you the answer is no. You have to consider what Neleah would want—"

"I don't care what she would want! I care about what *I* want."

"You sound like a tiny faeling," Dax scolded.

I didn't know what had come over me, but I shoved him.

Hard.

His eyes went wide before his expression morphed into anger. "You want to go?"

"Yeah," I seethed through gritted teeth. "I want to go."

Before I could register his movement, he lunged forward—his arm going between my legs and the other going around my back to lift me high in the air and body slamming me into the ground. The air left my lungs, and my eyes bugged out of their sockets as I tried to breathe. Loathe to admit it, but his strength, even after such trauma, took me by surprise. The bastard. I punched his bicep over and over as he held me by the throat and summoned his trident, bringing the tip of it to my neck and causing me to still. "Stop this!" he yelled.

"I'm not giving you her trident!"

"You are!"

"No, the fuck, I'm not!"

"What in the realms is going on here?" a gentle female voice called from the door that had opened unbeknownst to us. I twisted my head as much as I possibly could with Dax's fucking trident at my neck to find Reneah and her horrified expression, her gaze taking in the two of us on the ground.

"I was just teaching Cathan a lesson in responsibility, Leader Diaz," Dax had the audacity to inform her.

My head snapped to him. "Responsibility? The balls on you to reprimand me!"

Dax leaned down, his nose nearly touching mine. "You need a good reprimanding."

Reneah tsked. "This is no way for grown males to act. Off the floor. The both of you."

We glared at each other a moment longer before listening to the only voice of reason in the room. When I swatted his outheld hand before rising to my feet on my own, he pointed a meaty finger at me. "You'd better make your peace with her trident. Asherah will eventually need to train. That's my number one responsibility. I don't care what your feelings are on the matter." With one final parting glare, Dax left the room—the silence enveloping Reneah and me where we stood in the middle of the living room. I couldn't bear to look at her. I dropped onto the couch and buried my face in my hands, trying desperately to restore my breathing to something normal and failing. My shoulders shook as the uncontrollable sobs commenced.

Of course, Asherah would need the trident. I wanted her to have it. The entire realm depended on her to take the lead, to guide our people into the next Ice Age. That's what Neleah intended, what she believed. But her trident... Her trident was the last thing holding her memory to me. It was a reminder that I loved her immensely.

It was a weapon against the *Tanama* bond.

I felt Reneah's presence before she perched on the couch next to me, rubbing circles on my back. I couldn't take the comfort. I didn't want it at that moment, which was why I said, "Leave me."

Her hand stilled. "Are you sure?" I heard her ask in a low, compassionate voice I didn't deserve. "I can get you some tea."

"Just leave!" I bellowed into my hands, which were still covering my face—my pride refusing to let her see me this way. A moment later, I heard the front door click shut.

That was days ago.

And now, I sat in my darkened living room, with the drapes pulled tightly closed, only a sliver of light breaching the space as I stared at the tumbler of whiskey that had barely remained empty as the sun rose and set these past few days. Neleah's trident lay over the chair across from me. It was as if her spirit was bidding farewell, some sentient being within the object telling me to let go.

That's the thing about grief. You think you're over it one day, and the next day, the most minor thing can trigger a response. It was like poking a sleeping dragon and not being able to deal with the consequences of it when it woke up.

But I wanted the dragon to stay with me, if only to remind me that my mate had been real.

I willed the dragon of grief to roar at me, to hold me firmly within its teeth until it left me numb and weak right where I currently sat, taking in the shining, golden trident as I drained the rest of my whiskey. I'd only moved from the couch to relieve myself and stuff the barest contents into my stomach for sustenance.

It was only twenty-four hours ago that I'd reached out a hand to grab the parchment from the Guardian Dax had sent, the act of stretching out my weak arm to take it still fresh in my mind. So, it was no surprise when the front door opened. I filled my tumbler with another dram of the amber liquid to douse the pain. I refused to meet his gaze. I simply stared at the low coffee table before me as he padded across the room to stand beside the chair holding Neleah's trident. His long sigh reached my ears. "I'm sorry."

"No. You're not," I croaked, my voice raspy with the lack of use and assault of alcohol down my throat for days on end.

"No. I'm not," he admitted. "But that doesn't mean I'm not here for you, my brother."

My throat tightened anew. I watched in my peripheral as he gently lifted the trident from the chair and quietly left the room.

And the sobs came again.

RENEAH

CHAPTER 6

Depression is a beast the soul has difficulty battling. It acts as both friend and foe, nurturer and murderer. When it sinks its claws into you, you both *want* the beast to sink its claws even further and let go of you entirely. I'd been there when my father passed away. I understood the beast better than anyone, so I'd respected Cathan's wishes when I'd received his letter three days prior saying he'd rather be alone. I'd given him a few days to grieve, to let the beast within scrape at his soul and try to convince him that there was nothing left to live for in a world without his bondmate. But seclusion be damned, I'd remind him that he had good reason to be here. Deep down, I was confident he understood he couldn't leave Asherah in this world without him, but the beast always had some magical reign over the senses that convinced you otherwise.

So, I had to remind him.

I figured the best place to start was with Atlantis' esteemed Secretary to the Sovereign, a male Neleah trusted with everything she had. My knuckles rapped upon the door to Myles' and Aurelio's quarters, the latter of which opened the door with a flourish to greet me—his fashionable velvet red robe, with its golden filigrees already donned for the new day. I had to admire him for his commitment to fashion, even though the Fae hardly wore clothing. His head, with his perfectly combed black hair, tilted to the side as he appraised me. "Reneah. To what do we owe this unexpected pleasure?"

"I need your help. Both you and Myles," I said on the tail end of a sigh.

Aurelio moved aside, motioning beyond the door with a graceful flourish of the hand. "Come in."

I stepped into the beautifully decorated living area, with its gleaming white modern rug in a beautiful contrast to its dark leather couches and comfy armchairs. Myles stood in the sleek kitchen, the rich aroma of coffee drifting across the room as he poured a cup for himself and his mate, looking exceptionally composed as always. I assumed he'd have to be, as Secretary to the Sovereign. When I noticed the faint dark circles under his eyes, my heart filled with empathy for him. I couldn't imagine what he must have felt, having spent every living day serving his Queen with a dignity and grace that would be studied by potential Secretaries for centuries to come, to suddenly having his Queen gone from the realms. If he was suffering, he certainly didn't show it. Myles Anthysius prided himself in perfection in every way, and he prided himself on being the perfect bondmate, as well, a role he held with a deep sense of duty and honor.

As he placed the coffeepot on the counter, he finally realized I stood before him. "Reneah."

I cast him a warm smile. "Good morning, Myles."

"What brings you here this fine morning? Coffee?"

I waved him off. "I'll bounce off the palace walls if I drink another cup. But thank you."

"Well, take a seat and tell us why you're here," Aurelio said as he plopped down on his leather armchair.

I joined him, sliding into the chair across from his. "I'm worried about Cathan and Asherah," I confessed. "They've been holed up in their rooms for days now. It can't be healthy for them."

Aurelio cast Myles a pointed glance. "See."

Myles carefully handed him his coffee, breathing a long sigh as he settled beside his mate. "Yes, we've noticed. It's been a constant theme of our arguments over the past couple of days."

My brow furrowed. "Do you not think we should do something about it?"

"I want to be respectful of their space," Myles admitted, ever the professional.

"There's a difference between being respectful and being there for the two of them," Aurelio admonished. "It doesn't look good that the Council has issued their expectations, and they've been holing themselves up in their rooms for days. I understand they're grieving, but Melysah is a conniving wench. You know she's using every angle to further her wicked motivations."

"He's right," I cut in. "She's up to something. The entire palace staff can sense it, and they have every right to be concerned. Melysah... She could be a completely different person when Neleah was in the Above World."

Myles rested his chin in the cradle of his palm. "Oh, I'm aware. Neleah was aware, as well." He pinched the bridge of his perfectly sculpted nose. "What do you propose?"

Aurelio tsked. "I've already told you, my love. She needs to be fitted for her dress for the Elemental Ball," Aurelio insisted. "It's the perfect excuse to get her out of bed."

"Yes, that covers Asherah. What about Cathan?" Myles asked.

"I think I have an idea," I intervened. "It'll take some time for Aurelio to get Asherah's measurements. Perhaps Cathan can go for a stroll in the gardens with his daughter and get some fresh air. I'm sure both of them would enjoy that."

Myles dipped his head in approval. "That's an excellent idea."

"I'll go straight away," Aurelio beamed. He sprung from his chair, his coffee splashing over the rim of his cup.

Myles expertly used his water magic to gather it before it could hit the pristine white rug and issued the fallen drops of coffee into the kitchen sink. The move was so practiced that I wondered how often he'd done that for his mate. What I wouldn't give to have magic to clean like that. "Leave her be, darling. Just until the afternoon."

Aurelio placed his perfectly manicured hands on his hips. "Absolutely not. I'm heading over there now."

Myles and Aurelio glared at each other in a battle of wills. Before I could get involved in a lovers' quarrel, I decided to make my exit. I cleared my throat as I rose from the couch. "I'll leave you all to it, then. Once I have Cathan up and ready for his stroll, I'll send him to Asherah's quarters."

I proceeded to the door with a smile, wondering which of the two would win that particular argument, but as I closed it behind me, I didn't miss Myles' defeated sigh.

I wrung my hands at my middle, blowing out a long breath in front of the door to the Queen's quarters. Mother would think me insane. Perhaps I was. But I couldn't let this male suffer any longer.

His daughter needed him, and if Cathan needed me to remind him… well, so be it.

I knocked and entered the rooms without permission. When I stepped over the threshold, I was met with pure darkness; not a single faelight breached the void before me. All the curtains had been drawn tight. If it weren't for my muscle memory, I would have likely tripped over something en route to the bedroom. "Cathan?"

All I received back was a muffled, "Yes?"

I stopped in the doorway, gathering my courage before bee-lining for the long velvet curtains blocking the sunlight. "It's time for you to get out of your funk, Your Majesty," I demanded as I threw open the velvet curtains and wheeled around.

My breath left me.

It never occurred to me that Cathan would sleep in the nude as he was now, save for the heather-colored sheet, reaching just above the 'v' of his abdomen, that thankfully covered the lower half of his body. His beautiful olive skin, blanketing his muscular, toned body, almost glowed. My gaze traveled up his torso to his weary brown eyes, observing me from where I stood by the window. If I had thought Cathan Rosahan Delmar was beautiful in his Fae form before, it would be nothing compared to how magnificent he was in his skin.

My gaze drifted to the unfilled bondmark on his chest, and it was a splash of cold water to my senses.

I shook my head to dispel those thoughts—those really, really inappropriate thoughts—and placed my hands on my hips, giving him my most Leader of the Palace Staff look. "You need to get out of bed," I demanded.

"You know… I was never really a fan of being told what to do in the bedroom. I much prefer the telling."

Dear goddess, the heat that rose to my face was certain to scorch my skin. "Oh? Well, sorry to disappoint you, but this female *will* tell you what to do in the bedroom for your own good."

"For my own good, eh?" he teased, the corner of his mouth twitching.

I breathed a sigh. "Get up, Cathan. Please."

He groaned and threw a pillow over his head. "Do I have to?"

"Yes, you have to."

"But I don't want to," he murmured.

"Sometimes, we have to do things we don't want to do. Have you ever cleaned the toilet of a visiting dignitary trying Atlantian food for the first time?"

Cathan lifted the pillow to give me an aghast scowl. "That's just terrible."

I nodded. "Well, then. You shouldn't complain now, should you? It's time to get up. Your daughter needs you."

Cathan threw the pillow on the other side of the bed. I had to suppress a laugh at how undignified he was at that moment. He was an entirely different Cathan than the world beyond the doors witnessed. "It's just…"

Sensing his need for someone to listen, I padded toward the bed and perched beside him. "Just what?"

He held his gaze on the ceiling and swallowed. "I feel like I've fallen into such a dark place. I don't know how to get out of it or how to be strong for Asherah, for the queendom. I don't know how Neleah did this for centuries on end. The weight of it, it's suffocating."

I shook my head. "Forgive me. You must think I'm being inconsiderate of your feelings."

Cathan gently grasped my hand, which lay next to his, sending the tiny hairs on my arm to new heights. "You're not being inconsiderate."

I grimaced. "I just wanted you to get some fresh air. It'll do you some good to get outside. Asherah's getting her fitting done for the Elemental Ball. Why don't you take her for a stroll in the gardens? Neleah always loved the gardens. I'm sure she'd love for her daughter to see them."

He let loose a long sigh. "You really know all the right buttons to push, don't you?"

My eyebrow lifted to my hairline. "Is it working?"

"It's working. I... I don't think I should be alone anymore."

I sat a little straighter at that. "You're not alone."

He motioned around the room. "I mean, in here. Alone. By myself all day. It's not good for my mental state."

"I can come by and check on you often if you would like?"

What am I saying?

His face lit with a small ounce of hope. "You would do that?" he asked.

I shouldn't. "Of course."

"You'd stay at the palace for a while? Keep me from my troublesome thoughts?"

There was no turning down the look of hope in his eyes. "I can stay in one of the guest rooms in the staff wing."

"Stay on my floor."

My eyes widened as I shook my head. "I don't think Kristos would approve."

"Fuck Kristos."

"Not my type."

Cathan huffed a laugh before he squeezed my hand. "Please? Only for a while. I don't want to be alone. And I... I like your company." His deep brown eyes searched mine, beseeching. He had no idea the effect he was having on me with that look.

And he never would.

I let loose a long, defeated sigh. "Very well. But you may want to send the request to Kristos yourself."

The smile that spread across his handsome face was like I'd given him a lifeline. "You're the best, Reneah. I'll send him a message right away." Cathan beamed. He threw the covers back with a smile, utterly unaware of the small glimpse of his manhood I caught before he donned his scales and headed for the bathroom.

I quickly averted my gaze as I rose from the bed and bolted for the door. "Asherah should be ready soon."

The hiss of water spraying from the showerhead reached my ears. "Oh, Reneah?"

I paused, looking over my shoulder as Cathan peeked his head, riddled with dark, disheveled wavy hair, out of the bathroom door. My eyebrow rose. "Yes?"

"Thank you."

I couldn't hold back my smile. "Anytime, Cathan."

As I busied myself with throwing open the living room curtains and setting the coffeepot to brew, I had to question the sanity of living on the same floor as my King.

But there was no turning back now.

RENEAH

CHAPTER 7

CATHAN SENT A MESSAGE to Kristos as promised, and as expected, Kristos nearly had a heart attack. I couldn't blame him. It was unheard of for any of the palace staff to stay on the same floor as the royal family, but Cathan had insisted it wasn't for any other reason but to keep me close for their transition back to Atlantis. Kristos let loose a long exhale through his upturned nose before telling me, "Do not disappoint me, Leader Diaz."

"Now, why would I disappoint one of my favorite people in the world?" I'd replied in a cheeky tone.

Kristos only huffed and turned to tend to whatever poor soul he planned to scrutinize next.

And that was that.

I went home to gather my belongings under the watchful eye of Mother's lifted eyebrow. "I don't have to tell you this is highly unusual."

I tucked my feather-soft undergarments into the corner of my luggage. "No, Mother."

"And I don't have to tell you... no... warn you not to disgrace this family, do I?"

I lay the set of neatly folded work pants on my luggage and turned to her. "My King asked me to be there for him and his daughter. What would you have done if you were in my silk slippers?"

Mother breathed out a sigh. "I would have rushed home to pack my bags."

I motioned to my luggage on my bed before placing my hands on my hips and giving her my best admonishing look.

Mother's dirty blonde hair shifted as she tilted her head back and forth. "Very well. I see your point."

I turned and resumed my packing. "I don't know why you think the worst of me."

"It's not you I'm worried about."

I paused. "Why would you worry about the King?"

"Because he's a male, and males will do anything to pull out of a funk. And you, my darling daughter, are not exactly hard on the eyes."

"Nonsense."

"How so? You're a gorgeous woman."

I wheeled around and plopped on the bed beside my fully packed bag. "I get it from you."

"Why thank you, dear," she said, her face softening.

"But that still doesn't mean you must worry about him doing something. I'm well below Cathan's station. If he wanted to get over his grief, there is a herd of females living comfortably in the Royal Quarters of Borinke'n who'd be happy to satisfy his cock pocket."

"Language, Rennie. And since when do you call him by name?"

My shoulders lifted in a shrug. "Since he asked me to. Anyway," I continued as she opened her mouth to protest, "I'm just speaking the truth. Besides, I respect my King, and I... I loved Neleah, in my own way. I owe it to her to help Asherah and Cathan move past this. If I fear anyone's disappointment, it's hers, reaching me from beyond the Veil."

Mother appraised me in a moment that stretched before her head dipped in a nod. "Very well. But you do the best you can to stay out of the way. Always remember perfect status."

The corner of my mouth lifted in a grin. "Always."

With my things safely packed into my travel bag, I said my good-byes to both Mother and Tobias. The latter promised to visit me in the Royal Wing, but I expressly forbade it. No matter how close they were to me, I wouldn't bring anyone to my temporary home.

Unfortunately for me, there was no refusing Millie and Gina, who bombarded my new quarters as I settled in. "How in the world did you pull this off? The Royal Wing?"

"I'm not cleaning your porcelain throne," Millie declared with a grin as she scanned the room.

My eyes rolled to the back of my head. "I'm not asking you to."

Gina straightened the bedding, saying, "It's mighty fine of the King to invite you here. I think it's sweet."

"Well, it's certainly unheard of," Millie said as she perched on the chair with an air of uncertainty, unsure if she was allowed to get comfortable.

I lengthened my spine. "In my eyes, this changes nothing. I'll still be expected to complete my palace duties and ensure you all do yours. It's not like I'm his mistress or anything. And do not give me that look, Millie. I'm no Scarlett May. The male is mourning, and I'm here for him and his daughter to make sure that they're okay. I do this for Neleah."

Gina gave me a sad smile and perched on the arm of Millie's chair. "We're only teasing, Rennie. We know how much Neleah loved your family, and you, her."

I blew out a sigh. "I'm sorry. I just left my mother."

"Oh, that must've gone splendidly," Millie mused.

"About as well as you can imagine."

Gina fluttered a hand in the air. "Don't give her any mind. We know your heart. It's in your blood to take care of others, and we love you for it."

My throat suddenly tightened. "Thank you. For saying so."

A mischievous smile broke through the moment. "Of course, if you did bed the King, I, for one, wouldn't breathe a word in exchange for all the salacious details."

Millie swatted Gina's leg. "You mustn't joke of it."

"What? Our Rennie has cobwebs gathering down below and hasn't seen a penis beyond her mind's eye, with all the descriptions in her romance books."

Millie leveled her with a look. "But it's *the King*."

"And he's in mourning," I added. "You saw him and Neleah together, the kind of love they shared."

"Actually, we never saw him and Neleah together," Millie corrected. When I tilted my head, she added, "We've only taken a little over twenty trips around the sun. We're younger than the Heir. He's been in the Above World all this time."

My brow furrowed. "I hadn't thought of that." It made sense. This was the first introduction to the King for most of the younger humans in Atlantis. I was only a child when they left for the Above World; my own memories of them were vague.

"They say the goddess encourages love beyond the death of the mate," Gina continued, "as a sort of grievance blessing for the Fae to allow them to find love again."

Millie scoffed. "Sounds ridiculous."

A deep 'v' formed on Gina's brow. "How so?"

"Because if I found love and they passed away, I wouldn't want to get over it so soon," she told us, crossing her arms indignantly.

Gina glanced down at her lap with a sense of sadness that was uncharacteristic of her. "But the goddess opens their heart to hold love for both their former mate and their future one. I think it's remarkable."

Millie's eyebrow rose to her hairline. "And you know this due to your extensive knowledge of being a Fae yourself?"

Gina's shoulder lifted in a shrug as a twitch pulled at her lips. "I haven't been a Fae, but I've had one inside me."

I gasped. "Gina, you scandalous little chambermaid. Who was it? And when did this happen?"

"And why didn't you tell us?" Millie added, eyes wide.

Gina's mouth tipped in a grin as she inspected her nails. "If you all ventured with me to Sinkers more often, you would know I've taken on a lover."

"But who?"

"Yes, Gina. Who?"

Now, Gina's teeth peeked through her smile. "The owner."

"Of Sinkers?" I asked in shock.

Millie's brow furrowed. "The good-looking one with the perfect brown hair?"

Gina nodded as her face lit with a joy I'd rarely seen on her. "That very one."

"And how long has this been going on?" Millie inquired, with a hint of offense in her tone.

Gina waved a hand in the air. "A few months now. The point is, Jimani—that's his name, by the way—has a hollow bond."

My smile suddenly dropped. "Oh no. I'm so sorry to hear that."

"He would welcome your condolences, but it happened centuries ago. He told me, when he lost his mate, at first, he experienced grief. But as the days passed, it was as if the goddess herself walked with him, healing his heart and leaving him with only the happiest of memories with his mate. And as the years and decades passed by, there was less hurt. He became open to all the possibilities as if the goddess was encouraging him to open his heart, knowing he would move on when ready." Gina's gaze went distant. "Jimani said it was almost ritualistic. Even now, since he and I started... whatever this is, he not only feels the support of the goddess but of his former mate beyond the Veil."

My eyebrow rose. "This sounds like more than a tryst."

Gina straightened out a pleat on her pant leg. "I'm human. It can never be anything serious."

My heart sank. I *did* know it couldn't be anything serious. Humans were but a speck in the fabric of a Fae's life. It was why it was incredibly taboo for a Fae to be with a human and severely frowned upon. I tried to give her my most encouraging smile. "There's nothing wrong with enjoying his companionship, Gina."

Millie grabbed her hand, squeezing it gently. "She's right. You enjoy your Fae."

"And we'll enjoy the free drinks at Sinkers." I winked.

We all shared a moment of laughter before I resumed unpacking, and Gina and Millie departed for the Princess's floor, to tidy up her space. My mind drifted to the King and the hollow bond mark on his chest. I wondered if the goddess had walked with him in the gardens earlier today, providing him with the healing I knew his heart needed.

Reneah

Chapter 8

I WIPED DOWN THE kitchen countertop to a shine so pristine my own reflection stared back at me with a grin. I rested my hands on my hips and inhaled the fresh lemon and lavender scent that permeated the room just as the front door opened. Cathan entered with a somewhat perplexed look on his face. I tilted my head a little. "What's the matter?"

Cathan shook his head. "I... Goddess. I don't even know where to start."

"That sounds like quite a story to tell," I remarked.

Cathan let out an amused huff. "You'll never believe it."

"Well, take a seat. Coffee?"

He crossed the room and plopped down in his plush sitting chair, one of two affixed by the large arching window. "Maybe tea?"

"Coming right up."

I wasted no time preparing Earthos' finest green tea before joining him in the neighboring chair, the steam from my teacup tickling my nose as I sipped. An unusual feeling of familiarity settled within, a natural familiarity of being in his presence, like he wasn't my King, but a friend.

I didn't know what to make of it.

Cathan stared into his cup like it might reveal his future. "Well?" I prompted.

"I think... I think my daughter may have a mate."

The teacup paused halfway to my mouth. "Say what?"

He ran his fingers through the wavy locks of his dark hair. "This is so strange."

"Who? And why do you think this?" I asked as I set my teacup on the side table.

"Commander Eliron met us in the gardens. He's requested to guard Asherah."

My brow dipped. "Isn't that—"

"Well below his rank? Yes. Way below."

I shook my head in disbelief. "What did he say was his reasoning?"

"He said he was the best person to protect her from the Akani."

"I don't see anything wrong with that," I said carefully. "And he's right. I feel better with him guarding Asherah."

"As do I, but it was the way he looked at her." The corner of his full lips lifted in a smirk. "I've been a mated male before. I know the look. He tried to avoid eye contact with her, but when he couldn't avoid it, I could see something passing between them."

Commander Eliron was one of the finest Guardians in Atlantis. He was a Champion and, if rumor was true, one of the most lethal Guardians in the realm. "Are you upset by this match?"

He traced his fingers over a scale on his thigh. "No... I... well..."

I smiled sheepishly at him. "You're not ready."

He huffed. "No, I don't think I am. She's my daughter—my little peanut—my little girl. Forgive me if this sounds selfish, but I'm not ready for her to find her mate yet. Some Fae wait centuries to find their match. My daughter is only twenty-three."

"There's nothing selfish about that. The bond between father and daughter is a unique one. I'm sure a part of you wishes she could've stayed a tiny faeling forever."

Cathan took a long sip of his tea. "If this is what I think it is, I'm not upset by the match." He shook his head. "By the goddess. Draevyn is an amazing Guardian. He may possibly be the best in the history of Atlantis."

"Save yourself, right?" I teased as I hid my smile behind my teacup.

Cathan let loose a glorious laugh. "I think not."

"I think you're being modest."

His face contorted in a grimace. "I'm being honest. I haven't trained in centuries. All of that stopped the day I became Neleah's bondmate and King," he remarked, a shadow passing over his features.

I appraised him as it dawned on me. "You had to give up quite a bit of yourself to be with her."

The light filtering in from the window highlighted the determined gleam in his eyes. "And I'd do it all again, of course. But, I did have to give up my life as a Guardian." He turned his attention beyond the window as he stared off into the distance, a wondrous grin breaking across his olive-skinned face. "Being a Guardian, those were some of the happiest days of my life. The constant ache in the bones, the hundreds of hours of training. They all became a ritual for me. My calling always sings to my soul."

I tilted my head. "Perhaps you should take up your trident again."

Cathan actually flinched. "I couldn't."

"Why not?"

He turned his gaze on me then. "I have to be there for Asherah."

"Sounds like she has one of the best mentors in the realms there for her, but I do understand what you're saying. Perhaps you can slowly get back into training."

He shook his head. "Not with all the meetings with the Above World delegation. There's not enough time."

I reached out and patted his arm. "Don't be too hard on yourself. You're doing the best you can. When Asherah takes the throne, it will alleviate some of the burden you're carrying. And if I may be so bold to assume, a burden you've been carrying since you mated with Neleah. You'll have plenty of time just to be you."

He rested his hand on top of mine, and I pleaded with my blood not to rise to my face. "Thank you, Reneah. I... I don't know what I'd do without you. I feel so much better with you here." Our gazes held for a long beat.

"It is my honor, my King."

"Cathan," he murmured.

"I'm sorry?" I asked a little too breathlessly.

"Cathan. Call me Cathan."

"Right. Cathan."

There was something passing between his dark brown eyes and mine—the little light flecks playing tricks on my eyes. It made me feel... things. I cleared my throat and rose from my chair, gathering the empty teacups. "Would you like any more tea?"

"No, I think I'm good."

I washed the cups in silence, trying desperately to suppress the nagging feeling inside me, the one that had me starting to feel some-thing I had no right to feel. I wouldn't become the next Scarlett May.

I had to remember my place.

CATHAN

CHAPTER 9

Damn the goddess.

Damn her and the hollow bond now sitting empty on my pec. My deliberate unpreparedness for life after the loss of my mate amplified its meaning. The floodgates of emotion and awareness of a world without Neleah overwhelmed every nerve-ending in my body. She'd warned me, but I'd refused to listen because my mind couldn't conceive of a life without my bondmate.

I breathed a long sigh as I beheld myself in the bathroom mirror; the male staring back at me, weary with exhaustion from the grief he'd been carrying—dark circles blanketing the skin underneath his eyes, eyes that remained dimmed and had once held light. That grief had morphed into scalding hot anger, burning so fiercely that one would melt from a single touch. I scolded myself once again for feeling such awful feelings toward my dead mate. The vision of her that day, commanding me to leave, amplified my inner turmoil. I could have helped her. Yet, I understood the importance of helping our daughter escape to safety. Despite the understanding, the fact that she was right all along had my fury burning as hot as the mythical lava fields of Corenathia.

When a recent conversation I'd had with her drifted into my mind, I skewered the reflection of the hollow bond on my best with an unflinching look. Her voice came clear as day, like a phantom memory plaguing me.

"You'll need to move on, is what you'll do," she'd said.

"Never," I'd told her defiantly.

"You will."

My brow dropped in a deep furrow. "How can you say that?" I'd asked as we sat on the dock of our home in the Keys, admiring the warm shades of orange and pink blanketing the late afternoon sky. The sun had begun dipping below the horizon, and our feet dangled toward the canal but were still too high to touch it.

"Because that's what the goddess wants," she'd told me confidently, the long strands of her beautiful dark hair rustling around her face.

I reached out and guided her chin to meet my gaze. "That's not what *I* want."

Neleah huffed a humorous little laugh I could still hear in my mind. "The goddess hardly cares what you want. You've known our bond is... different. You can't deny what passed between us at the bonding ceremony. You know how the *Tanama* bond works. There are some things you must learn to accept."

"And you know I refuse to accept it," I protested, dropping my hand away from her in offense.

Her expression grew stormy. "That's blasphemous. Do not say such things, Cathan. We must hold great reverence and acceptance for the role the goddess has given us." She cast her gaze on the final rays spreading across the sea in the distance. "I've long accepted that my life will be cut short."

I reached around her, pulling her closer to me, as if, somehow, that would dismiss the ominous prediction. "Stop saying such things."

"I mean it," she said in a low tone. Her slender neck bobbed on a swallow with some suppressed feeling. "And you should be prepared for what it means for you and Asherah." She turned to me then; her beautiful blue eyes—eyes I had been captive to for centuries before that moment—grew grave. "You are a great male and a wonderful mate. I couldn't have asked for a better companion in this life."

Imposter mate. I dashed the thought aside and reached up, brushing my thumb across her cool cheek. "You speak like you'll be gone tomorrow."

She placed her hand over mine. "I wish with everything in me that I could stay forever, but when the goddess visits me in my dreams, she reminds me of my mission in this life."

I shook my head defiantly. "Could be just a dream."

Neleah laced her fingers through mine, placing our combined hands on her lap. "I want you to promise me something."

"Anything."

"You must find someone else to share your life with after I'm gone."

I jerked back. "You know that's not possible."

"Yes, it is."

"No, it is not. You're fully aware of what the bond means. No one will take me as a mate."

"We've been careful about others finding out about the bond. You're using that as an excuse."

"Why are you saying this?"

Her eyes welled with unshed tears. "Because you and Asherah deserve a mate and a mother who can be there for you, who can take care of you the way you deserve."

"You take care of us plenty," I reassured her, gripping her tighter to me.

"Come on, Cathan. We've never lied to each other before. Let's not start now."

My brow dipped to the point of pain. "Why are you so insistent on this?"

Neleah blew out a breath through those beautiful lips I'd loved and kissed so many times. "Because you know what the *Tanama* bond will do once I'm gone. You've heard the stories. So, you must move on. Do not deny the goddess's call to another because you feel some sense of loyalty toward me. You've sacrificed so much as my bondmate. No, don't open your mouth and try to deny it. You know it's true. And I love you so much more for that sacrifice. But when I'm called from this life, you need to move on."

"You never know. The bond works both ways. It may be me who's called to die."

"I think we both know it's not." The bond within my chest hummed in agreement, and I wanted to tear it out. "Find someone who makes their life about you; pampers you."

"You pamper me plenty."

Neleah snorted. "Pampering you with a honey-do list while I meet with human dignitaries and the Queens is not the same as pampering. You deserve so much more than I've been able to give. You have my blessing... to move on."

When the sun had long set, I remember I kept insisting that she was mad for suggesting such a thing, refusing to acknowledge that blasted hum within my chest. But if it meant something to her to hear the words, I would.

So, I made the promise.

Little did I know, the bond bestowed upon us would call her a couple of years later. But she knew.

She *knew*.

Now, as I stared at the male in the mirror, I wished desperately that I hadn't made the promise to her that day. That declaration was an oath to the hollow bond and all the possibilities after her passing, possibilities I had no right to entertain, like the sweet encouragement, gentle curves, and sweet smile of a certain human chambermaid, who had grown on me despite the heavy weight of grief I'd refused to let go of.

In truth, my mind raced with all the ways Neleah and Reneah were different—with Reneah's gentle, calming, comforting qualities outweighing Neleah's—and I hated myself for it. The thoughts assaulted my mind, flickering through like a spark in the dark I couldn't pull my gaze from. I slammed my hand onto the stone sink in frustration. It was much too soon for this; perhaps my time in the human world had smothered my innate Fae instincts. We were a different species. Our cultures were different.

And the Fae couldn't bond with humans.

Even though my mate had given her blessing long ago because of the *Tanama* bond, it still felt like a betrayal to look at Reneah in any way that might seem... inappropriate, especially because she was a *human*.

My eyes roamed over my features in the mirror before locking on the hollow bond. A faint crawling tickled inside it. I threw my reflection a look of disgust. Neleah... She'd been exceptional. And although our bond was *different*, we shared a certain camaraderie and laughter that was special to us, a passion that had taken us to our knees when we had first mated.

Just as the stories told, and as she predicted, that passion, the love and emotion I'd felt for my bondmate, slowed from a low boil until the water cooled painfully in my heart, still there but not active. The bond truly was a curse.

And the masses would flee from me if they knew. But they wouldn't know...

Ever.

I let loose a heavy sigh and finally, *finally* pulled myself away from the mirror—stepping into the shower to prepare for my trip to the Above World.

I'd been so preoccupied with my thoughts that I'd forgotten I needed to pack human clothes. Or else I'd give the human delegation a scare with my scales. I rinsed off the soap hurriedly and toweled myself off in a frenzy. There was little time. Chancellor Matthews, the President of the human delegation, was a pain in the ass when anyone arrived late. Dax and I would swim through the heavily monitored waters on our way to Washington, D.C. They were always the trickiest, no matter what sort of magic we used.

I donned my scales as I exited the bathroom and began rummaging through my closet, noticing my duffel bag and a few other key items missing. My brow furrowed until I caught the faint humming drifting to my ears from the living room area. I followed the siren call until I found Reneah carefully steaming my suit with a magicked steaming apparatus I'd missed desperately in my absence from Atlantis. I leaned against the door jamb as I watched her skillfully rid my long-sleeved, crisp white button-up shirt of any and all wrinkles.

She stood back, giving the shirt a final scan from where it hung on a decorative sconce before giving an approving nod. She carefully placed the shirt and the gray slacks in a garment bag. When she pulled the zipper to the top, she turned and was startled. "Cathan," she breathed.

"So sorry to scare you."

She fluttered a hand. "No need to apologize. I barely notice the world around me when I'm in packing mode."

Packing mode, indeed. My duffel bag sat on the couch—shirts, pants, and boxers stacked neatly within. Apparently, I needn't worry about preparing a single thing. Reneah had already done that. I tried not to look too closely at how the simple gesture of gathering my belongings brought me comfort, a task that had often been mine as Neleah's bondmate. "You didn't need to do that," I said.

"It was no burden at all." She cast me a warm smile as she carefully zipped up the bag. "Your everyday shoes are at the bottom of the bag, and your weird shaver thingy is also in there."

I bit my lips to hold back my laughter. "My Norelco?"

"Yes, that Above World contraption. I put it in that protective case next to your toothbrush and other toiletries." She turned to me with a grand look of accomplishment. It made the corner of my mouth twitch in a smile. "You should have everything you need."

I casually strode further into the living room. "And if I don't, should I complain to management?"

Reneah's face morphed into mocked offense. "My dear King. You wouldn't."

I huffed a laugh. "No, I wouldn't. I'm sure you did a marvelous job. Thank you, Reneah. I thought I'd be late because, somehow, I forgot to pack."

"You don't need to worry about a thing. While you're here, I'll take care of you," she told me, her gentle tone like a soothing serum.

There was something about the way she said those words, something that went beyond the duffel and the perfectly prepared garment bag. The way she held my gaze, just the two of us in the personal confines of my quarters, and the way it felt so right... It was like a warm blanket on a frigid night.

A timer dinged in the kitchen, breaking our spell, and a smile lit her face. "Your breakfast is ready."

My eyebrows rose to my hairline. "Breakfast, too? You *are* spoiling me."

She strode before the oven. "You keep throwing appreciation my way, and I'll be inclined to spoil you forever," she teased as she bent over to remove a pie plate from the oven.

Goddess help me. I was entirely grateful she couldn't see me scanning the wonderful curves of her perfectly plump ass through the pants of her uniform, how she bent in such a way that accentuated the way her lower back curved into her waist so dramatically. Reneah's petite form differed from Neleah's tall, slender frame. And I... liked it.

My gaze roamed over her as she set the pie on the range and turned. I didn't want to know what sort of look I was giving her to cause such a beautiful blush to spread across her cheeks, the strength to alter it withering away.

A knock on the door interrupted us, and Dax strolled in a moment later wearing a t-shirt two sizes too small and jeans vastly inappropriate for a meeting with the human delegation. "What in the world are you wearing?"

"What?" Dax lifted his arms and gave a twirl. "Isn't this what the hip kids are wearing these days?"

"Maybe in nineteen eighty-two," Reneah teased.

A deep laugh left me. "She's not wrong, Dax. We'll need to get you sorted before you leave."

Dax slid into the high chair next to mine at the kitchen island. "It hardly matters. I'm just going to guard you. I've got no one to impress up there."

"It certainly matters. You'll need to change."

Dax grumbled.

"There, there." I patted him on the back. "You'll get through it. Eat first. There's plenty of breakfast quiche. Are you hungry?"

Dax perked up at that. "Always."

"Perfect!" Reneah beamed. "Because it's cool enough to eat."

Reneah served us plates heaping with steaming quiche, placing everything we needed before us: silverware, hunter-green cloth napkins, and two glasses of the freshest orange juice Atlantis had to offer. When I rose to grab some cheese from the fridge, she leaped into motion before I could lift my ass from my chair. I don't think I'd ever had freshly grated cheese on my eggs, but here I was, enjoying it because Reneah made it so. She waited on us, leaving us wanting for nothing.

And this was just breakfast.

Reneah wiped off her hands with a kitchen towel as she said, "I'll be leaving you all to it."

My brow furrowed. "You're not eating?"

Reneah dashed a hand. "No, no. I ate earlier this morning. Eat it all if you'd like. If there's anything left, I'll put it away when I return to tidy up. I need to check on the Princess."

And now, she was checking on my daughter, too. "You are a marvel."

She smiled radiantly as she placed her hands on the dip of her hips. "I'm just doing my job."

"Hah, I'll try that one on Gina and Millie," Dax mused. "I can barely get them to tidy my room when I'm on palace duty, let alone make me a quiche."

Reneah snorted. "Good luck."

My brow dipped. "Millie and Gina?"

"My staff, and best friends on my crew," Reneah answered as she set the towel on the rack to dry. "They have a... thing against the Guardians when they come to stay in the palace. It seems some of them leave quite a mess behind."

Dax cast her a look of mock offense. "I would never, my dear Reneah."

She gave a very ungraceful snort. "On that note, I'll go check on Asherah."

"Give her my love."

Reneah smiled kindly. "You've got it."

An hour later, Dax and I left for the Above World, and I could still see the reflection of the hollow bond in the mirror.

"That's it, Cathan. Give me another inch."

"I've given you a fucking inch."

"I want just a little more."

"Fuck off, Dax."

The sweat slowly dripped down my forehead as I reluctantly slid down the wall of the hotel gym where Dax was currently putting me through my paces. I'd made the mistake of voicing that I may want to start training for the Guard again. Dax pounced on the idea, but not in the way I wanted.

Wall sits.

In the Above World.

That was his initiation back into the Guard. He didn't even grant me the decency of training with a trident. He said I was way too rusty.

"You know," Dax began, "this is an effective way to pass the time in the Above World."

I scoffed, wincing against the burning pain in my thighs. "As if I didn't have enough problems with the human delegation."

"Yes," Dax mused. "I did want to punch Chancellor Matthews in the throat a few times during that meeting."

"I want to punch you in the throat," I gritted through my teeth.

Dax tsked. "One more inch for that remark."

"You bastard."

"Aye." Sweat trickled into my eyes, blurring his face with its shit-eating grin as he bent at the waist. "And I'm about to be your worst nightmare."

"Fuck."

He rose to full height. "Ten more seconds."

I didn't think I could last one more second, but I gathered the will to press against the wall. They were the longest ten seconds of my life.

"Rest," Dax commanded.

I slid to the floor, my breath pumping out of my lungs as I shut my eyes against the pain. It was only when the cool surface of a water bottle pressed against my cheek that I opened my eyes. "Thanks," I said before ripping the cap off and gulping down the contents in one go.

Dax crouched down in front of me. "It'll get easier."

I tipped my head back against the wall. "Nothing about my life has been easy."

Dax let loose a sigh. "Do you want to talk about it?"

Did I want to talk about it?

Shame immediately consumed me. There was so much that I wanted to tell my best friend, so much that I wanted to let him know about Neleah that I hadn't told anyone before because... well...

It made me feel like an imposter mate.

A mate, but... not.

And the feelings developing for the human deep within me that I couldn't control, other feelings I wanted to grip on to, but couldn't because of the damn bond. It was enough to drive a male mad. But I couldn't tell anyone. I wouldn't.

Sweat flicked onto my shoulder as I shook my head. "I can't."

Something akin to disappointment flickered across Dax's features. "You know I'm always here if you do want to talk."

I winced. "I do know, brother. I'm sorry."

Dax rose and held out a hand. "Don't be sorry. You'll know when you're ready."

As he lifted me to stand, my thighs aching with the effort, I didn't think I'd ever be ready to tell him. To tell anyone.

RENEAH

CHAPTER 10

P ALACE MEETINGS WERE ALWAYS a nice reprieve from our daily duties. They were a chance for us to catch up with one another or perhaps bitch and groan about the day. The palace staff were sort of a family that way—a well-oiled unit. But, when Kristos mentioned my assignment to the royal wing, since I was, in fact, staying there, I couldn't help but notice a few gazes lingering in my direction. I willed myself not to blush like I was guilty of doing anything but what I'd been asked to do, while trying to arrange my face in a professional manner. I had done nothing wrong. The King asked for me specifically. And I was doing my duty.

I was doing my duty.

Just doing my duty.

It wasn't until the room emptied—with the week's tasks assigned and everyone off to their respective floors—that I let loose a breath I hadn't realized I'd been holding.

"Leader Diaz."

I turned toward Kristos, his perfectly sculpted dark brows dipping down. "Is everything alright?"

I nodded more insistently than necessary. "Why wouldn't I be?"

His dark brown eyes scanned me for a moment before answering, "No reason. How is everything in the royal wing?"

I straightened my spine. "So far, they're both healing, I think. Cathan has gone to the Above World. From what I understand, the Princess has already begun her studies. She's looking forward to the Elemental Ceremony, if only to finally have her mark. Commander Eliron is guarding her, which brings peace and relief to everyone in the palace."

He tilted his head. "And you? Are you... comfortable there?"

"Where, sir?"

"In the royal wing?"

I shrugged nonchalantly. "Of course, sir. Why do you ask?"

Kristos sighed as he leaned against a long wooden break room table. The morning light from the tall, arched window reflected off the shiny brown skin of his shaved head. "I just worry, is all."

The corner of my lips lifted. "Why do you worry?"

"Because I don't want the King to take advantage of you in a moment of grief," he said in a tone that indicated the obvious.

And there it was, the plain-as-day worry weighing down on the space between us, like a heavy blanket in the middle of a hot summer night. I cleared my throat. "You don't have to worry about that."

His eyebrow lifted to his non-existent hairline. "Oh?"

I threw my hands up in frustration. "Why does everyone keep thinking the King will take advantage of me? My goddess."

"We keep asking because the request is highly unusual, Leader Diaz. The difference between everyone and me is that everyone else won't be held accountable if something were to happen on their watch, and the King could land himself in hot water. He has a Council to answer to, you know. And Councilor Velafyn is closely monitoring for any... cracks in the royal foundation, if you catch my drift."

I *did* catch his drift. Melysah Velafyn was a tyrant and a nuisance. In addition to her constant harassment of the staff in the absence of the buffer, otherwise known as Queen Neleah, her sense of entitlement prompted her to request all sorts of things from the palace staff, things that Kristos had managed and elegantly dismissed with expert skill. There was a reason he was the head of our staff. I blew a long sigh. "I'm sorry for losing my cool."

The corner of his mouth twitched. "I've known you since you were a child. That was not losing your cool, but I accept your apology, anyway."

"You say that like you're so much older than me."

"Seven years is plenty more superior," he said. I snorted, causing his dark-toned lips to lift in a smile. "I take you at your word, Reneah. But the second anything happens, you let me know. I don't want you in any uncompromising position."

"I promise."

But as I quickly slinked out of the break room, I had to wonder why he sounded so sure that something *would* happen. I was a professional. I refused to let that happen.

Something in my soul smirked at that.

I traced my fingers over the beautiful teal fabric, instantaneously jealous that my birth rank wasn't higher. I loved all the glitz and glamor of the balls in Atlantis. The Elemental Ball would be no different, except that I couldn't attend because I was... well... just a chambermaid. I let loose a sigh of longing.

"Why, pray tell, are you so glum?" Aurelio asked as he pulled another thread through the fabric with expert precision.

I'd come immediately to his office after I was through with my tasks in the royal wing, finding comfort in all the beautiful rolls of cotton, silk, wool, and velvet fabrics lining the walls in various colors of blue, pink, and green, the jars of pointy sewing needles, and the hum of his sewing machine. With Asherah and Cathan's quarters being utterly spotless and Asherah somewhere off with her Commander, it left me with time to daydream. "I want to go to the ball."

"And I want to go to the Oscars in Los Angeles, but you don't see me breathing heavily over incredibly expensive fabric," he wittily replied without missing a beat or a stitch.

I dropped said fabric immediately.

He glanced up at me with a gleam of mischief in his brown eyes, the corner of his mouth twitching. "I was kidding, Reneah. And why can't you go to the ball? I'm sure Kristos can take you. It's not like he has a date."

I tsked. "Kristos doesn't do social events. And if he did, of course, he wouldn't have a date. Have you ever seen him look lustfully at anything but his clipboard?"

Aurelio shrugged his shoulder with an amused look on his face as he returned his attention to the beautiful garment in his capable hands. "He's a mysterious one."

"Well, I'll leave him to that mystery."

"You could always sneak in."

I tsked. "Nonsense. I don't want to risk it. No, I think I'll keep the idea of what a Royal Atlantian ball would be like and stay in my quarters reading until I'm needed," I said as I picked at a stray thread on the fabric. Aurelio's eyes narrowed on my movement, and I quickly snatched my hand back.

"Perhaps your King will ask you," he said, the corner of his perfect lips tilting up in a smirk.

"My *grieving* King isn't going with anyone but his daughter."

"His daughter seems to be preoccupied with a certain Commander."

"Yes, she does. They'd make a lovely couple, wouldn't they?"

"I'll consider your deflection a sign that I shouldn't ask how things are going in your new quarters."

"Everything is fine in my new quarters."

"Just think," he continued as if I hadn't spoken, "if the King *did* ask you, it would be like a true Cinderella story."

"Funny, I'm not in the mood for a Cinderella retelling."

"But you could be." Aurelio set the fabric down on his work table with a short huff of breath. "Really, Rennie. Just sneak into the ball. Find yourself a hot sauce, high-ranking Guardian, and clear the cobwebs. There's a fierce, flaming dragon hiding somewhere in there. I can feel it."

I pointed at him. "You leave my flaming dragon out of this."

"What?" he asked in mock offense.

"You know what."

Aurelio actually let out a whimper of displeasure. "But Rennie, I need some entertainment in my life. Some true palace scandal that will grace the pages of all the Atlantis gossip columns."

"My love life is hardly entertaining and will certainly not be gracing the gossip columns."

"But it could be. That's the point," he said, dragging out the last words before sighing heavily. "Fine. Ruin my fun." He stood from his chair and held up the dress. "She's going to look amazing."

"Just like Neleah," I nearly whispered. Princess Asherah was a beautiful young woman filled with all the perfect characteristics of her parents—Neleah's mesmerizing eyes, Cathan's strong cheekbones, Neleah's endless, silky hair. The gown held reverently in Aurelio's gentle hands was sure to be the talk of the ball. "It's pure perfection, Aurelio."

His amber eyes roamed over every inch of the dress. "I'm sure I'll find something wrong with it. An artist is never truly satisfied with their work. Even when I've declared it complete, I seem to find even the littlest of things to fix."

I wondered, not for the first time, what it would be like to have an artistic calling, to actually live out my life as a royal seamstress and designer like Aurelio. I absolutely adored fashion and had spent many hours chatting about fabrics and designs with Aurelio. His office was a refuge of mine, whether he realized it or not. I loved his company, and he never seemed to mind when I lingered or simply observed him. I wondered what it would be like to be his apprentice, his protege, but I wouldn't dare to ask. I wouldn't even dare to dream. As far as I knew, Aurelio didn't have an apprentice and didn't have any plans to take one. So, I'd take whatever knowledge I could get. "And what are you wearing to the ball?"

Aurelio straightened and waved his hand in the air with a dramatic flourish—his golden bangles jingling. "It is a fabulous surprise. I simply can't divulge any of the details."

"Ooooh. That good, huh?"

"You'd better believe it is better than good. Come to my quarters after the party. We'll drink faery wine and gossip about who left with whom and who wore what."

I smiled wide. "You got it."

And despite my dream of going to the ball, I'd take any kind of Elemental Ball celebration I could get, even if it was just my friend and me.

RENEAH

CHAPTER 11

I STOOD ABSOLUTELY PETRIFIED in the center of my deceased Queen's enormous walk-in closet, my mouth agape, my mind a puddle of nerves. The chandelier twinkled against the rows and rows of various gowns in every shade of sea blue, soft yellow, sea green, and light lavender—the tiny jeweled accents winking at me like they were in on my little charade. It was entirely overwhelming, but I had to select something and select something quick because...

"Couldn't I just invite you to be there? As my guest?"

My heart had nearly dropped out of my ass when Princess Asherah asked me to go to the Elemental Ball with her. My dear, sweet, new "friend"—according to her because I would never presume—asked me to go with her to the ball.

A Cinderella story indeed.

Selecting a dress on the fly was not easy. For one, Queen Neleah had been considerably taller than me. Secondly, my hips had a little more... ahem... flare than hers. Thirdly, there were so many beautiful choices. A trove of dresses was displayed before me in so many different colors: pastel pink, dark navy blue, crimson red, and emerald green. Some were long, and others were short. I wanted to try them all, but I'd have to be quick. Only a handful of hours remained until the ball, and who knew what sort of alterations the dress would need?

My hand drifted over different textured fabrics, some soft, some gritty beneath my fingers. I stopped at one with a mesmerizing ruby-red color. I'd never worn such a bold color, but tonight seemed the perfect night to try. I quickly kicked off my work slippers, the thick beige carpet caressing the soles of my bare feet as I unbuttoned the light blue tunic of my uniform and placed it on the plush settee sitting in the center of the enormous closet, followed by my stark black uniform slacks. While reciting prayers to the goddess, I carefully slipped the dress over my head, the soft fabric coasting over the skin of my torso until it settled across my hips. The hem of the dress tickled my toes, but with some heels, it was sure to be the perfect length. "Must have been a tea-length dress on her," I murmured. I swished the dress back and forth; hundreds of diamonds worth more than my entire existence glimmered in the faelights. I couldn't suppress the smile on my face as I dashed out of the closet. "I think I got it!"

I gave the dress a last-second straightening before I looked up. I stopped in my tracks. "Oh, my goddess." I immediately dropped into a curtsy, wholly mortified to be rummaging through Cathan's mate's closet—his *dead* mate, who he'd been endlessly grieving. "I'm so sorry, Your Highness."

I should have asked for permission. I should have asked him if it was okay, and here I was in Neleah's dress. I'd been too comfortable around them. I'd been too comfortable around *him*. I'm just a chambermaid, for crying out loud!

He's going to fire me.

This is it.

I'm done.

"You look beautiful, Reneah," Cathan said softly, instantly putting me at ease. I rose and brought my gaze to his beautiful brown eyes, trying desperately not to swoon in front of his daughter. "Neleah would have loved to see you in her dress. *And* going to an Elemental Ball. She would've been pleased. Thank you for accompanying my daughter. You can steer her clear of all the busybodies and the troublemakers."

I nodded vigorously, my nerves getting the absolute best of me. "Absolutely, Your Highness. I've got her."

As Asherah let loose a sigh, Cathan's eyes scanned me briefly. If I'd blinked, I would have missed it. "Ugh. Now I'm even more nervous. Can't we just do the Elemental Ceremony?"

"And miss all the fashion?" I exclaimed, bringing my palm to my throat. "Blasphemous!"

Asherah gave an amusing grunt, and I inhaled deeply. "I'd better change back into my clothes." Without sparing another minute, I turned for the closet and rushed to put my uniform on. On shaky legs and shotty nerves, I strolled back into the room with the ruby-red dress draped over my arm. Asherah waited for me by the door with a smile. I spared a glance in Cathan's direction, and the corner of his sensual lips lifted. "See you this evening, Reneah."

I gave him a quick curtsy and followed Asherah out of the room, the King's small smile staying with me as I exited the room without caving to the need to look behind me. I prepared myself for something even more challenging and made my way to Kristos' office.

My knuckles rapped upon the thick wooden door of Kristos' office.

"Come in," he called a moment later.

I drew a long breath before turning the cool glass knob and entering, trying desperately to prepare myself for the reaction Kristos was certain to have. As I entered, I was greeted with a flood of mid-afternoon light; the rays glistening off the top of Kristos' head as he remained focused on the tablet before him. I paused for a moment, appraising him. I considered myself incredibly lucky to have Kristos as a mentor. His family had been with the palace just as long as mine had, both of us taking pride in our lineage in every facet of our work. He was a mysterious man. Many of the staff had tried to crack the nut to get a peek into his life, but had failed. I'd only been provided with a glimpse because my mother was his mentor, and I caught snippets in passing. Out of respect, I kept those details to myself.

Kristos Morales lived a few blocks away from our townhome. He diligently and honorably cared for his parents, making sure they lived a comfortable life in retirement. He had no significant other, or none that we could tell of, anyway. It seemed he was more invested in his palace role than he was in finding someone to share his life with. It was an achievement when any one of us could get him to crack a smile, a skill I excelled at. I'd keep trying until the day he retires.

At my silence, he finally glanced up from his tablet. "Leader Diaz. To what do I owe this rather unexpected interruption to the middle of my day?"

Did I mention he was a little prickly? It was like trying to hug a cactus in the High Desert of Earthos. "I... um... need to inform you of something," I began as I gently closed the door behind me and slid into the suede upholstered chair before his large oak desk.

Kristos's perfectly sculpted dark eyebrow rose. "Yes?"

I cleared my throat, my hands fidgeting in my lap. "Princess Asherah has invited me to the ball as her guest," I said.

His face softened. "That's kind of her to ask. I'm sure it was very difficult for you to decline. I know how much you love events like that."

I grimaced. "Um... well... I didn't exactly decline."

Kristos's steely stare bore down into my soul. "You didn't, what?"

"I... uh... didn't decline."

Kristos buried his face in his hands. "Goddess divine."

"We immediately went to the Queen's closet—"

"Oh, goddess. Don't tell me—"

"And I picked out an amazing ruby-red dress. You have to see—"

"I don't want to see it."

"And then the King expressed his gratitude for planning to escort his daughter."

"Of course he did."

"And so, I had to come to you straight away and let you know that I'll be going to the ball this evening."

Kristos's hands dropped with a thump on his desk as he glared at me. He had the uncanny ability to make me feel like I was twelve. It was incredibly impressive. "Do I need to remind you how inappropriate all of this is?"

I gave my head a tilt. "*All of this*, sir?"

He raised his hand and began counting off with his long, elegant index finger. "You've been invited to stay in the royal wing, which is completely unheard of." Middle finger. "The King has requested that you, and you alone, take care of Asherah and his quarters." Ring finger. "The Princess has invited you as her guest to the Elemental

Ball, in which she is the main reason for the celebration, and you accepted, so you'll be seen by any number of people while attending." And last but not least, the pinky. "And you've rummaged through our beloved Queen's closet, receiving a glowing approval from the King to accompany his daughter to the ball." He cocked his head. "Did I get all of that right?"

I let loose a gentle scoff. "Well, when you put it like that, it sounds dreadful."

He threw up his hands in a very uncharacteristic gesture of frustration. "That's because it is, Leader Diaz."

My shoulders sagged. "You say this like I've done something wrong. What am I to do? Deny the Princess? Deny my King? I can't exactly do that now, can I?"

"Let's be honest here, Reneah. You didn't even try to decline."

I lifted my shoulder in a shrug. "I would think it would be incredibly impolite to deny them anything."

His frustrated stare bore into me as he exhaled. "You are walking a fine line."

"I understand the line I'm walking just fine."

"You'll remember your place this evening. Remember, you represent the palace staff at all times—*my staff*. Please do not disappoint me."

"You have my word."

Kristos nodded in defeat before his eyes flicked up to me. "Well, what are you still doing here? You have a ball to get ready for."

I squealed with delight, much to Kristos' annoyance. "Thank you, Leader Morales." I leapt from my chair and placed a sloppy kiss on his shiny head before he batted me away.

"Go. Go. I have work to do," he demanded, the corner of his mouth twitching ever so slightly.

I rushed out of the room and made my way to the one person who would share in my excitement. The door to Aurelio's workshop was wide open, and my cheeks hurt as they held the smile that had been affixed for the entire two flights of stairs it took to reach it. His amber eyes lit as I bolted into the room. "What is it, Rennie?"

I jumped on the balls of my feet. "I'm going to the ball."

RENEAH

CHAPTER 12

I T WAS A DREAM.

It had to be.

I pinched myself, for the millionth time, to make sure I wasn't dreaming, and my breath escaped me double that. I smoothed out the fabric of my ruby red dress as our canoa ambled through the streets of Borike'n—the immense interloper feeling consuming me. On the short ride back to the palace for the Elemental Ball, the gazes of dozens of humans tracked us in passing, cementing that feeling.

The ceremony was held without interruption—thank the goddess. I waited by the canoa with Braeliah—our royal commuter—during the ceremony, just in case we needed to flee the scene with the Princess. But no such drama happened.

As we neared the side entrance of the palace that led to the ballroom, I kept a careful eye on Asherah. At present, she gently rubbed at her new mark on her wrist in awe or fear—I couldn't tell. I reached over and patted her arm. "Don't be nervous."

She snorted.

I huffed a laugh. "I know. Easier said than done, right?"

"We've arrived!" Braeliah called from the front.

Asherah blew out a breath as she rose to exit the canoa.

The more time I spent with Asherah, the more I understood that she didn't really enjoy being the center of attention. She didn't really like attention at all. It was as if she'd give anything to squirrel away in her quarters away from everyone, which is why when we found ourselves in front of the ballroom doors, I said, "Okay, I'll be waiting for you in the corner of the room." I rested a hand on my hip, dreading this next part. "You and your father will have the first dance. And don't make that face," I admonished when she winced. "You'll be just fine. Myles will introduce you to the crowd. The dance will be over before you know it, and then we can find some fabulous faerie wine, dissect people's fashion sense, and stare at all the handsome centuries-old Fae males from the corner of the room all night long."

She breathed in deeply. "Okay. I can do this."

My gaze slid over her shoulder, and my breath caught. Cathan, in his Fae form, was stunning, but Cathan in a midnight black tuxedo almost caused me to whimper at how dashing he looked. His beautiful black hair was perfectly combed back—his entire aesthetic making the golden streaks of his brown eyes stand out in stark contrast. The corner of my lips lifted when I noticed he was just as nervous as his daughter, his hands fidgeting over his cufflinks repeatedly. "Speaking of handsome males, here comes your father."

Cathan glanced up from the cufflink he was fussing with and finally noticed Asherah before him. He positively beamed with fatherly affection that made my heart squeeze. "There's my girl," he said as he wrapped her in a gentle embrace. He pulled back and swept his gaze over her dress. "I didn't have time to tell you before the ceremony, but you look wonderful, Sher. So much like your mother," he said with a bittersweet smile. Cathan's gaze carried over her shoulder to where I quietly stood like an intruder in their father-daughter moment, his smile of pride putting me at ease. "You did a fantastic job."

I could feel the heat creep across my face. "Thank you, Your Highness." I tore my gaze from him, not wanting to let him see the effect he had on me, and peered into the ballroom. "Looks like Myles is ready for you all. I'd better get inside." I slipped my hand into Asherah's and gave her a reassuring squeeze. "Remember to breathe, Ash. Keep your back straight and shoulders back. Posture is everything." I dipped into a quick curtsy, my traitorous eyes needing one final look at the handsome King before I ventured into the awaiting crowd beyond the open doors of the ballroom.

My heart kicked in my chest as I carefully squeezed between bystanders wanting to see the Heir. I prayed to the goddess for protection against any damage to Neleah's dress. I gingerly gathered the fabric in my hand, pulling it tight against my legs to avoid others trampling it. When the corner of the room came into view, I exhaled in relief. I turned, facing the room, just as Myles's voice boomed over the crowd, "It is my honor to present his royal highness, King Regent Cathan Rosahan Delmar and Princess Asherah Delmar Rosahan."

The applause echoed loudly in the immense stone room. Cathan led an incredibly nervous-looking Asherah to the center of the dance floor with ease, Asherah grabbing onto her father like a lifeline. It wasn't long before the quartet's music filled the room, and they began twirling in a traditional Atlantian dance. I couldn't suppress my smile as they passed the side closest to me. Asherah danced with her father like she'd done it a million times before.

"Faery wine?" I glanced at the server, who approached my side just in time to see his eyes widen. "Reneah?"

"Tobias."

His baby-blue eyes scanned me incredulously. "What on Earthos are you doing at the ball?"

I lifted my chin as I grabbed a crystal goblet from his tray. "I'm escorting the Princess this evening."

"The Princess?"

"Yes. That's what I said. The Princess."

Tobias, impeccably dressed in a bright white dress shirt, black cummerbund, and pants, gave a woman who approached him a gentlemanly smile. He lowered the tray so she might grab a glass and returned his attention to me the second she departed. "But how?" he said in a harsh whisper.

I took a small sip of my delicious faery wine before saying, "Princess Asherah found it odd that I wasn't going to the ball. She wanted me to accompany her so that I could keep her company. The King insisted." My shoulder lifted in a casual shrug. "And so I accepted."

"Does Auntie know?"

I glared at him in warning.

He sighed heavily, his free hand reaching to thread through his light brown hair before he thought better of ruining his perfectly combed strands and dropped his arm to his side. "She'll find out, you know."

"Not if you don't say anything." I gave him a shooing gesture. "Now get going. I don't want to distract you from your duties."

"Don't do anything reckless," he hissed over his shoulder, offering the next cluster of guests a drink with a practiced smile.

"Why does everyone think I'm going to be reckless?" I murmured to no one.

Cathan and Asherah were speaking to each other now, and it seemed that some memory was passing between them. I greedily sipped my wine to calm my nerves, my gaze fixed on father and daughter. I couldn't keep my eyes off of them, off of *him*. As they whirled closer again, my gaze dropped to the way his lower back dipped before his delectable backside flared into two perfect globes.

"And who do we have here?" a slithering male voice that made my spine stiffen said from beside me.

I tore my gaze from the dance floor to find Kane Ruema, Councilor Velafyn's Guardian and bitch boy, standing beside me. When his chilly look traveled over my body, the faery wine in my stomach churned. "I didn't realize they let chambermaid filth in this evening."

"Oh, no? Seeing how they let in Guardian filth such as yourself, I'd think you would have realized my presence would be perfectly acceptable."

A growl emanated from his throat, causing a few guests to turn and cast him an admonishing look.

I sighed heavily through my nose. "What can I do for you, Ruema?"

"You can do nothing for me except polish my shoes."

I took another casual sip. "I'm afraid I'm off duty at the moment."

"Filth such as yourself is never off duty," he sneered. "I'm hungry. Go fetch me something to eat."

I flicked my head toward the buffet table behind us, laden with savory eats. "Go fetch it yourself."

His brows rose. "You dare not to serve me?"

"Yes. I dare. Last I checked, you're a Guardian, not a King."

I stood my ground as he leaned down into my personal space. "You are below me in every way. Don't forget that as you sip your wine and enjoy the festivities this evening. You're nothing but a petty little human."

I shrugged nonchalantly. "Okay," I said, my reply garnering the exact response I sought from Kane, as he bared his teeth at me. With one final glare, Kane turned and disappeared into the crowd. My shoulders immediately sagged with relief. Oh, how I despised that male.

When I noticed the telltale sounds of the end of the song, I grabbed an appetizer plate off the buffet table behind me and loaded it with rich empanadas, a few crackers with cheddar cheese slices, and plump green grapes. Asherah was sure to be hungry. I waited patiently as I watched her scan the crowd. The look of relief when she finally found me was rather comical. I handed her plate over as she reached my side. "You danced beautifully."

"Thanks," she replied while practically inhaling a tiny empanada. She pointed toward the dance floor with the tip of her second one. "You're not going to dance?"

I lifted a shoulder. "Maybe. I'd much prefer to analyze dresses from afar, though. I can never get enough of the fashion. We never see enough of it on the Fae."

Asherah smiled at that. "You truly love the fashion world, huh?"

"Oh, without a doubt. And what's not to love? Being able to make people feel beautiful through something that I created? That's power. Of course, I'm nowhere near Aurelio's level, but I enjoy makeup and design like him."

"Does he know this?"

"Of course. He's the ultimate fashion buddy."

She popped a green grape in her mouth. "You've never thought of learning from him? Perhaps doing more of the design work?"

I held up my wrist for her inspection. "I have no mark. No calling. Humans in Atlantis generally follow the lineage of employment their families have been given. Although it's not frowned upon to seek a different line of work than my ancestors, I've always known my place is to serve you and your family. There's honor in that, as well."

A severe crease appeared between her eyebrows. There was no other way to describe the emotion, but I was touched that Asherah saw me—the real me—and actually cared about my passion, even though there was little I could do about it. "As honored as I am for your help, you should ask him. See if he can teach you a few things," she insisted, placing her appetizer plate on the neighboring table.

My brow furrowed. "Ask who? Aurelio?"

"Ask me what?" Aurelio asked as he approached arm in arm with Myles. The curious gleam in his kohl-lined amber eyes immediately caused me to panic. Asherah was about to bust my world wide open, and she didn't even know it. She scanned Aurelio from head to toe.

"Yes, Princess. I will take all the gawking this evening," Aurelio teased with a hand at his hip.

"I can't help it. You look fucking hot," Asherah complimented.

I couldn't agree more. Long, dark sleeves graced his slender arms. A midnight black flare-collar dress shirt rested over a single-breasted indigo vest. A train that flowed in one continuous piece of fabric from his vest carried behind him and perfectly complimented his black slim-legged pants. The indigo and diamonds of his stiletto heels glimmered as he sashayed before us. He dipped into a bow with a flourish of the hand in perfect Aurelio dramatic fashion.

"He looks absolutely radiant," Myles said. Anyone would be lucky to find someone who looked at Aurelio like Myles looked at his mate. Just once in my life, I wanted to know what that felt like.

"If you keep talking like that, my love, I'll show you just how radiant I can be," Aurelio teased as he placed a chaste kiss on Myles' lips, causing the color to bloom from his neck to his face. Myles straightened his matching indigo vest, and I smiled at how perfectly they matched.

"You both look marvelous," I complimented.

"Thank you, love," Aurelio said before his perfectly plucked eyebrow curved toward his equally perfectly set hair. "Now, are you going to tell me what you were going to ask me? Or do I need to dump the faerie wine down your throat until you divulge?"

My panic returned when I caught Asherah's mischievous grin. "She was going to ask if she can be your design protégé."

Aurelio gasped. "My protégé?"

I waved my hand. "No, no. I couldn't."

"But you can. I insist," Aurelio retorted.

"There's no reason you couldn't do both, Reneah," Myles assured me. "I believe it's important to stay current on the latest fashions, especially with the influx of humans entering the queendom soon. Aurelio will need all the help he can get. And I'm sure the Princess wouldn't mind."

"Not at all," Asherah confirmed, beaming like she'd won a battle.

They looked at me in anticipation. This was not something I had intended. My position within the palace was an honor many of the chambermaids would die for. A part of me felt guilty for entertaining this side of myself. It felt selfish. If I was being honest, I felt selfish for my mere presence in the royal wing. And here I was about to do the most selfish act of all. I prayed Mother wouldn't find out, as I gave a solemn nod. "Very well. I'd be honored to be your protégé, Aurelio." And with the recognition that I'd given my answer and... well... there's nothing I can do about it now, a smirk lifted my lips as I beamed. "I can't wait to work with all the fabrics and colors, and—oh!" I glanced around Aurelio as my gaze caught on a shocking ensemble. "What in the world is she wearing?"

Aurelio's eyes drifted toward the entrance where I was gaping—his face morphing into a scowl. "Oh my. She didn't."

"She did," I breathed in mortification.

Melysah Velafyn strolled into the room as the sea of people parted. A pale peach dress drowned her pale skin. I couldn't tell where the fabric began, and her complexion ended.

"But someone should have told her that color is drab on her. Who let her out in that?" Aurelio asked, aghast, bringing his hand to his throat.

"Her complexion is far too fair for that color."

"Is she blind?"

"Blind or delusional," I said, peering up at Aurelio—his lips twitching. We burst into laughter.

"Well, now that I have a protégé, I'm stealing you away." He grabbed my hand. "Let's go take a closer inspection." He peered back at Myles. "You don't mind, my love, do you?"

Myles smiled warmly. "Not at all, my dear. Go on. We'll be here."

Aurelio threaded his slender fingers through mine and pulled me through the crowd, for which I was grateful. Being petite made getting through a sea of people far more difficult, but Aurelio's height and expert glare were quite effective when anyone dared to get in our way.

When we finally reached the other side of the ballroom, we expertly positioned ourselves for the show that was Melysah Velafyn. We grabbed a fresh glass of faery wine from the tray of a server I didn't recognize, giving him a smile of gratitude.

For most of us in Atlantis, Melysah Velafyn's motivations had been as clear as the dome sky on a bright, cloudless day. Rumors swirled about her Council meetings and how she'd even attempted to talk down to Queen Neleah, something only the brave ventured to do. While many thought she simply wanted power, I knew better. Those of us who'd witnessed the Akani's anti-human posters blanketing sandstone buildings and propaganda pamphlets littering the sidewalks and streets of Borike'n hailing the rise of a new royal line knew better. She wanted to be *queen*, a notion that sent a wicked chill throughout my entire being. She had about as much empathy toward humans as an ant beneath a shoe.

"So, are you going to tell me why you never said anything about becoming my protégé?" he asked, pulling me from my troubling thoughts. I should have seen the question coming the second he and I were alone.

I glanced down at the floor. "I know you haven't taken an apprentice."

"So, you want to be my apprentice, not my protégé?"

"Protégé is fine."

"Mmhmm."

"I swear."

"Yes, and somehow, I don't believe you."

I lifted my gaze to the crowd before me, unwilling to meet his eyes. Melysah had somehow made her way to Commander Eliron and a group of high-ranking Guardians. Draevyn barely acknowledged her. And yet she threaded her arm through his—the action causing Draevyn's face to distort in an insult. I didn't miss Kane quietly seething behind them, which made me smile. With a grace few possessed, Draevyn disentangled himself and moved to the other side of the group, the other Guardians catching his drift and blocking Melysah—the perplexed look on her face with pure satisfaction.

Get a clue.

After a minute of feeling Aurelio's stare on me, I finally conceded and glanced up at him. "You know I can't leave my position, even if I wanted to."

Aurelio tsked. "Says who?"

My eyebrow lifted. "Have you met my mother?"

"I know your mother very well."

"Well then, you know that I can't entertain living a life other than the one set since I was born."

"Come to think of it, I didn't even know that I *could* take on an apprentice," he continued, tapping his finger to his chin as if I hadn't just said that there was no changing my fate.

"And there would be no one to replace me," I told him, sipping my wine.

"It's a grand idea—an apprentice," he mused, a conspiratorial smile overtaking his face. "It sounds so official. I like having you as my apprentice," he said with a cheeky wink.

"But I'm *not* your apprentice," I deadpanned.

"You are now."

I pinched the bridge of my nose. "Goddess above."

"Leader Diaz?"

Every muscle in my body went rigid. As I dropped my hand, Melysah and Kane appeared before us—the latter grinning with evil delight. Melysah's gaze traveled between me and Aurelio. "What exactly are you doing here?"

"Councilor Velafyn," I addressed her as I dipped into a short curtsy. "I'm here as Princess Asherah's guest."

With how her face pinched, you would have thought I'd told her I had just swallowed a live snail. "But you? A chambermaid?"

"What does it matter to you?" Aurelio asked, coming closer to my side.

Her steely gaze sharpened on him. "It matters to me because we must have order in our palace. It's quite literally my job."

"It may be your job, but there's nothing against Reneah accompanying Asherah."

Melysah's thin lips pressed tight before she returned her attention to me. "You're tending to my quarters this week," she demanded.

I stiffened. "I-I'm afraid I can't do that, Councilor."

She tilted her head. "And why not? I've given you a directive and expect you to follow it. My word is bond, chambermaid." She seethed. My gaze flicked behind her to Kane's smug expression—his muscular arms crossed over his chest with anticipation.

"I've been assigned to the royal wing."

"Assigned to the royal wing?" she asked amusedly.

"Yes, Councilor."

"Well, then. As of this moment, consider yourself reassigned."

"I'm afraid you can't do that, Councilor Velafyn," called a deep male voice behind me. General Dax Lumeya's large form came into view as he drifted to my side, glaring at Melysah. "The King has requested Reneah's presence in the royal wing. She's to remain there and take care of them until he dismisses her. I'm sure Leader Morales will happily make other arrangements for you."

Melysah skewered Dax with an unflinching look before grabbing Kane's hand. "I'd like to dance," she declared as she pulled her boy toy behind her.

I blew out a long breath. "Thank you, Dax."

He smiled at me warmly. "It's my pleasure."

"Let's head over to the safe zone on the other side of the ballroom," Aurelio suggested, his hand threading through mine. "This side is growing rather boring."

As we sliced through the crowd, I felt a presence looming behind me like a tangible thing. I spared a glance over my shoulder, and my breath caught. The King's mesmerizing gaze met mine from where he stood behind Dax, and it followed me until the crowd swallowed me whole.

Aurelio and I continued scanning the crowd for the best and worst dressed in attendance while tucked away with Asherah and Myles in the corner of the room. I tried to rid myself of the image of Cathan looking at me like he did.

Tried, but failed.

My goddess. It was so unlike the way he'd usually regarded me. And I... didn't know what to make of it.

As Aurelio pointed out one of the Council member's stunning heels, someone approached out of the corner of my eye and snagged my attention. King Cathan strode toward us, his powerful gaze locked on mine. My entire body froze as a sea of people parted for him until he came to stand before me with his hand held out. "May I have this dance?"

I forgot how to speak.

No, truly.

I fucking forgot how to speak as this wonderful, beautiful male just asked me—a nothing chambermaid—to dance.

"This is the part where you take his hand," Aurelio whispered.

Asherah's hand pressed into the small of my back, pushing me forward. I carefully placed my hand in his, and something... *something* passed between us. I couldn't say what it was, but the reassuring twitch of Cathan's lips had me following him until we were out on the dance floor—his warm, large hand against my lower back, and my hand raised in his and ready for the dance. I carefully placed my other hand on his firm shoulder, gazing into those mesmerizing brown eyes.

And then we moved as if in a dream, one I wished would never end. His gaze dropped to my slightly parted lips before he asked, "Are you okay, Reneah?"

"Okay?"

"Yes. From earlier? Melysah should've never spoken to you that way. Not now. Not ever."

There was an intensity in his eyes that had me glancing away. "Oh, I understand now. Well, yes. I'm okay," I told him as he expertly wound us around another couple. "That's not the first time that's happened, and it certainly won't be the last."

"It will if I have anything to do with it," he declared.

I returned my attention to those beautiful eyes so full of some emotion I wasn't prepared to acknowledge. "It means a lot to me that you care," I confessed.

Cathan gripped me a little closer to him. "As soon as I overheard her tone, I sent Dax to you."

I blew out a breath. "Thank you."

"It was the least I could do." His eyes searched mine. "And are you enjoying yourself?"

My lips spread into a wide smile, which he dashingly returned with a radiant smile of his own. "Immensely. I feel like I'm in a dream."

"Well, that makes one of us."

I huffed out a laugh. "Not enjoying your Kingly duties?"

"Not in the slightest," he said, my dress fanning out as he turned us around the floor once again. "I forgot how stuffy some of these people are. It makes me long for my time in the Above World, when things were much simpler. Now, I'm forced to listen to Councilman Reyes spout off about the importance of having a successful town hall, what to do and what to say. And when I say spout off, I mean just that. Half of his sentences involved spittle, that speckled my face every four or five words. I had to excuse myself to clean up in the washroom and stealthily avoid him for the rest of the evening."

I giggled. "Well, I hope your present company makes things a little better for you," I teased as he twirled me with ease.

"I find that my present company is making things infinitely better."

My eyebrow rose. "Oh?" I asked with a teasing grin.

My breath caught when he leaned down close to my ear. "In any case, your ruby red lips are far more appealing than Councilor Reyes's." His breath crested across my cheek as he righted himself, an absolutely sinful expression flitting across his face. I could feel the heat rising to my cheeks, and there was little I could do about it.

Judging by the smirk lifting those beautiful, sensual lips, it seemed to please him. "My, my. Your blush is so lovely, Reneah Diaz."

A deep sense of confusion crept down my being. The male had been grieving. Most Fae had difficulty moving on from their bond-mate in the event of their death. It could take centuries before they entertained taking another lover, let alone another mate. But the look in Cathan's eyes seemed to suggest that his mind wasn't on his dead mate. His eyes, eyes that were held firmly on my parted lips, seemed to suggest that his mind was on... me.

And damn if my curiosity didn't get the better of me.

I cleared my throat and glanced away. "Yes, well. If you keep talking to me like that, I'll be a tomato by the end of the evening."

His hearty laugh sent a zing to my heart. "I'd love to see that, so perhaps I'll keep it up."

"Lucky me."

His smile dropped slightly. "In seriousness, though, you look divine. The dress was the perfect pick. I hope this isn't untoward, but I'm having trouble keeping my eyes off you this evening."

Did the King just say that to me?

I was dreaming.

I had to be.

"I... uh... I'm having trouble keeping my eyes off me, too. I mean—you. I'm having trouble keeping my eyes off you."

You bumbling idiot!

Cathan pressed his lips together to suppress his laugh. "Is that so?"

"Yes," I replied a bit breathlessly. *Is it getting hot in here?*

"Well, I feel honored to have those beautiful eyes on me. They're welcome to look anytime."

I might melt into the floor. A tingling sensation spread throughout my core, and my knees went weak when his nostrils flared—his pupils widening through the sea of gold and brown of his irises.

What in the realms is happening?

A light murmur of familiar voices cut through our moment—Cathan's gaze traveling over my shoulder. His expression morphed into one of pure anger. "Fuck."

I turned to see what he was glaring at. Melysah stood a few paces away from Asherah and Draevyn, seething. "Shit."

Aurelio expertly positioned himself close enough to Asherah but kept his distance while Myles scanned the crowd, presumably looking for Cathan.

Cathan's groan vibrated against me. "I'll go and intercept."

I held him back, the firm ridges of his chest digging into the palm of my hand. "Let her fight her own battles. She can handle Melysah, and she'll have to, in any case, if she's going to rule this queendom."

As I watched the drama unfold, Cathan's hand gripped my hip. My gaze slid back to him, his beautiful eyes searching mine. "Thank you," he whispered.

"No need to thank me, Cathan. I'm here for you. And for her."

Before I could get lost in the touch of that hand on my hip or the way he looked at me, I cleared my throat. "I'd better take the Princess back to her quarters, or perhaps take the party elsewhere."

"That's a good idea. But wait," he said as he leaned down and brought his soft lips to my heated cheek, pressing a gentle kiss upon it. "Thank you for the dance."

My lips came so close to his as he pulled away. I grabbed all the strength within and replied, "Thank you."

And as I left the ball with Aurelio, Asherah, and Draevyn, I could still feel his lips on my skin.

RENEAH

CHAPTER 13

I DREAMED OF HIM.

Even in my dreams, I could feel the heat of his body against mine as we danced, his strong arms holding me close. It was the only space for a chambermaid such as myself to experience a King's affections. I awoke the following morning with a smile on my face—the fabric of Neleah's ruby red dress scraping across my skin as I stretched. I'd refused to remove the dress and may have been a little too tipsy to do so. As my eyelids opened, that smile immediately dropped. A familiar figure leaned over my bed.

I gasped. "Mother."

She glared at me in a way I hadn't seen since I was fifteen and snuck back into the house after venturing to Muse for the first time. After that incident, I didn't leave the house for an entire month, save for schooling. She planted her hands firmly on the curves of her hips. "You went to the ball," she said in the exact tone she'd used when I had leapt into the window from that night out on the town so long ago.

I pulled myself up to sit, resting my back against the headboard, and mustered all the courage I possessed to face my mother. She was terrifying when she got like this. "I did."

Mother scanned my dress, now wrinkled with a good night's rest. Her eyes went impossibly wide. "That's Neleah's dress."

"Yes. It is."

"And why, dear daughter, are you wearing it?"

"Because Asherah and Cathan insisted," I told her, my voice and bravery getting smaller by the second.

"That's *Princess* Asherah and *King* Cathan. You are a royal chambermaid and have no business calling them by their first names," she seethed through gritted teeth.

My lips pursed. "What are you even doing here?"

Her dirty blonde eyebrow lifted. "You need to ask that?"

I sighed heavily. "Tobias."

"Yes, Tobias. Good, well-mannered, *always does the right thing*, Tobias," she said, raising her voice an octave. She began pacing beside the bed. "Have you lost your mind, Reneah?"

I fidgeted with a thread on the duvet cover. "I don't see what the issue is. Asherah asked me to go to the ball as her guest. Cathan was grateful for it."

"Don't be cute," she scolded, folding her arms and glaring. "You know, that's not why I made the trip up here this early in the morning."

My brow furrowed. "How did you get in, anyway?"

"This palace was my home for many decades. Its doors will always be open to me. Don't try to deflect the point."

"What point, Mother?"

"What point? What *point*? The point of you dancing with the King. The point of you looking very intimate with him, according to my sources. And mind you, my sources are *always* correct."

"Your sources must be blind. It was just a dance."

She scoffed. "It was just a dance? Reneah, do you think I was born yesterday?" She motioned with a petite arm around the room. "Look at where you are. King Cathan has given you a room in his wing, for the love of the goddess. None of this is normal."

"I never said it was," I said firmly.

"You're being reckless."

"Enough." I threw the covers off and dashed toward the bathroom, hoping it would create some distance between us. "I'll not be scolded like a twelve-year-old."

No such luck. She followed me into the bathing chamber. "Perhaps you need a good scolding," she called through the water closet door.

Couldn't a woman use the toilet in peace?

Again, no such luck.

When I emerged, she was leaning against the long stone sink, waiting for me with her arms tightly crossed over her middle. Her glare cut into me as I washed my hands and began brushing my teeth.

"You're playing with fire."

"I-w ah-w n-ah."

"What?"

I spit out my toothpaste in the stone basin. "I am not." I quickly rinsed my mouth and exited the chamber. "They invited me, and I went. And I had a good time. Thank you for asking."

"You frolicked around the ball like a fool, and now Councilor Velafyn is on your tail."

I whirled to her. "What do you mean?"

Her gaze turned severe. "After making a mockery of her in front of everyone, you didn't think you'd get away with it, did you?"

"How did you hear about that?"

A worried expression grew across her features, so at odds with the anger she held a moment ago. "Everyone heard about that. It's all the palace staff can talk about. Why do you think I'm here?"

I pinched the bridge of my nose. "Holy goddess."

"Yes, holy goddess, indeed. She'll be aiming for you now."

I turned and began straightening the bedding, unable to grasp the situation fully. "I'll handle it," I said.

"That's the thing. You *can't* handle it."

"And why not?"

"Because you're a chambermaid, Reneah!" she yelled. I paused and sat on the bed. A deep feeling of dread spread throughout me at the desperation in her gaze—her worry a tangible thing I felt in my soul. Her shoulders sagged as she huffed out a breath. "I don't want anything to happen to you. She's... she's evil, that female."

"I know, Mother," I breathed.

She padded over to me and dropped onto the bed by my side, her arm coming around my shoulders. "I'm worried," she said with motherly affection I probably didn't deserve.

"I know," I whispered.

"The King certainly has his charms. Don't even try to deny that. Do you remember when you were a little girl, and I used to bring you to work with me? I used to catch you staring at King Cathan's portrait when you thought no one was looking."

I glanced away from her so that she wouldn't see the blush on my face. "Could you blame me? He's handsome."

"A fact that every heterosexual Fae female and human woman with eyes acknowledges. And some of the males, too."

"So, I used to look at his portrait. So what?"

"So, I worry that your infatuation might cloud your brain and that his... behavior toward you might give you false hope."

"What I feel for Cathan is not an infatuation at all."

"Isn't it?"

I sighed. "Mother, it's not. He's handsome. But Cathan has become my... friend."

"Chambermaids cannot be friends with Kings."

"Is that what Neleah would say?"

Mother opened her mouth to speak, but the words wouldn't come out. She blew out a breath. "No. No, she would not say that."

"Then why are you being so... bigoted?"

Mother jerked back. "I'm not bigoted. I'm simply concerned. There's something bigger going on than just balls and palace duties. I can feel it."

I placed my hand on hers. "Mother, nothing is going to happen. Cathan and Asherah—and that's what they've asked me to call them, so don't start—wouldn't let that happen. I've grown close to them, and I care for them deeply. Trust that everything will work out."

She cast me an anxious look before placing her other hand over mine. "All I ask is that you be careful."

"I will be," I promised her, but as Mother departed and I readied for the day ahead, my thoughts were plagued with the future that awaited me now that I'd gone and stirred the pot. Melysah Velafyn was not one to trifle with.

And trifle I did.

RENEAH

CHAPTER 14

MOTHER'S WARNING KEPT REPEATING in my head over and over and over. As much as I hated it, I kept it strictly professional upon seeing Cathan shortly after Mother's departure. I could still feel his gaze on me despite giving all my attention to my cleaning. It turns out that would be our last interaction for a while. His sad smile as he said goodbye before leaving for the Above World was still fresh in my mind. Oh, how I wanted to tell him how much I loved our dance and our time together, how I wanted to let him know that I was feeling... things.

Regardless of those *things*, I desperately needed to remember that he was grieving, that he couldn't possibly be feeling anything for anyone, let alone a human. And not so soon after his bondmate's death.

It was unheard of.

It was why I welcomed the distance between Cathan and me, in order to suppress my emotions. While he was away in the Above World, I continued straightening his room in his absence and checking on Asherah to ensure she had everything she needed. It turns out Melysah was indeed on the warpath. The morning after the ball, I wasn't the only one with an unexpected visitor. I'd welcomed Dax into Asherah's quarters so that they could have a "talk" about her relationship with Draevyn.

"It's horseshit," I told her once he'd left the room. "What she's doing is pure harassment."

"Luckily, she didn't succeed," she said, sipping her *Dirty After Dark Roast* coffee from Fae Flings Bookstore as she sat at the kitchen island. I gifted her a bag and was thrilled she loved it so much. It was just another thing we had in common.

A smirk lifted my lips. "Yes, indeed. You still have your Guardian." I wagged my eyebrows. The deep, scarlet blush that crept across her face had me bellowing with laughter. It was beautiful to see the beginning of... whatever it was between the two of them. Being raised in the Above World, she likely didn't understand what she was feeling for her Guardian. I would have told her, but the poor thing had been inundated with new traditions, terminologies, and a completely different way of life. Best to take these things one step at a time.

Her father would likely want to hear of this development, though. It was a delicate dance between friend and favored chambermaid I attempted with Cathan and Asherah. I didn't want to breach Asherah's trust, but I didn't want to keep anything from him, either. I'd have to do my best to satisfy both intentions.

A few days later, as I was sweeping my rag over the kitchen counter—the pristine shine winking faelights—the front door opened in a flurry. Cathan hurried into his quarters. I paused, unable to move, not knowing how to react when his gaze met mine. "Hello," I said a little breathlessly.

I'd never tire of the gentle smile he gave me. "Hi, Reneah."

"Did you have a nice swim back?"

The door closed behind him with a deafening click. "Yes, no issues at all. I thought I might be late for Asherah's first Queendoms Council, though."

"Not at all," I assured him, placing my cleaner and rag underneath the sink. "I'm heading down to her quarters soon to bring her a heavy coat and make sure she's not freaking out."

Cathan snorted as he plopped down on the plush couch. "Oh, she's freaking out."

"Yes, well. I'll be there to calm her nerves," I said as I hung the dish towel on the oven handle and moved on oddly shaky legs to stand before him.

We took each other in for a long moment, and my pulse began to speed. It was then I realized just how much I'd missed him since the ball, just how much of an impression he'd left on me. Cathan patted the space next to him. "Sit."

I pointed with a thumb in the direction of the kitchen. "Do you want anything to drink?"

"No, I'm good. Sit with me," he said, his gaze imploring.

I slowly lowered myself beside him—his beautiful scaled legs just inches from my clothed ones.

His firm, muscular arm came to rest on the back of the couch, just behind my head, and the gesture kicked up my heart rate. "So," he began. "What's new?"

I huffed out a laugh. "Everything. You've missed quite a bit of drama."

A frown appeared on his face. "What kind of drama?" he asked.

"Melysah."

"Oh, for fuck's sake," he groaned as his head dropped back on the couch—my eyes immediately going to the enticing line of neck, to the stubble that peppered his jaw. "She's insufferable."

"Understatement."

"What did she do now?"

"Well, for starters, Asherah had issued an order at the ball. Melysah wouldn't alert Dax and complain about Draevyn's 'proximity issues,' as she called it. But Melysah found a way around that order and had Kane do her dirty work for her."

"Of course she did."

"So Dax and Asherah met the morning after the ball. She insisted that there wasn't anything going on between them and Draevyn was just doing his duty."

Cathan cast me an amused look. "She doesn't truly believe that, does she?"

"I don't think she knows what she *is* feeling. Remember, she doesn't understand mates and what it means to have one. I think she's just confused."

He rubbed his free hand down his face. "I'm doing an awful job of helping her," he said.

"Well, in fairness, no young woman wants her father explaining mates in detail. That's best left to friends," I said, pointing at myself. "Besides, I'd bet Draevyn's likely breaching the subject. He has to know what she is to him."

Cathan grunted.

I tilted my head at him. "Are you... are you upset at that?"

"No," he replied too quickly.

I poked him in the side teasingly. "Yes, you are. You're upset."

He shifted uncomfortably. "I'm not upset. I just..."

"Just what?"

"I just believe in certain traditions, even though I'm not entitled to them. That's all," he confessed.

"Like?"

"Like asking for permission to court my daughter."

"Ah," I said, nodding in understanding. "So, you're upset that he hasn't approached you?"

Cathan fluttered a hand. "Again, I'm not upset. I'm just bothered. I get it. It's a different day and age and all that. Plus, she's a grown female now. She's likely had plenty of boyfriends I don't know about."

"She has."

He winced. "Don't tell me."

"I won't," I promised, giggling.

His shoulders sagged with a sigh. "I'm sure he'll come to me, eventually." His thumb suddenly brushed the back of my neck, and my skin pebbled. "What else?"

I forgot how to breathe, let alone talk. I cleared my throat. "Well, Melysah also paid a visit to Kristos." His thumb paused as his chiseled jaw clenched. I immediately missed the slight caress. "Despite Dax's directive, she went to him anyway and insisted Kane monitor for anything unusual." I shook my head. "So, I guess he'll be around more frequently."

"I don't like it."

"I don't, either."

"But you'll be able to stay with me?"

I shouldn't have enjoyed the sound of 'stay with me' rolling off his tongue so much. He's supposed to be grieving his dead mate, not looking at me with such longing that it made my heart flip. I shouldn't harbor feelings for him this way.

But I did.

Damn it. I did.

"Kristos advised that I'd stay as your chambermaid per your orders."

"You're no chambermaid to me," he bit out, and I shrunk under the intensity of his gaze.

"But I am," I reminded him in a low voice.

Cathan turned to me, setting his thigh at an angle on the couch—his knee digging into my thigh as he reverently took my hand in his. "I understand what your title is, Reneah. I understand the honor in it, the history of your role, and the one within your family. The Diaz Family is one of the best in all of Atlantis."

"Thank you."

His finger traced over the back of my hand, causing my breath to hitch. "But... when you are here with me, you are the same as any other royal, the same as any other Guardian. You are not beneath me. You are beside me. I'd even go as far as to say you're above me. This is who you are to me. So, please. Do not refer to yourself as a simple chambermaid. You are so much more, both to Asherah and to me."

My throat closed with emotion. "Thank you," I whispered.

Cathan's gaze suddenly searched mine with urgency. "Have dinner with me."

I froze. "What?"

"Have dinner with me this evening. And don't you dare say that you can't or that it's inappropriate. Just say yes."

I *had* been about to say it was inappropriate, but... for once in my life, I wanted to do something just for me and not for Mother, my family, for Kristos, the palace, a Queen, a Princess, or even a King—although it was for his benefit, too, I suppose. I didn't understand what was happening between us, this thing. And my curiosity wouldn't let it rest. So, I said, "Okay."

A smile parted those sensual lips, and his beautiful brown eyes lit with a boyish charm. "Great. That's great. Meet me here around eight. That should leave plenty of time after the Queendoms Council to prepare."

"Shit!" I leapt from the couch. "Asherah. The Queendoms Council."

Cathan stayed where he was with a wry grin emerging. "Yes?"

I rushed into the closet, grabbed the heaviest woolen coat I could find, and emerged a second later. "She needs a coat. I need to meet with her before she departs for the temple. And it would be best if you made your way to meet with the High Priestess as well. You only have twenty minutes."

He rose with patient grace from the couch. "Don't worry. That's plenty of time."

"Don't test fate," I warned, opening the door.

"Reneah?" his soft, melodic voice called. I paused and glanced over my shoulder, meeting his cheeky gaze. "See you this evening," he said with a subtle wink.

I shook my head. "See you this evening." I closed the door behind me and couldn't help but smile.

I breathed a series of short breaths as I beheld myself in the mirror—a woman shifting from foot to foot, wearing the sixth possible outfit for this evening, stared back at me. Keeping in line with my rebellious theme, I chose a long, royal blue strapless dress that held tight to my skin and threw on a jean jacket to conceal my bare shoulders and arms. I thought it looked appropriate for... whatever this was.

"This isn't a date," I murmured for the millionth time that day. I shifted my attention to the pile of clothes on the bed. They ranged from "super chill" to "super rock star" to "super risqué." They perfectly described how muddled my emotions were about all of this. I was all over the place.

I glanced at the clock on the bedroom wall. Only five minutes left. I blew out a breath. "Too late now, Reneah." I gave myself a final look before heading out the door.

I willed my jelly-like legs to carry me to Cathan's quarters at the other end of the hall and knocked on the door.

"Come in," I heard his muffled call.

I sent a prayer up to the goddess and turned the doorknob.

The most amazing smells assaulted my nose when I stepped through the door. Savory with hints of basil and garlic—was that parsley? A current of freshly baked bread—my stomach growled in anticipation.

Cathan stood before the oven, hunched over a pot of steaming yumminess I was dying to try. He glanced over his shoulder. "Hello there," he greeted, that beautiful grin emerging. "Want to try some?"

"If it tastes as good as it smells, I'd be happy to." I strolled over to the kitchen as Cathan held out a spoon with his other hand underneath to keep the substance from dripping onto the floor. When I came to stand before him, I opened my mouth. He placed the spoon on my bottom lip and tipped it until the most delicious sauce graced my tastebuds. Piping hot, a light kick of pepper, hints of tomato, creamy but not too heavy. Herbs that blended so perfectly together. I closed my eyes and moaned. "This is divine." I'd never tasted any sauce so flavorful in my life.

When I opened my eyes, Cathan's gaze held to the movement of my tongue swiping over my bottom lip—a certain hunger causing heat to pool in my lower belly. It drifted over the panes of my neck and lower to the curves of my breasts, just visible through the opening in my jacket, and lower still over my abdomen until the sound of splashing water broke the spell.

"Shit," he exclaimed, dropping the spoon on the counter and immediately turning down the heat on the boiling pasta.

"Need help?" I offered.

He fluttered a hand. "No, no. Just got... distracted."

It was my turn to smirk. "I see."

With the momentary crisis over, he turned to me fully with an almost shy, boyish charm. "You look beautiful, Reneah."

"Thank you," I replied. I noticed his dark hair was shorter on the sides and freshly trimmed but still long on the top. He donned a flare collar with his scales shaped in a sleeveless tunic that revealed just a hint of his muscular, defined chest. "You look handsome. Fresh cut?"

He motioned over himself while shifting from foot to foot—the nervous energy rolling off him. "There's not much a Water Fae can do to get dressed up for a special occasion, but I did my best."

So, this *was* a special occasion.

Noted.

I motioned over myself in return. "I wasn't sure if we were going out or not."

"Oh. Did you want to go out? I just figured—"

"No, no. This is better than going out."

Cathan breathed a small sigh of relief. "Oh, good. Good." Were those nerves I saw across his features? "Wine?" he asked.

"Always."

"Red or white?"

"Red."

"My kind of woman," he murmured in a soft tone. When he heard my breath hitch, he cleared his throat and deftly retrieved two wine glasses from the cupboard—removing the cork with a skill only a seasoned wine drinker could have. Moments later, he handed me a glass—the deep burgundy wine shimmering against the kitchen faelights. "Why don't you make yourself comfortable in the dining room?"

My head gave a slight tilt. "Are you sure you don't need my help?"

"No, truly. It's my pleasure to serve you," he said with a wink as he pulled two plates from the top shelf. "Go on. I'll be there in a moment."

I reached for his wine glass. "At least let me carry the precious cargo."

"Deal," he said.

I carefully padded to the dining room on the other side of the kitchen wall, the soft sounds of jazz sounding through the magicked speakers on a small table on the far end of the room—tunes from the Above World many of the folk in Atlantis enjoyed. The long, oak table gleamed against the dining room lights as I set Cathan's wine glass at the head and placed my jacket on the neighboring chair.

It was a modest table for the Queen's quarters, but then again, it was only intended for those closest to the royal family. Three chairs sat on either side, one at each end of the table. Two more chairs sat against the wall in the rare event of more than eight guests at a time. The windows in this room reached high, providing the perfect view of the palace gardens during the day with all of its beautiful flowers of pinks, and oranges, and blues. The dome constellations winked back at me as I admired the night sky beyond the window.

The sound of plates being set on the dining room table had me spinning around. Cathan pulled out the chair at the head of the table and gestured to it. "Your dinner awaits you." I didn't overlook the act of having me sit at the head of the table—a chambermaid—but I kept that part to myself since he'd likely scold me for voicing it. Tonight, I was his guest, not his chambermaid, but...

'Damn. I did an excellent job making the table shine to perfection,' I thought to myself as I slid into my seat—Cathan pushing me closer to the table with ease.

"Be right back," he said, exiting the room. A moment later, he reemerged with the bottle of wine, silverware, and hunter-green cloth napkins, setting them in their perfect place before taking the seat beside me. I regarded him in pure amusement as he took such pride in ensuring everything was in order. It only made him all the more attractive—this King, who can cook and serve with precision and pride. Satisfied that everything was in its place, he looked at me then—that beautiful smile kicking up the corner of his lips. "May the goddess bless this meal."

"Indeed, may she bless this deliciously crafted meal."

Wasting no time welcoming the first bite of vodka sauce and pasta into my mouth, I observed him then. There was an undercurrent of nervousness I couldn't quite place. As I tried desperately not to leave any sauce on my face, I wondered why this male, who was so typically confident and put together, fidgeted in his seat, risking the occasional glances my way. All those thoughts were dashed aside when all the herbs and spices hit their mark. By the third or fourth bite, I elicited a moan. "Who knew my King could cook?"

Cathan gave me a pleased smile. "You like it?"

"No, no. I don't like it. I *love* it. Where in the world did you learn to cook like this?"

"Nonna Maria. A kind, Italian woman. She was our neighbor in the Above World who took pity on a stay-at-home dad and taught me everything she knew."

"Goddess bless her."

"She *did* bless her with a long, long life. She passed away a few years ago," he informed me, his gaze distantly sad.

"I'm sorry to hear that," I told him sincerely. "That must have been difficult."

He nodded as he swallowed a mouthful of pasta and brushed his mouth with his napkin. "She was a lifeline for me. As you can imagine, being mostly alone up there with Neleah, tending to her duties wasn't easy. Nonna Maria was fantastic company. I consider myself lucky." The corner of his mouth twitched up in a grin. "So, tell me, Reneah. If you weren't a chambermaid, what would be your dream job?"

My finger traced the rim of my wine glass. "A designer."

His eyes popped wide. "Really? I could have sworn you would say Head of Staff, like Kristos."

"Yes, that's a logical assumption, given my family's history."

"Does Aurelio know?"

"Yes, he knows. And..." I had to be careful—so very careful. Revealing this to Cathan might propel my career in a direction I couldn't come back from, but I... wanted to tell him. "He's offered me an apprenticeship."

Cathan reached for my hand, gently patting it before pulling it away. I didn't look too closely at the thrill his touch sent through me. "That's wonderful, Reneah."

"I-I haven't accepted," I told him, with a huff of a laugh. "Not entirely, anyway. I promised I'd study with him as long as I'm still assigned to the Royal quarters."

Judging by the smile that lifted those breathtaking lips, that was the wrong thing to say. "Then, you must pursue it; Royal quarter duties be damned. If you find inspiration in something, that's the goddess talking."

I slowly sipped my wine, wondering if asking for details regarding his relationship with Neleah was appropriate.

The corner of his mouth twitched. "What did you want to ask?"

My brow furrowed. "How can you tell I wanted to ask something?"

"You have a twinkle in your eyes that tells me so."

"I'm not twinkling."

He laughed heartily as he grabbed his wine—his plate nearly empty. "Ask me anything, Reneah. I'm an open book to you."

That comment sent comfort through me, knowing he trusted me the way he did. I gathered my final few noodles with my fork and asked, "Was it difficult to deny your elemental calling to raise Asherah on your own in the Above World? Without Neleah there?"

Something like pain flickered across his features. "I won't lie to you. Yes, it was difficult for so many reasons. The least of it was denying my calling, longing for it. Being a somewhat single dad had its challenges. And I don't mean that in the "poor male has to raise a child on his own." That part I did gladly. Being a father is one of the greatest honors of my life. And Asherah is a remarkable daughter. But Neleah and I... We were..." A shadow came across his face. Whatever he had to say had to be the source of some kind of pain, as evidenced by the far-off look in his eyes.

I set my fork on the now empty plate. "I'm sorry. You don't have to—"

"No, I... I want to. I've never told anyone about this." He glanced up, and the pure, pained expression marred his handsome face, slicing deep into my soul. "You would be the very first person I've ever told. Not even Dax knows."

I felt a crease emerge on my dipped brow. "Surely you know you can tell me anything."

For a moment, his beautiful brown eyes hung on me. Thinking. Agonizing. His shoulders suddenly sagged, like the fight had gone right out of him. "I know. I wasn't expecting to divulge this over a meal, but I've realized there's no good way to reveal this. And I fear what I'm about to say will sound wild. Irrational even." His expression grew grave. "It can ruin everything. For me. For Asherah."

Tension climbed down my spine. "I won't breathe a word," I promised.

His head dipped in a nod, as if deciding. "What do you know of a *Tanama* bond, Reneah?"

The question raised the hairs on the back of my neck. "It's the butterfly bond."

"And you know what it means when mates are cursed with it?" he asked, his hands clenching on top of the table where they lay.

"I know that the bond is short-lived, just like the life of a butterfly, because one of the mates will meet an untimely death. It's solely a bond of duty and honor to the goddess, but cursed by Maboya. The feelings and memories of the dead mate are suppressed, and the curse compels the living mate to bond again quickly. But potential mates avoid them like the plague, fearing their bond will also be cursed."

"Everyone is so damned superstitious," he threw out defensively. In truth, I understood his reaction. The *Tanama* tale was one we'd learned of early in life, a Fae folklore passed down by generations of Atlantians, both human and Fae. The bond was an ancient magic named after the ancient Atlantian word for butterfly. It's a bond born of necessity and duty to the goddess, not of love. And it guaranteed a certain death for one of the mates, in a mission for the goddess. When one of the first *Tanama* mates dies, they forget their mate and are immediately called to another.

It was the tale of the broken mate.

Millennia ago, a couple presented themselves before the goddess. When a wave failed to crest during the ceremony, the high priestesses already knew what they were, having been told by Atabey in a vision. But when Maboya, the Great Evil Spirit and former lover of the Goddess Atabey, learned of this special bond and mission to defeat him, he lured the couple into a trap and cursed their bond forever. As sure as the dome sun rises, one of the bondmate's lives was cut short.

Because of Maboya's curse, the living mate knew he'd be drawn to another, and his feelings toward his dead mate became muted. Forgotten. It drove him to madness. It was just as Maboya had intended. Everyone loathed the mate left behind for moving on so soon. Hated him even. The broken mate became a pariah in society. Maboya wanted those who were called for a mission to the goddess to be cursed, for the descendants to be cursed. Despised. And because the longing, the need for his next mate, consumed him, he eventually died of a broken heart at the refusal of the bond.

It is said those with the *Tanama* bond were cursed with it forever. No one wanted to risk mating with someone with a *Tanama* bond, or anyone in their family, for that matter.

It was a bond of death.

But Cathan was right. We wouldn't know if the *Tanama* bond was hereditary or if it was simply bad luck...

Because no one has ever mated with someone who'd be cursed with a *Tanama* bond.

"But... you and Neleah didn't... couldn't—"

"The Bohiti Semaya created the wave during the ceremony," he confessed.

The tips of my fingers rose to my open mouth. "Oh my goddess."

Cathan closed his eyes on the tail end of a wince. "I know."

"I'm sorry. I just don't understand. You and Neleah loved each other."

"Very much. Despite Neleah feeling called by the goddess, it turns out *Tanama* mates can experience a bond of love," he quipped.

My mind raced with all the possibilities of what this could mean for him, what it could mean for Asherah, especially with everything developing with her Guardian. "And of your feelings for Neleah now? Please tell me that's not true."

His throat worked on a swallow. "Muted," he whispered.

My mind couldn't fathom what he must be feeling. I instinctively reached for his arm, giving it a gentle squeeze. "There's no way—not in this realm or the next—that I would ever let you forget about Neleah. And neither will Asherah. She was too good of a soul and meant too much to my family for her to slip away from your consciousness. The countless memories you have as a family, those treasures will be Asherah's to remind you. You can always rely on us to remind you of that, to remind you of who she was at her core, regardless of your muted feelings."

When Cathan's pained gaze landed on mine, something *clicked*. A growing sense of dread grew in my gut, something my human heart wasn't entirely prepared for. I slowly pulled my hand away. If the part of the tale about muted feelings was true, then the other part was as well.

Cathan would likely feel called to another.

To a Fae.

Goddess. Why did the thought of that happening feel so *wrong*?

I closed my eyes to fight the rising tide of embarrassment. Of course, thinking this male was interested in anything more than friendship with me was silly. He'd be called to solidify the bond with a Fae and may have already felt compelled to. My lids slowly opened. "And of the other part of the tale?" I ventured to ask, straightening the skirt of my dress.

His chair screeched against the floor as he rose to stand at my side. He crouched down, bringing himself eye-level with my gaze. "The next part doesn't make any sense, Reneah. None whatsoever." He reached for my hand, taking it in his large one. "I have felt the call."

"You have?"

"Yes, I have."

"She must be a really lucky female."

"I haven't been called to a female."

My eyebrow rose to my hairline at that. "Male, then?"

His soft chuckle had my body easing a bit. "No, not a male. A woman. A human woman."

I drew in a shallow gasp. "That's impossible."

"But it is," he said, dropping his scales to his abdomen and placing my hand above his hollow bond. "For weeks, I've been feeling drawn to you in a way that's inexplicable. I..." he shook his head, "I don't understand it. Can't make sense of it. We're not supposed to mate with humans."

"Because we're just that. Just humans."

"You're not *just* anything, Reneah. Not to me."

"Cathan—"

Before I could utter any more denials, lips as soft as a fallen rose petal and as puffy as a drifting cloud on a warm summer day moved against mine so slowly, so reverently, that I nearly became faint with want. What was this magic? What was this... feeling? I could barely place it, but I knew within my warring heart I was losing a battle I couldn't win. And didn't want to. I grasped his forearms, bracketing my head, holding on for dear life as my toes curled in my sandals. His soft, warm tongue slipped over mine like a slow caress.

When the feeling of him hit an unbearable peak, I moaned in his mouth with desperate need. "Cathan."

He pulled back and gazed at me with hooded eyes. "Goddess. The way you say my name, the way it falls so beautifully from those mesmerizing lips."

The spell broke, and I closed my eyes, my forehead coming to rest against his. I hated myself for the words about to leave my lips, especially after he'd poured out his heart to me, but it couldn't be helped. "This is all... this is all too much. I think I need space," I breathed out.

My meaning immediately hit him. Cathan drew back, his gaze traveling over my face, before dipping his head in a defeated nod and rising from the floor to full height. "Of course," he whispered resolutely.

The sudden urge to escape overwhelmed me. I rose and gathered my jacket before coming to stand before him. "Thank you," I said, my voice seductive even to my ears.

The longing in Cathan's gaze held me captive. "You never need to thank me." Suddenly, he wrapped his arms around me, and I sank into his embrace. I wanted to bottle up the warmth of him. I was a puddle of desire and confusion. I turned out of his hold and fled for the door, refusing to look behind me. But his pleading voice stopped me in my tracks. "Reneah?" I reluctantly glanced over my shoulder, his soft expression slicing through my willpower to leave. "It is I who should be thanking you."

"For what?"

"For helping me remember what it feels like to be alive again."

And, of course, my traitorous heart leapt at that. I wheeled around to the door before I could do anything stupid. My thoughts assaulted me, and I was crippled beneath them as I practically ran down the hallway. I was just a human. A human. What was happening? I entered my quarters with my nerves firing at all ends, but I paused within the entryway. A fresh bouquet of ruby red roses in a crystal vase sat on the kitchen counter. Carefully, I plucked out the note, scanning the handwritten note, my walls immediately falling:

My Dearest Reneah,

If this evening went as planned, then I've told you something near and dear to my heart. I pray that whatever you decide, we'll still remain close. I couldn't bear to lose you. I couldn't bear losing my friend.

~Your King

CATHAN

CHAPTER 15

I TAPPED A FINGER on my tablet for the hundredth time in a minute, attempting to review the notes I'd jotted down during my last meeting with the human delegation. I'd read the same paragraph three times now and the one before one more than that. My thoughts were heavy with a particular human woman, the way her lips felt against mine, the way something clicked in place.

And yet, didn't.

I shifted in my seat to adjust to the growing ache in my cock, which had been a constant companion since Reneah left that evening.

Time.

She needed time.

And who could blame her? I'd bared my entire soul, every inch of the secret I'd been hiding at her feet. None of it made any sense to me. I doubt it made any sense to her.

That is why I welcomed the meeting with the human delegation despite hating all the previous ones. It gave Reneah the time she needed, the space. I could give her that, even though there was a building ache from missing her.

A beep sounded from the hotel door, jarring me from my thoughts.

Dax entered, his eyes immediately finding me where I sat on the couch of our two-bedroom suite. We hadn't had much time to chat since our arrival to the Above World; swimming through the ocean's dark depths, with the Akani growing traction amongst the Fae, always kept us vigilant. We couldn't afford casual conversation with tensions on the rise. Once we had arrived, I reluctantly entered my meeting while he stayed guard outside the posh hotel meeting doors—a meeting filled with the thickest kind of tension one could imagine. Theories about whether we were telling the truth, threats about exposing the Fae to the humans in the Above World, large sums of money offered to save an entire country over the next. Some of the filthiest, most disgusting things transpired during the human delegation meetings. In truth, it was no better than the council meetings in Atlantis, with Melysah's faction splitting the council down the middle. When I emerged from the human delegation meeting, bone-dead and exhausted, Dax left for the gym, leaving me to rest.

Now, as he returned from what was clearly a grueling workout with his clothes drenched in sweat and his face blotched in red patches so stark against his cream skin, there was a hint of some-thing in his eyes I couldn't quite determine. Surprise? Judgment? It had been Dax I entrusted with the task of delivering the roses to Reneah's room as she and I were dining that evening. Given that he was so close to both Neleah and me, it was a risk. Normally, there was nothing that I couldn't tell my best friend, who was more like my brother. But this secret? This shame? I shouldn't tell him. Yet, I'd been considering it, given that I'd pulled him into my mess.

My *Tanama* bond mess.

Dax dipped down into the armchair across from me as his blond eyebrow arched, not even mustering the energy to ask. I already knew his question.

I exhaled slowly. "I care for her."

He gave me a brisk nod. "Yup. I gathered that."

"I know what you're going to say," I told him, casting him a look short of an eye roll.

His knowing eyes scanned me. "Do you?"

"Yes, it's too soon after Neleah's passing, and she's a human."

Dax settled back in his chair, somehow making it look smaller than it was with his massive size. "Can you blame me?"

It was on the tip of my tongue, the truth of it. I traced a scale on my knee with my pointer finger. "I can't blame you, but then again, you don't know the whole story."

A shrug. "So, enlighten me."

"I'm afraid the answer will come off as a bit of a shock."

"I've been around a long time, Cathan. There's very little that shocks me anymore."

I blew out a steady breath, forcing those two words past my lips. "*Tanama* bond."

Apparently, there was still something that could cause a shock for Dax based on the way his eyes widened—his pupils shrinking to a pinpoint within his cobalt blue eyes. "That's a load of bullshit, Cathan. We would have known the night you and Neleah bonded."

"We may have had some help from a certain priestess in creating an illusion and keeping it secret."

Dax froze, a flutter of uncertainty cresting across his face. "Tell me everything. And don't you dare leave anything out."

And so I did.

I confessed everything to my best friend, a friend who, over the centuries, had become closer to Neleah and me than any other being on the planet. I told him how I'd been a mate but wasn't, how we were basically mates on borrowed time. My once roaring feelings for Neleah, which had brought me to my knees with how I felt about her, were muted, as if they didn't exist at all. How, if the legend was true, I didn't have much time left on this earth. And, more importantly, how my *Tanama* bond was calling to a human woman I couldn't solidify it with.

A pure tragedy all around.

Dax rubbed the stubble of his chin as he gazed off in the distance. "How did I not know?"

"You couldn't have."

He sighed heavily. "I am so sorry, brother."

"You don't have to apologize."

"But I do. I came back from the gym, blowing off so much steam that I practically broke a few of those human machines, wanting to judge you for moving on so soon, wanting to tell you a dozen things for having me prance around the palace with roses. I'm ashamed I felt that way without knowing the truth."

I fluttered a hand in the air. "Think nothing of it." Dax's mouth opened several times as if trying to form words. I arched an eyebrow. "Yes? Spit it out."

"I'm sorry. I know all of this must be very hard for you, and I empathize with your plight. Forgive me for adding to it, but have you thought of what this might mean for Reneah?"

I glanced out the floor-to-ceiling window with a furrowed brow. "You mean with her position in the palace?"

"Of course."

"Goddess," I admonished myself. "I'd been so consumed with the bond, with the feelings raging within me, that I'd been an ass for not thinking of what this meant for her."

Dax's expression softened. "Reneah's family's role is a prestigious one. The idea of feeling a bonding call to a human is unheard of, but if you two decide to cross this line, she'd be risking it all. For you."

In truth, I barely understood what a relationship between Reneah would do to those around us if it were ever discovered. Reneah took a lot of pride in her work; that much I knew for sure. But given what she divulged about her passion for design, I had to wonder whether she was happy with her role or if she was doing it out of obligation to her family. Either way, I didn't want to jeopardize what she ultimately chose for herself. I shook my head. "I hadn't given it as much thought as it deserves."

"You should. Her family has held that palace role for centuries. You need to ask yourself exactly how much she means to you because if you continue this and it doesn't work out? It'll be too late. Her family's role will be stripped and given to another family, and they'll be homeless."

"I wouldn't let that happen."

Dax winced. "And Asherah? What's she going to say about all of this?"

I shook my head. "Explaining the *Tanama* bond to her, it will break her heart—for her mother, for the possibility of her own bond being different. Trying to explain how I'm being drawn to a human she's grown close to will be even harder."

"Is Reneah worth it?"

"Yes," I answered immediately. I thought about our time together thus far, the way she smiled, the way she took care of not only me, but of Asherah. "She's worth it. And there's very little I can do, given that the bond is pushing me toward her every second of the day. I can't help it, Dax. You know how it works."

He held his meaty palms up in surrender. "Forgive me. I have no idea what it's like to be mated, even with a cursed bond. You have my full support, brother. Whatever you need, whatever secrets you want held under guard, I'm here for you."

My shoulders sagged. "Thank you."

"And speaking of secrets, that's the reason I'm here."

"Oh?" I asked with a lift of my eyebrow.

"Of course, if this isn't the right time—"

"No, no. Please. I welcome the distraction."

Dax ran his hand through the long locks of his blond hair with a sigh. "I was training Asherah in the training center, and something... odd happened."

I sat a little straighter at that. "Like what?"

Dax shook his head, his expression of awe intriguing my interest. "I'd never seen anything like it, Cathan. She... she stopped the flow of water." He provided every detail of the event. Asherah didn't fully understand because she didn't know it wasn't common.

My brow furrowed. "But that's impossible. No Water Fae has the ability to stop the flow of water."

"That's what I said, but there I was watching her do it. I told her I'd let you know, but I think it best not to tell anyone until we understand why it happened."

I rubbed the stubble on my chin. "Yes, I think you're right. What do you make of it?"

He huffed a laugh. "I have not a damn clue. It's clearly... something. The goddess doesn't give gifts like that to anyone."

My mind raced with the possibilities. "Is Asherah okay?"

Dax beamed like the proud instructor I knew he was. "More than okay. She's fantastic. A complete natural and a fast learner. She'll do splendidly."

Pride coursed through my veins. "I know she will."

With that, Dax left the room to shower. Asherah stopped the flow of water, and I didn't know what to make of it. I didn't know what to make of Reneah Diaz, either. I let loose a sigh. Dax's warning about Reneah's position weighed heavily on my mind. It was no wonder she fled from my quarters as she did. Was she debating whether to risk it all?

I wanted to know.

Needed to know.

Reneah

CHAPTER 16

W ITH CATHAN ONCE AGAIN in the Above World and Asherah with Draevyn visiting the Fotuto outpost, I found myself in Aurelio's workshop, nervously presenting some of my designs for one of the wealthy Fae planning an extended vacation to Greece. He immediately sat me down and ordered me to sketch a collection.

Three of them.

I'd never been so excited to actually put my designs to use. Someone would actually wear the clothing of my creation. Elation immediately coursed through me at the thought.

"I spy with my little eye someone who is holding a secret."

I paused in my sketching and gave Aurelio a side-eye. "What secrets do you think I'm holding?" I replied, curious.

Aurelio set down the violet silk garment he'd been sewing with a smug smile. "My sources tell me that a certain blond Guardian was spotted carrying roses to Cathan's floor. Now, unless some miracle has happened and Dax is now into males—something gay males all over Atlantis would rejoice in, mind you—it could only mean they were intended for the only other occupant on that floor."

So, that's how Cathan got the roses to my quarters. I tried to school my face of mock fascination. "You know, Dax and Cathan have been spending a lot of time together. I think they'd make a lovely couple."

"I'd bet," he continued, "that if I were to go up to *your* quarters, I would find those roses in your room."

"Oh?" I replied, the corner of my traitorous mouth twitching.

"Spill it."

"There's nothing to spill," I said. I was on shaky territory with this subject. When I glanced up from my notebook, he cocked his eyebrow at me. I sighed and dropped my charcoal pencil on the table. "Dax isn't courting me."

"So, what was he doing bringing roses to the royal wing?"

I promised I wouldn't tell anyone, but I desperately needed to confess how I was feeling inside. This wasn't just Cathan's secret anymore. This was... bigger. If I could tell anyone, Aurelio would be the one I would trust. "He was bringing them on behalf of someone else."

"Oooh!" He placed his elbow on the table and propped his chin in his palm. "Is it another Guardian?"

I twisted the pencil between my fingers as my lips tipped up in a smile. "Technically, yes. He's a Guardian."

Aurelio tapped his lips in thought. "But I haven't seen you with a Guardian. If one *were* courting you, I'd have seen him ask you to dance at the ball. Come to think of it, the only person you danced with at the ball was the King, and technically, he *is* a Guardian, but he wouldn't entertain a lover, not so soon after his mate's death."

"Not unless his bond was... *different*," I provided.

Aurelio paused, his amber eyes widening and his spine straightening. He let loose a long, dramatic gasp. "Holy sh—"

"What you have likely deduced is correct."

"But... you're a human."

"Keep your voice down," I hissed, my eyes flicking to the open door of his workshop, knowing anyone could overhear.

Coming to the same conclusion, Aurelio leapt from his chair, closed the door, and wheeled around to me. "I want every detail."

I winced in anticipation. "You have to promise this will stay between us. Seriously, Aurelio. If this gets out, it can be very, very bad."

Aurelio blinked. "I never keep anything from Myles."

"Try. Please. Because what I'm about to tell you could ruin Cathan. It could ruin Asherah. And me."

Aurelio nodded and slid back into his seat across from me. "Does he have a *Tanama* bond?"

"Yes," I said, my heart aching as I pushed the confession past my lips, "but there lies the confusion because, as you can tell," I waved a hand from my head to my toes, "I'm human. We don't know how this is possible."

His amber eyed gaze was fixed on my every word. "If anyone were to find out, they would crucify poor Cathan. And you."

I swallowed past the lump in my throat. "And Asherah."

"I take it your move into the royal wing wasn't of a professional nature."

"Well, it was, initially. For me, anyway."

"But?"

"But..." my shoulder lifted in a shrug, "I started feeling drawn to him for some reason, even though he'd just lost his mate. My guilt nearly consumed me whole. It still consumes me. It's not right."

Aurelio cast me a look of pure empathy. "It's the *Tanama* bond, Rennie. I'm not judging you one bit. There's little you can do about it when it calls the cursed mate to his next one."

I shook my head. "But I'm not a Fae."

"The goddess must be up to something," he mused, tapping his chin in thought.

"I... I don't know how this happened. I just know that I'm in deep."

"Just how deep are you in?" he asked with a wag of his eyebrows.

I threw a sewing chalk at his head, which he deftly caught. "Be serious, Aurelio. Not deep like that. He just... kissed me."

He gasped, bringing his hand to his throat. "My dear little Reneah, you kissed a King!"

"Keep your voice down," I hissed, "or the whole palace will know, and I'll be deemed the next Scarlet May, and our family will be out on the streets."

"Then you can come to live with Myles and me."

I snorted. "We'll be banned from the palace. Plus, I'm sure Myles wouldn't appreciate it."

"Quit trying to avoid the deets, my apprentice."

"I'm not trying to avoid the deets, and I'm not your apprentice."

He fluttered a hand, his bangles clanking. "Semantics. Now spill."

And so, I told Aurelio everything, from the moment I started feeling something for Cathan to his request that I move into the royal wing, our dance, the night he informed me of the *Tanama* bond.

The kiss.

When I finished, Aurelio stared at me, gooey-eyed. "This is like a real-life fairy tale."

"I suppose it would be if the entire thing weren't dripping with scandal and a cursed bond. For starters, I'm a chambermaid with a family lineage to uphold. And secondly, there's the small little fact that I'm a human."

"Well, you'll be a chambermaid for as long as you deny the apprenticeship. So, that little fact doesn't matter. And the other? Yes, you're human, but the goddess, in her divine wisdom, *must* be up to something."

I blew out a breath. "I'm just a temporary human distraction for him."

Aurelio cast me an admonishing look. "Rennie, I've known the King all of my life. He's an honorable male. If he's drawn to you, there's nothing you can do about it. Enjoy it."

I shook my head. "I don't know how we'll keep what we feel for each other a secret from the world."

Aurelio cocked his head. "You care for him."

"Deeply. I... I think he's an incredibly easy male to fall for. And I shouldn't," I scoffed. "I'm nothing but some human side piece that can never bond with him."

Aurelio rose and came around the worktable, crouching at my side as he took my hand. "Reneah, you are such a magnificent being. I won't have you talk poorly of yourself. You are one of the greatest palace leaders of all time. I'd dare say, even greater than your mother."

"You'd better pray she never hears you say that."

He tsked and continued. "It's the truth. Your heart is so big. You're a fierce friend, one I'm proud to call mine. You care about everyone even when they don't deserve it, and your staff loves you for it. You even put your duty to your family before your own desires and before everything you want in your life. We may not understand why this is happening, but take this moment for you. Enjoy it."

"What if everyone finds out about his bond?"

He cocked a brow. "Have you all agreed to go public?"

"We haven't talked since that night."

His head dipped in a nod. "Then we'll cross that bridge when we get to it." His eyes held a certain seriousness I'd never seen in my friend's gaze before as he said, "You don't have to have all the answers. You just need to live for today."

Aurelio was right, of course. I didn't have to have all the answers, and I'd never dared to just… live. I wasn't sure who this Reneah was, and while it was entirely uncomfortable, I wanted to explore who she was without the expectations placed on her. And didn't that just make the decision easy? I nodded in resolution. "Okay. Live in the moment."

Aurelio's beautiful, show-stopping smile emerged. "That's my apprentice."

I gave him my best dramatic eye roll. "I'm not your apprentice."

"You are. And I expect you here daily to give me all the details of your romance." His brow furrowed. "It's times like these that I wish I were a writer. This would make a really fantastic book."

I couldn't suppress my laugh. It *was* like a romance. Right there in Aurelio's workshop, I vowed to let it sweep me away.

Broken bond be damned.

Reneah

CHAPTER 17

THINKING IT BEST TO keep myself occupied in my King's absence, I spent a few days at Mother's townhouse in Borike'n. I filled those days full of distractions, which included my training duties here in the palace for all new staff members and my regular check-ins with my team to ensure everything was running smoothly. I welcomed the perfect distraction that kept me from thinking about his kiss. His soft, full lips and how they felt against mine flashed in my mind and occupied my days. I was *still* thinking about it as I strode down the hallway to his quarters after finding the note on my floor upon my return. Hopefully, the note hadn't been there long.

I lightly knocked on the door and entered when Cathan summoned me. His beautiful smile nearly knocked the wind from my lungs, and I couldn't help but return it.

"Hi," I murmured.

Cathan stepped toward me—slowly, gracefully, keeping his eyes on my form the entire time. I didn't know how he made me feel like a goddess, even in my unflattering uniform, but here I was, wanting to remove every layer to feel the press of his skin against mine—wondering what it would feel like. I remained stock still as he cupped my face, studying me with a steady gaze. "I thought I'd never see you again."

I rested my hand against his forearm. "Oh, I don't scare that easily, my King."

Cathan chuckled lightly as he brushed his hands up and down my arms. "Are you okay?"

Guilt immediately reared its head from the pit of my stomach. Perhaps I'd put a little too much distance between us, given everything he'd revealed. "Of course. I just... needed time."

He nodded after a beat. "Of course."

"I... uh... got your letter."

Cathan threaded his hand through mine, the act causing heat to pool in my lower belly. "Sit with me."

On unsteady legs—which seemed to be the norm around this male—I joined him on the couch as he turned to me, never letting go of my hand. His gaze dropped to where our fingers were intertwined, his mouth opening and closing a few times. Whatever he had to say couldn't be pleasant. Fear traveled through my body as he said, "It's okay if you don't want any part of this. The bond. Me. Asherah finding out. The realms finding out. It's a lot. And... I'll make do. I understand."

I jerked back. "Understand?"

"That you'd rather not pursue," he motioned between us with his free hand, "whatever this is. I understand."

I felt my eyebrow arch. "Did I say I didn't want to pursue this?"

His shoulders lifted in the most ungraceful shrug. "I mean, no. But you have a lot at risk. Your position. Your family. I'd only considered my feelings and this strange pull I have to you." His fingers carefully lifted my chin. "I've been selfish. For that, I must apologize."

I snorted. "You have not."

"But I have. I didn't consider what you'd be risking."

"In all fairness, it is me who makes that decision. It's me who has to ponder the consequences."

"And have you?" he asked with a careful look.

I blew out a long breath. "I have." There was so much a stake. My job. Our home. My friendship with Asherah. My mother's wrath. The realms finding out about his bond.

My heart.

I refused to give voice to those things at such a tender moment.

Cathan reached up and cupped my cheek and I leaned into his warmth, closing my eyes as I succumbed to it. "And you're willing to take the risk?"

It was a question that I'd asked endlessly in my head. While I thought I had an answer one minute, I'd change it the next. But as the weeks pressed on, there was only one answer now.

"Yes," I whispered.

The look of relief and pure joy that flitted across his face was everything. Cathan brought his mouth within an inch of mine, and my breath caught—our lips nearly touching. His minty breath crested softly against my skin, eliciting a growing ache in my core. "We're in this together, you and I. I'm grateful to have you by my side as I overcome the challenges of this cursed bond. You honor me, Reneah. And I plan to honor you in equal measure." Cathan swallowed my gasp as his lips finally reached mine—his arms wrapping around my middle, causing me to sag into his embrace. I was wholly consumed as his tongue rolled with mine like gentle waves upon The Shingu. I never wanted it to end.

But Cathan suddenly pulled back in alarm. "Shit. I hear Asherah coming," he whispered in a hiss, leaping from the couch in a flourish.

Thank the goddess for Fae hearing.

The front door suddenly flew open, and Asherah rushed into the room. Her shoulders sagged in relief when she saw me sitting on the couch. "Oh good! You're both here. I need help."

I immediately rose to my feet, praying to the goddess that my tender lips didn't give anything away. "Whatever you need."

"What's going on?" Cathan asked.

Asherah ran her fingers through her dark hair. "There's a hurricane about to hit our home in the Above World."

Cathan's face softened in understanding. "I see. And you want to...?"

Asherah huffed and threw her hands in the air. "I want to help, of course."

Cathan placed his hands on his hips, looking as fatherly as I'd ever seen him. "Sher Bear, I understand you want to go to the Above World and help, but you could be risking a lot of questions from our neighbors and friends."

She looked at him incredulously. "Do they not deserve an explanation?"

"You cannot tell them of your mother's passing."

Her blue eyes widened. "They don't know that Mom passed?"

Cathan shook his head. "They can't know."

"Why?"

"It's too soon."

"What do you mean, too soon?"

"Asherah, just trust me, huh?"

Asherah let loose a frustrated sigh. "Fine. So, they can't know about Mom. Can we at least help them? We won't mention anything."

Cathan's eyebrow rose. "We?"

Asherah stood a little straighter as she answered, "Yes. We. Draevyn is coming with me to help."

The corner of Cathan's mouth twitched. "Is he now?"

Father and daughter glared at each other with somewhat eerily similar expressions. Before a battle ensued, I gently intervened in the most Reneah way possible. "I think it's wonderful he's going with her, my King."

Cathan's attention swiftly wheeled in my direction at the use of the formality—a deep crease forming on his brow. I threw him an imploring glance, knowing that it was best to treat him like the King he was in front of his daughter.

"So? Can I get some help?" Asherah asked, drawing our gazes.

Cathan sighed heavily. "Of course. We'll need to find Myles. He's always the best at organizing aid."

Asherah happily skipped backward toward the door with a smile on her face. "I'm already on it. I'll run down to his quarters. Meet you there?"

"Yes, we'll be there in a minute," Cathan assured her, and she was gone a second later.

"She's going to make a fine Queen," I remarked, my gaze held to the door where she disappeared. My heart swelled witnessing her passion and care for helping the Above World humans, something so rare in Atlantis.

"That she is."

I returned my attention to Cathan as he closed the distance between us, snaking his arms around my waist. "What is this 'my King' business in front of Asherah?"

With my finger, I lightly brushed against a scale on his chest. "I think it's best if we stick to the formalities in front of her."

He pressed his lips against my cheek, traveling to my jaw as he said, "She wouldn't mind if you called me Cathan." His lips brushed against my ear, causing my skin to pebble. "And the only time I want to hear 'my King' fall from your lips is when I have you crying out in ecstasy."

"Goddess," I whispered.

"Yes, you are," he said, taking me in an intoxicating kiss that left me weak in the knees. He drew back, looking his fill. "I wish you could come with me."

"Go with you, where?" I asked, slightly dazed.

"To the Above World."

I sighed. "How I wish I could."

His thumb brushed over my cheekbone as a smirk emerged. "Wishes do come true, you know?"

"Clearly, not *all* wishes."

He chuckled. "We'll see." His smile suddenly fell. "I feel like I just got home."

"That's because you did just get home."

He let loose a sigh. "I want to stay."

"But you need to go."

"I know."

I pushed him toward the door. "Go help Asherah. I'll pack your things and meet you in Myles' quarters."

As he exited, he cast an endearing glance over his shoulder. "What would I do without you?"

I shook my head, refusing to answer him.

As I began setting out his clothes, I knew that one day, he'd find out exactly what he'd do without me. If I were a Fae and we were properly mated, and that bond turned out to be yet another *Tanama* bond, the curse would ensure one of us would perish. But a death bond wasn't necessary. As a human, only one of us would leave this realm.

My death was inevitable.

CATHAN

CHAPTER 18

WALKING THROUGH THE FRONT door was like coming home to an old friend—the hinges creaking a little from the years of saltwater abuse from the neighboring canal. The home still smelled of Neleah, still held all the same decor. I half expected to find her sitting at the kitchen table going over paperwork, which had been her norm whenever she was here.

However, as Dax and I entered the living room, a whole other smell infiltrated the space. It was the faint scent of the male currently making the moves on my daughter. And damn that goddess, if he was truly her mate, there was little I could do about it. That didn't mean I could make him sweat.

Just a little, of course.

"Well, doesn't this look fun?" Dax chided, glancing at them over my shoulder.

Draevyn sprung from the couch like something bit his ass, bowing. "Regent."

"Draevyn," I drawled in amusement. "How nice to see you here. Alone. With my daughter."

"Dad," Asherah scolded in a tone very reminiscent of her mother, pinching the bridge of her nose.

And being the father I was, I planned to have as much fun at her expense as I could.

I know—cruel faery.

I fluttered a hand. "I get it, Sher. You're a grown woman. Etcetera, etcetera." My gaze returned to Draevyn. "I'm not about to tell you how to do your job or that she's still in a shitload of peril."

"I understand, Your Highness."

"Good. The other Guardians are on their way."

Asherah looked absolutely appalled. "Like, right now?"

I jerked back dramatically. "You didn't think we'd have our future Queen up here with just one Guardian, did you?" I may or may not have gone a step further than usual in hopes that I could entice Draevyn to hang with his Guardian buddies and drive a wedge into the speed at which these two stars appeared to be colliding.

"The Blue Fin is an amazing establishment," Dax's muffled voice called, scanning the interior of the refrigerator. "Fine food. Fantastic music coming out of those speakie thingies. Ah." Dax's face lit with pure joy as he cracked open a Fizzy Finny IPA, taking a long gulp. "And *delightful* refreshments." His brow furrowed, casting me a questioning gaze. "How come you never brought us any of these? They're fantastic."

"Because a beer run for the Guardians wasn't exactly a top priority," I murmured.

Asherah let loose a sigh and rose from the couch. "I better get to bed. I'm going surfing in the morning."

"Then, I best be off to bed as well," Draevyn announced.

I folded my arms, watching which direction Draevyn intended to go.

"I'll show you to the guest room," Asherah finally directed, breaking the tension.

"Or the man cave with the other Guardians," I suggested.

Asherah scowled. "That's downstairs."

I nodded. "Yup. And Dax is sleeping on the couch, so you'll be well protected."

"No. Draevyn stays near me." She glanced at Dax. "Not that I don't trust you or anything. No offense."

Dax raised his beer. "None taken."

Traitor.

"I feel more comfortable with Draevyn," she pleaded, and there was little I could do when she gave me the puppy-dog eyes. "It's not like he's sleeping in my room. He'll be in the room next door."

I sighed in defeat. "Fine. Okay. You still good on the couch?" I asked Dax, who seemed to be nearing the end of his first beer in the span of a minute.

"Of course," he replied with a knowing grin.

"Good night, Dad. Dax," Asherah said swiftly as they disappeared down the hallway.

Dax dropped into Draevyn's vacated seat and found his favorite toy: the TV remote. Short whistles and the clash of helmets blared from the football game on the television mounted on the wall as I grabbed a beer of my own and joined him.

"You're going to give poor Draevyn a heart attack."

"Fae can't have heart attacks," I said dryly.

"If they could, he would have one by now. You know you can do nothing about it if they are what we suspect?"

I groaned. "Yes," I grumbled, taking a swig of my beer.

Dax leaned closer. "Does Asherah suspect anything between you and Reneah?" he asked in a low voice.

"No. And I'd like to keep it that way for now."

His brow furrowed. "Until when?"

"What?"

"Until when? You can't expect to keep your bond a secret from her forever," he whispered in a hiss.

How did I explain to my own daughter that I was forgetting her mother? That the once fierce passion I'd held for Neleah seemed non-existent? That the bond was driving me mad to mate with a human who couldn't complete the bond? That I was falling for her friend? I ran my fingers through my hair, an uncomfortable feeling crawling down my spine. A deep sense of selfishness settled in my gut. Asherah finding out about Reneah would cause a riff between them, between us. "I don't know what to do."

"Well, it might be time to think about it, Cathan," he mused with a chastising expression. "This whole thing is going to blow up in your face."

"Thank you for the ominous warning," I said in a low, weary tone.

He shrugged. "I'm just trying to look out for you."

I cast him an apologetic look. "I know, buddy. It's just... When I'm with Reneah, I'm the happiest I've been in a long while, regardless of the bond. And I know it sounds terrible." My brow lowered in a furrow. "Those last couple of decades with Neleah, they were challenging for us. We knew what was about to happen. I could feel Neleah distancing herself from me, never from Asherah, of course. Just me. Perhaps it was in an effort to lessen the blow, but it made me sad, nonetheless. Reneah, she makes me truly smile again. She makes me *feel* again."

"Don't think I don't want those things for you, Cathan," Dax assured me. "I do. I just want you to think of the consequences because if you don't confess to Asherah about your little human and the *Tanama* bond, things are bound to unfold in a bad way. You'll need to be there for Reneah, and you need to be prepared for what you'll say to your daughter. They've become close. I'd venture a bet that Reneah wouldn't feel comfortable keeping secrets from her friend."

I rubbed a hand down my face. "You're right."

Dax emptied his can and placed it on the coffee table. "Have you... you know?" he asked, waggling his eyebrows.

The corner of my mouth lifted in a smirk. "No, you scandalmonger."

"I don't know how you're managing. Your little human has a nice—"

"Finish that sentence, and you'll sleep on the dock tonight."

"And she's so tiny, too. I imagine she'd be perfect for lift—"

I punched him in the leg, even as my cock twitched with the thought. "Enough."

Dax flashed me an innocent look. "What? I'm just stating the obvious."

I shook my head and finished off my beer. "Want another?"

"A punch? Or a beer?"

"The first depends on you talking about my woman like that again."

"I'll take a beer, then."

"Wise decision."

As I ventured to the kitchen to grab a couple more Fizzy Finnys, I realized it was the first time I'd called Reneah my woman.

And the bond hummed within me.

RENEAH

CHAPTER 19

THE MUSIC PUMPED IN a slow beat from the jukebox sitting in the corner of Sinkers—the cold bite of the frosty pint glass numbing the tips of my fingers as I stared at the frothy bubbles of my brew. I heard Gina let loose a long sigh across from me in the dark booth tucked away in the corner where we couldn't be bothered.

"Won't you tell us what's going on?" she implored.

"She probably can't tell us, Gina," Millie hissed. "Not if it's about who we *think* this is about."

"Is that true, Rennie? Is this…" she began, leaning forward with a hopeful glint in her chestnut-colored eyes, "is this about the King?" she asked in a whisper.

I couldn't hold back my wince before looking around the room—my gaze snagging on a pair of beady eyes coming from a burly Fae sitting at the bar. His glare didn't look friendly in the least, causing me to shift my attention back to my friends. "You know I can't tell you."

"See? Told you," Millie admonished.

I sighed heavily. "I wish that I could."

"But you look so sad. Did he hurt you? Because, King or not, I'll cut his balls off," Gina threatened.

"That is not only treasonous but blasphemous," Millie scolded. "Thou shall not touch the royal balls."

"I think it's a little too late for poor Rennie."

I grimaced. "I didn't touch his balls."

Gina's brow lifted. "But you touched something? Tell me you did."

"Gina, you're being ridiculous," Millie hissed. "She's probably preoccupied with having to help the poor male grieve his dead mate, not having a tryst as you're implying."

I decided not to answer and took a long sip of my amber beer, the cold biting my throat in its descent as I remembered Cathan's soft lips against mine, feeling wholly unworthy of them. In Cathan's absence, my thoughts were heavy with the idea that if it weren't for some stupid cursed bond, he'd likely not even look in my direction, probably wouldn't have noticed me at all.

And didn't that make me feel inadequate?

In addition to those really awful feelings, it had been a few long, long weeks without him. I... missed him. How I longed to kiss those lips again. How I wished I could scream from the rooftops of Borike'n just how much I cared for Cathan. But I couldn't. No one could find out about his bond. No one would understand how the memories of his dead mate were fading or how he was being called to a human.

Being called to me.

Beyond feeling desperately and wonderfully attracted to him, I hadn't felt what the Fae did when they called to their mate. There was no tingling sensation on the left side of my chest, as was typical for mates. But goddess, my need for him, the longing for him to take my body, devoured me.

"Oh, by the looks on that face, I just may be right," Gina remarked, the corner of her lips lifting.

Millie gave a dramatic roll of the eyes. "For the goddess's sake, Gina. Not everyone is a horny toad like you. We shouldn't imply such things in public and especially not in your lover's bar."

I glanced over my shoulder once again and the same burly Fae had his eyes fixed on us... once again. I swallowed a good gulp of my beer to stifle the panic rising within me.

Gina's face brightened as something caught her eye in the distance. "Speaking of lovers..."

Jimani, the owner of Sinkers, cut through the Fae's line of sight as he strode over to our booth with a tray of freshly poured beers, the liquid spilling over the rim of the closest pint glass as he set the tray on the table. "You ladies look like you could use another round," he said.

"Perceptive as always, babe," Gina complimented with a bat of her lashes.

Jimani smiled warmly at her, placing a pint in front of each of us. "It's my job to observe the mood of my patrons. This one is on the house."

"You don't have to do that," I told him.

"I insist," he said with a kind smile, and I could see why Gina was enamored by the male. He was pretty handsome.

I shifted in my seat. "Uh... Jimani. Mind if I ask a question?"

His facial expression betrayed his surprise and interest. "Of course."

I flicked my head toward the bar. "Who's the big, burly Fae at the bar throwing eye daggers our way?"

Jimani's brow dipped in a furrow as he briefly glanced over his shoulder. "Oh. That there would be Froryn."

"And just why is he looking at us like we've offended him?" I asked, my eyebrow lifted in an arch.

He let out a heavy sigh and leaned against the table, bringing him lower for our ears only. "He's an Akani sympathizer. He's been here a few times, toeing the line with his disparaging comments. If he keeps it up, he'll no longer be welcomed in my bar. I won't tolerate that type of shit in here." He realized the table held on his every word with a growing fear in their eyes. "Not to worry, ladies. Nothing will happen to you while you're here. Even if one of our trusted patrons walks you home, we'll make sure you're safe," he said, putting us immediately at ease. He glanced at Gina with a smooth smirk and pinched her chin affectionately. "Enjoy, ladies."

"See you later?" Gina asked, as he was about to turn away.

"I'm counting on it," he said with a wink before leaving us to our drinks.

Gina sighed with a wistful look I fully understood. It brought a rare smile to my face, one I hadn't felt like wearing since leaving Cathan's quarters at his request. "You've got it bad."

"That she does," Millie murmured into her pint.

Gina playfully slapped her arm. "Oh, stop. I can't help it."

"I think it's wonderful," I said.

"Thank you, Rennie. Now, stop avoiding the reason we're here."

My shoulders sank. "You've been asking me for three weeks, and my answer is just the same. Everything's fine."

This was the line I'd stuck to like a mantra. How I wished I could tell my best friends about everything. They'd been persistently asking for a while now.

Millie threw me a dubious look. "You're going to need to lie a little better than that. You've been moping around King Cathan's floor in his absence with the most wistful look, while cleaning every inch like a woman possessed."

She wasn't lying. His quarters were entirely spotless. I'd even decided to stay with my mother in Borike'n for the company, the longing for him becoming too much. Did he miss me? It's a question I couldn't give voice to—a question I've asked repeatedly, but only to myself. The devastation of the bond wasn't the only reason I refused to tell Millie and Gina. The last thing I wanted was to subject them to any possible disciplinary action if Kristos somehow learned that they knew something was going on. I loved them far too much for that. But... oh! How I truly wanted to divulge everything to them. Everything was so overwhelming, and while I had Aurelio, I wanted their perspective as humans. My bottom lip wobbled, and I attempted to hide it as I took a sip from my pint.

Gina reached out and patted my other arm, resting on the table. "I know you can't tell us, but forget the details. We don't need them. Truly. The only thing we care about is if you're alright."

"What can we do to help?" Millie asked, the concern tangible on her face.

I gave them the best grin I could conjure. "You're already doing it. Beers at Sinkers do wonders."

"Maybe you could use a night out on the town," Millie suggested, her face brightening. "Why don't you go with Aurelio to Muse tomorrow night? He has all the connections. You could even take the Princess with you. I've heard she's a bit mopey as well."

Gina's eyes widened. "Oh, yes! That sounds like a great idea!"

I winced. "I can't. I have a shift the following morning."

Millie waved a hand. "We'll cover for you."

"For sure," Gina assured, vigorously nodding her head. "You never take any time off. And it's been ages since you've been to Muse."

She did have a point. Despite my love for dancing, I gave up going to clubs a while ago. Maybe it was the thing I needed, the perfect distraction. "I suppose I could ask Aurelio."

"That's the spirit!" Gina beamed.

"Let's make a declaration here and now," Millie said as she raised her beer. "To letting that shit go."

"Yes, let that shit go," Gina echoed, her beer waiting patiently in the air for mine.

I raised my glass because perhaps I needed a distraction. "To letting that shit go."

The clink of our glasses echoed like a signal to the world.

Reneah Diaz was about to let loose.

"Come in!" Aurelio called beyond the front door of his workshop.

I whisked into the room with a smile I felt on my cheeks. "Greetings, Accomplice."

Aurelio paused in his sewing and glanced up with an arched brow. "Accomplice? Whatever for?"

I braced my hands on the wooden worktable and leaned in. "We're going to Muse."

He gasped. "To Muse?" his brow furrowed. "Did someone put something in your Dirty After Dark Roast this morning?"

I rolled my eyes. "No. I'm just feeling... spontaneous."

"Spontaneous, huh?" he asked with an all-knowing smirk.

I blew out a measured breath. "Look, it's been a rough few weeks. I need a good distraction, and I felt Muse and some time with my friends would be the best remedy—unless you're not up for it."

He threw his needle on the silk burgundy garment he was sewing. "Oh, I'm always up for it."

I dipped my head in a single nod. "Good, because we're sneaking the Princess out of the palace to go with us."

A mischievous gleam sparked in his amber eyes as he rubbed his hands together. "This is getting better by the minute."

"She's been moping around," I told him as I cast an indifferent glance around the room, my gaze snagging on a pretty floral-patterned fabric with interest. "I think it's time for her to get out a bit. She needs a night out on the town just as much as I do."

"I agree. I grow tired of seeing her so solemn," he said, leaning back in his chair. "So, what's the plan?"

"I've obtained Braeliah's help. She'll be waiting in the moat at the side of the palace. I packed a dress in anticipation of this evening's festivities. If it's okay to get ready at your place, we'll head there now, and I'll get dressed."

Aurelio leapt from his chair. "Of course."

"There's just one small issue," I began as I followed in his wake.

He came to a halt and swiveled around with a furrowed brow. "And that is?"

"Kane Ruema," I winced.

Aurelio scowled. "Why is he a problem?"

"He's guarding Asherah's quarters."

"I thought Mayana was on duty?"

"Mayana's gone into heat."

Aurelio brought his hand to his collarbone. "Oh dear. Poor Mayana. Her nether regions must be sucking everything dry."

I snorted. "We'll need to come up with a distraction. Some way to lure him away from her quarters. Any ideas?"

Aurelio pursed his lips in thought for a few fleeting moments until his face brightened. He moved to the other side of the room and opened a tall cabinet, the clanking of tiny jars echoing around the room as he moved the items about. "Aha!" He returned to his worktable, wiggling a tiny bottle in the air for me to see. "We'll give him a little incentive to go to the toilet."

My expression slid into an amused frown. "But how's he going to eat it?"

"Easy," he said as he pulled open a drawer hidden in his worktable and fetched a cookie tin.

Not just any cookie tin.

Madam Malei's Double Rich Chocolate Chip Cookies. They were the best in all the realms. Just looking at the fancy tin made my mouth water. "I don't think Kane is worth those cookies."

His eyebrow arched, casting me a pointed look. "Do you want to sneak out to Muse or not?"

Ugh! But the sugary goodness was so good. I let loose a defeated sigh. "Fine."

With a wicked smile, he poured a few drops onto two cookies and pulled out a third. "While you're getting ready, I'll walk down Asherah's hallway like I'm looking for Myles while eating my delicious cookie. I'll offer him the rest. Kane will be shitting his pants within minutes. I'll hurry back when the coast is clear."

Without another word, I hurried to his quarters to prepare for the evening while he went to play his part. I had just finished applying my lip gloss when he rushed into the room. "He's gone. You need to fetch the Princess. Ooh! Don't we look like a scandalous little vixen?"

I straightened out my purple sequin dress. "I will take that as the compliment I intended to land."

"Well, hurry along as fast as you can!" he warned with a shooing gesture.

Without a moment to lose, I rushed to Asherah's floor and knocked on the door, rushing into the room. "You better get your ass off that chair if you want to escape that asshole Guardian and have a little fun tonight."

RENEAH

CHAPTER 20

I SHOOK MY HEAD with a fleeting smile on my face as my heels crunched on the cobblestone path leading to our townhome, my aching feet screaming at me for abusing them in the heels I'd opted for that matched perfectly with my sparkling dress. The evening was a complete success. I hadn't danced like that in so long. I didn't have a care in the world out on the dance floor. I hadn't thought about the looming threat of the Akani. I hadn't thought once about Cathan or how much I missed him. It was only when I noticed Draevyn slinking in from the front of Muse, wrapping his arms around Asherah in the most loving way, that my heart ached anew. What I wouldn't give to have Cathan's arms wrapped around me again.

I reached the front steps of our home and lifted the potted plant to the right of the door, where the spare key lay hidden. I was so distracted by the weight of the damn thing—my arms straining to lift it an inch—that I hadn't noticed the figure peeking out of the alleyway next to our home. "Reneah," a male voice whispered.

I jerked up wide-eyed as I beheld the cloaked figure before me, his face hidden in shadow. He reached for his hood and held it back slightly to reveal his beautiful face, a face I had missed so much. My shoulders dropped a bit. "You scared me," I whispered in a hiss.

"Sorry, I just got back. I had to see you," he said softly.

With a quick glance behind me to ensure none of my nosy family members stood by the bay window observing me, I disappeared into the alleyway with Cathan. My heartbeat raced as he slid his arms around my waist and buried his head in the crook of my neck, inhaling deeply. "Goddess, I've missed you so much. Being away from you has been agony."

His admission warmed my soul. He drew back and cupped my face, and I couldn't help but lean into his palm. I swallowed past my emotions. "I've missed you too."

"You weren't in my quarters or yours when I returned," he said, an edge of vulnerability creeping into his tone. "Millie said I would find you here."

A wince of guilt betrayed my feelings. "I was lonely."

"Ah. Understandable." He bit his delicious lower lip before asking, "Will you... be coming back?"

The corner of my mouth twitched. "What's in it for me?"

"Oh, Reneah," he began, his mouth coming within an inch of mine. "You have no idea how much I plan to show you what's in it for you."

Cathan captured my gasp of surprise with a kiss. Those soft, alluring lips consumed me, lips I'd thought of non-stop since he left for the Above World. My hands came to grip his cloak, the rough wool biting into my hands. I took my time relishing in the feel of his tongue slipping around mine and couldn't help the moan that escaped me when he pulled me tighter into him—his hardening length digging into my belly.

Cathan pulled back, his breathing erratic as his hungry gaze swept over me. "What exactly are you wearing?"

"Something appropriate for a foam party at Muse," I told him, flashing him an amused grin.

A deep groan emitted from his throat. "You look ravishing. Your skin—I want to lick every inch." He brought his lips down to mine again in the most possessive kiss—one I felt all the way down to my toes—before pivoting me and gently backing me up against the wall. I became wanton with need. I gripped his beautiful wavy locks between my fingers as his hands came under my thighs, lifting me with an ease that left me breathless. I instantly wrapped my legs around his waist, my hips moving on reflex against his rock-hard length. It parted the folds of my aching heat through the wool cloak pressed in between us. His lips dropped to my neck, peppering soft kisses down to my collarbone. "Mmm, I think someone is just as needy for me as I am for her."

"Yes," I breathed shamelessly, bucking against him.

"And how should I reward such a lovely response from such a lovely lady who is greedy for my touch?"

My hand dropped on top of his and guided it under the hem of my dress, right over my bare mound, causing him to groan. "Fuck. Are you not wearing any underwear, baby?"

"I didn't feel the need," I breathed against his lips.

His fingers parted my folds, gathering the wetness on the tips of his fingers. "So wet. Tell me, Reneah. Were you thinking of me out there on the dance floor when you were grinding up on someone else who wasn't me?" His delicious thumb swirled around my throbbing clit, causing my hips to thrust against him.

I gripped his cloak to steady myself and issued my response. "Yes."

Two fingers deftly entered my tight opening as he began to slowly thrust them in sync with his thumb, driving me to absolute madness.

"And was it only me you thought about as you shook that sweet, plump ass to the beat of the music?"

"You're all I ever think about," I confessed against my better judgment.

Cathan breathed out a sigh against my neck before placing a gentle kiss on my damp skin. "Then the feeling is mutual because I can't stop thinking about how much I want you in my life, even though I don't deserve you."

My need built as I shamelessly rode his hand. I moved to cup his face. "You deserve the world, Cathan," I rasped in a wanton voice I didn't recognize was my own.

His lips captured mine, drinking in every possible inch of me. "Come for me, baby. I want to feel you shudder against my fingers," he commanded.

And for my King, I'd do anything.

My hips bucked against his hand, my need building to an almost unbearable ache, and as my release finally crested, I threw my head back against the wall as he captured my moan between his lush lips. I couldn't hold him tight enough to me, and I never wanted to let him go. How dangerous was this game I was playing?

Lethal.

Because it was destined to be discovered, to tear our futures apart.

And I didn't care.

I couldn't bring myself to care.

Cathan ever so slowly slid his fingers from my heat and brought his fingers to his mouth, his tongue swirling around the evidence of my desire. "I will go to sleep every night dreaming of this moment," he said, his gaze laden with evident need. "And the way you taste."

I rested my head back on the wall, observing him, my vision blurring. The emotions I worked so hard to suppress bubbled over and broke the passionate moment between us.

He rested his hand against my cheek. "Why are you crying?"

"I know the reality of what you're going through, with your feelings for Neleah suppressed by that damn cursed bond. I can't help thinking... what if... what if you didn't have it? Would you even look at me? Want me?"

"Reneah—"

"It's true though, Cathan. You'd be grieving long after I'd left the earth. I wouldn't even be a passing thought in your mind."

A pained expression flitted across his face. "I can't ponder on the what-ifs, baby. I can't. This is the reality of my life, of this bond. This is the reality of my feelings for you. Yes, this cursed bond is inexplicably drawing me to you, but it doesn't feel like a curse when it calls me to someone who's become my friend, someone whose beauty leaves me intoxicated, someone I'm beginning to feel I can't live without."

"And yet, you'll have to live without me."

"And yet, I'll have to live without you," he repeated in confirmation.

I slumped in his hold. "This is all madness, but..."

"But?"

"I can't help the way I feel."

"How do you feel, baby?"

I sighed before dropping my legs from around his waist to the cobblestone street, shaking my head, and refusing him an answer.

He brushed my hair behind my ear. "You're not going to make this easy for me, are you?"

"I lack the will to resist you for anything you ask of me. Sounds pretty easy to me."

He let loose a light laugh. "You make it sound so bad."

"It will be extraordinary until the bottom falls from underneath our feet."

The tips of his fingers came underneath my chin, lifting my head to meet his imploring gaze. "It won't, Reneah. Please stop saying that. Please come back to the palace."

I couldn't help but brush my fingers across his chest, still covered in a cloak. How I wished there wasn't any clothing between us now. And how grateful I was that there was clothing between us. "I'll be in my quarters in the morning."

"I don't want you to move back into the spare quarters. I want you to stay with me. Stay with me, Reneah," he pleaded, his gaze boring into mine.

I tried to grasp his words and make sense of what he was proposing. "I couldn't."

"Why not?"

My eyebrow arched. "Have you met my mother? She'll have my ass."

"I'll have that ass." I playfully smacked his arm with a sigh, causing him to lean in and nip my lobe in retaliation. I melted into his embrace anew. "We'll keep your quarters open, but I want you in mine when you're there." His soft, warm lips pressed against the skin of my neck, my desire building yet again. "Why don't we go to the park for play night?" he asked.

"How can I say no to my favorite night at the park?"

Cathan leaned back, his face brightening with a hope that squeezed my heart. "Meet me at dusk?"

"Fine," I said, giggling in defeat. "I'll see you at the park at dusk."

His thumb brushed against my lower lip. "I'm so happy I got to see you. If only for a little while."

A flush of adoration rose on my cheeks. "I'm happy I got to see you too, my King."

Cathan gave me one more delicious, unforgettable kiss before he left me in the alleyway, the shadows of the street swallowing him whole as he disappeared into the night. I gathered myself momentarily, shifting my skirt a little lower, so I didn't look completely disheveled emerging from the alley. With all the remaining strength I could muster, I finally lifted that damn potted plant and retrieved the key, delighted to find that it still opened the front door.

But as I stepped through the doorway, my breath left me. Mother sat on the sofa with an accusatory expression cresting across her face, her arms crossed fiercely against her chest. "You're digging yourself into a hole you cannot escape, Reneah Diaz."

"Good Evening, Mother. What are you doing up so late?" I asked, closing the door behind me.

"I should be asking you the same question, but it turns out I don't need to. I can deduce exactly what you've been up to by the look on your face and the cloaked Fae male strolling back to the palace as we speak."

I'd debated getting my own place ages ago. That idea seemed very appealing as I faced my mother's wrath. I pinched the bridge of my nose. "I'm going to bed."

She rose from the couch. "The hell you are. We're going to talk about this. Now."

"Actually, we're not."

Mother tilted her head with a sneer, placing her hands on the curves of her hips. "Is that so? And just who do you think you are, talking to your mother that way, huh? The Queen? I have news for you."

I gave her my back as I headed for the stairs. "Can't wait to hear it," I murmured.

"You are *not* the Queen. You're a chambermaid, Reneah Diaz. And you have no business messing around with a King, let alone someone who just lost his mate."

It was absolutely amazing how Mother could make me feel like I was twelve again in the blink of an eye, even though she could never, in her wildest dreams, imagine what was happening between me and Cathan. "Mother, I appreciate your opinion, but it's unwarranted," I said, ascending the stairs to escape the conversation, knowing there was very little I could reveal to her about Cathan's bond.

"I don't care if you feel it's unwarranted. You're traipsing around town like some modern-day Scarlett May," Mother seethed, clearly not accepting my exit as dismissal. The padding of her feet in my wake set my nerves off. "You're embarrassing yourself if you think for one second that a male like that would be interested in you."

That gave me pause. I turned to her. "Why?" I dared to ask.

Mother's knuckles went white as she gripped the banister. "What do you mean, *why*?"

"Why do you think someone like that wouldn't be interested in me?"

I hated the look of pity that crested across her features. "Oh, Reneah. Please don't tell me you're falling for him."

A ball of apprehension filled in my stomach. "I just want to know why I'm not good enough. It can't be just because I'm a chambermaid."

Mother breached another step, that look of pity deepening. "Reneah, you'll never be good enough for him. You're fooling yourself if you think you are anything like Queen Neleah. She was a phenomenal female who was loved by all."

"I know this. I loved her as well," I bit out.

"Which is why you know deep down in your heart that Cathan could never love you more than he loved her. You're nothing but a passing ship that caught a breeze in the wrong direction, setting up space on a dock that's reserved for only one ship. He's playing with you, perhaps seeking out companionship of the flesh, but you'll never have his heart. That will always be Neleah's to have."

My vision blurred. "Are you done?"

Her eyebrow curved. "Are you?"

"With this conversation, yes. Goodnight, Mother," I said, turning in a desperate ascent for my bedroom door.

"If you continue on like this, know that you'll bring dishonor to our doorstep, and it will be entirely your fault," she called up the stairwell as I slammed my door behind me like they could dispel the truth of her words.

But not even a door could dispel them, their weight settling deep into my weeping heart.

RENEAH

CHAPTER 21

OU'LL NEVER BE GOOD *enough for him.*

As my feet carried me across the soft grass of Temple Park to meet Cathan, Mother's words kept replaying in my mind. I paused and searched the crowded park, my cloak tickling my ankles as a random wind moved it about. I gripped Cathan's missive with its specific instructions in my hand within my pocket. When I found the second willow to the right of the stage, I strode in its direction—my lips lifting in a slight smile. Plays in the park were a popular Atlantian activity. The vast space was packed with hundreds of friends and lovers alike, lying on blankets while sharing food, wine, and laughter. This was my favorite thing to do, and it was the norm to attend even if I didn't have anyone to go with, which is why when Cathan asked me to go with him, I couldn't refuse for selfish reasons of my own. It would be nice to go with someone else who enjoyed it as much as I did.

As I approached the majestic willow tree, the crowd began to sparse. I squinted in the darkness just beyond the green leaves that hung like a drape and found the male within, resting on top of a burgundy checkered blanket with his arms casually resting on bent knees and peaking through the opening of his cloak. I wheeled around, admiring the appeal of the second tree to the right of the stage. It was far enough up on a hill, which provided the perfect view of the play. I twisted back to him. "Secret spot?" I asked with a smirk.

Cathan's smile sent butterflies aflight through my stomach. "Actually, yes. I used to venture here when I was younger. It's been some time since I've visited. I'm glad to see the space wasn't occupied."

I moved forward and felt the telltale signs of a carefully crafted glamour surrounding me. I gingerly lowered myself next to him, his arm brushing against mine as I mimicked his position. "Hello."

Cathan's gaze roamed my face as he murmured, "Hello." He leaned in, bringing his lips to mine in a tender kiss. When he drew back, I couldn't help but smile at how relaxed he was, how happy. "Thank you... for meeting me here," he said.

"You don't have to thank me. I love play night at the park."

The corner of his mouth twitched. "Oh? Come here often, then?"

"Yes, actually. But I'm usually on the other side of the park. It's my go-to spot," I told him, flicking my wrist. "Creature of habit and all that. It's nice to see the play from this side." I glanced up at the canopy surrounding us. "I never thought this would be an ideal place."

He followed my gaze. "Yes, well. It's the perfect spot for a little privacy amongst the crowd." Ever so slowly, our gazes fell on each other again, and I became lost in the golden flecks amongst the swirls of brown in his eyes. Cathan reached for the tie at the top of my cloak and pulled it, the wool cloth falling in a heap around my hips. His attention moved over me, a hint of lust beginning to bloom in his gaze, stealing my breath. "You look lovely this evening."

I straightened my favorite lavender silk cardigan, which covered my spaghetti-strap chemise and long flowy skirt—a diversion from the Atlantian jumpers so many of the humans wore. "Um, thank you."

"You don't sound convinced," he said amusedly.

In truth, he wasn't wrong. I wasn't convinced. My mother's voice and her insistence that I was nothing to him kept playing on repeat in my mind. I gave a one-shoulder shrug. "It's nothing special."

A deep furrow emerged on his brow. "Well, you *do* look lovely."

My lips twitched into a reluctant smirk. "Is that so?"

"And beautiful."

I picked at a stray thread from the blanket. "You don't need to say that."

Cathan jerked back slightly. "What's gotten into you?"

I shook my head. "It's nothing."

"I'm not buying it. Tell me."

I debated the merits of confessing what happened between Mother and me to him. I didn't want to tarnish her reputation, having him think ill of her, but I didn't want to keep anything from him, either. I blew out a long sigh. "My mother... She... she saw you last night."

Understanding dawned on his face. "Ah, I see. And I take it she had some... opinions to share?"

I gave a very unladylike snort. "Yes. She did."

"Well, she must have been very effective with her word daggers if you're this down about it."

"I don't know if it's worth repeating."

The faelights around the park began to dim as the shuffling of feet sounded from behind the curtain. My breath hitched as his finger trailed down my neck. "It's obviously bothering you. Tell me. Please."

"She doesn't think I'm good enough for you," I blurted out, giving him a mock smile. "See? Not something worth repeating." I returned my attention to the stage as the actors for the opening scene of West Side Story took their places, ironically one of my favorite plays, despite the feeling that I was living in some fucked up version of it, with Cathan on the Jets and me on the Sharks.

I gasped as I was lifted from the ground and placed in the cradle of Cathan's thighs, his breath drifting across the shell of my ear. "Don't you dare waste another second listening to someone who doesn't have a clue about me and just how much I care about you," he breathed against my ear. "I think you're more than enough. You are perfect."

"But I'm nothing compared to Neleah."

Cathan eased me further into his lap, turning me toward his stoic face, leaving me breathless. "You're going to need to stop saying that."

"I'm only relaying what she told me. She's right, though. Neleah, she was—"

"I know who she was better than anyone." He cupped my face. "Why is there a need to compare? We can be respectful of my dead mate's importance to me and still respect *your* importance to me at the same time. It doesn't need to be one or the other." He scoffed, shaking his head. "I can't believe she said that to you. No one, and I mean no one, has the right to say such things to you. Only you and I know what there truly is between us. So, forget what she thinks. Let's just be us, okay?"

I nodded and pressed my lips to his. How could I deny him anything after that revelation? "Of course. I'm sorry."

"No need to apologize, except for missing the opening scene," he teased, tapping my nose. He settled me between his legs, and I leaned back into his welcoming embrace as we watched the story unfold before us.

It wasn't long before we reached the crescendo of Maria and Tony's tragic end to their forbidden romance. With the play over and the murmurs of people filing out of the park, reaching our quiet little cove of hanging leaves, I moved to get up, but Cathan held me in his arms. "Stay for a bit."

I cast him a questioning look. "Just what are you up to?"

I felt his glamour thickening over the spot where we lay as he grinned mischievously, his pearly white teeth gleaming in the darkness. "I'm not ready for this night to end just yet."

My eyebrow lifted. "Oh? And just what did you have in mind?"

"Perhaps it's better if I show you." Cathan brought his lips to mine, gently at first—his mouth slowly melding with mine, the warm slide of our tongues moving in a slow, sensual dance. It suddenly turned desperate, needy as he threaded his fingers through my hair. A faint feeling made my head light as he devoured me with his kiss. A tingling sensation spread throughout my body when he lifted me to straddle his lap—his thick erection bulging beneath his scales. I rolled my hips, desperate for the feel of him. He winced against my lips and growled lowly. "Goddess divine. The way you move drives me absolutely mad. I need to have you. Taste you. May I taste you, Reneah? Can I bring you absolute pleasure?"

His words left my mind muddled and clouded. I barely managed to get the next word past my lips. "Yes," I breathed.

With a strength that left me breathless, Cathan twisted me to lay me on the blanket, his wicked eyes scanning down my body.

Every muscle under his gaze tensed with anticipation. He ever so slowly leaned down and brought his soft lips to the base of my neck, peppering a trail of slight kisses to my breast—slowing those kisses to the point of reverence. Desire burned hotter in my throbbing core as he took the peak of my hardening nipple into his mouth through the fabric of my chemise, soaking it through. In a tiny fit of frustration, he pushed the chemise up and pulled my lace bra aside to suck my nipple fully into his mouth. My back arched as he swirled that delicious tongue in a torturous motion that fired every neuron in my core. Without missing a single beat, he moved to my other breast, giving my other nipple as much attention as he did the first. My breaths left me in a needy hitch, my fingers trailing over his cloak at his back. "I want to feel your skin, Cathan."

He quickly rose and stripped out of his cloak, his scales dropping to the 'v' of his lower abdomen. He reached for my cardigan and slid it off my shoulders, pulling my chemise over my head with the same desperation gleaming in his heated gaze. I was on fire everywhere for him, desperate with need, aching for him. Cathan undid the front clasp of my lace bra with ease and paused as his gaze roamed over my bare upper body. I nearly melted when he bit that luscious lip. "Goddess above. You are absolutely captivating." He ever so slowly took my bare breasts in his strong hands, gripping them with need. "I wish I could lick these all evening, but there are other parts of your exquisite body that need my attention." My breath hitched as he reached for the top of my skirt, pulling the stretchy material down my legs and discarding it in a heap of piling clothes. I lay under the willow, completely bare for this male holding me under some wicked spell that had me carelessly risking everything to be with him.

I couldn't bring myself to stop. "Part your beautiful legs for me," he commanded.

With my chest pumping in expectation, I slowly parted myself for his viewing pleasure. Cathan bit down on his knuckle, his gaze held on my sex, before declaring, "How I've been dying to taste you."

And then Cathan Rosahan devoured me.

He brought his mouth down to me, his tongue diving between my slick folds till he reached the sensitive nub, aching and ready for him. My head tipped back, and my mouth dropped open—his name falling from my lips, spurring him on as he masterfully licked me with eager anticipation. I brushed my fingers through the hair at the nape of his neck, desperate to hold on to him, desperate to touch him as the tip of his warm tongue swirled repeatedly over my tender clit in a mind-blowing rhythm.

Cathan breached my heat with one thick finger, thrusting with maddening precision as a second finger joined the first. My thighs came to clench around his head, my release rising to meet this incredible moment. My hips began pumping against his mouth, and my legs began to tremble—the sensations becoming too much all at once. "Cathan, I'm—"

My inevitable climax sent a fuse within him, the hum against my center sending me over the edge. I came with a heady moan that I tried desperately to silence behind my palm. My body shook as my release tore through my body.

My King came to feast.

And feast he did.

When I came down from the high, Cathan took a final slow lick through the evidence of how he affected me before he rose up my body and kissed me with gentle strokes of his tongue, the taste of me still lingering on his lips. I reached down to cup his length, but he stopped my hand, his eyes turning serious. "Tonight is solely about you."

"But I want to please you," I whispered.

Cathan shook his head before placing his warm lips against mine in a kiss that melted my heart. "You please me by existing. There will be plenty of time for my pleasure. Tonight is about you, so you know just how important you are to me."

I traced the contours of his cheekbones. "I feel like this is a dream."

Cathan rested his chin on my chest—still pumping with the last vestiges of our tryst—as he lay on top of me. "I assure you, baby. This isn't a dream, and I'll be happy to prove it to you over and over."

King Cathan Rosahan Delmar, the most unexpected person to enter my life and capture my heart whole, lay with me under the weeping willow, holding me tightly to him with the sounds of the dying night enveloping us outside the hanging leaves.

And I almost let myself believe in the dream.

RENEAH

CHAPTER 22

IT'S HARD TO FEEL confident that the bottom isn't going to entirely fall out from underneath your feet when you're riding so high on emotions that enthrall every beat of your heart, when happiness brings a smile to your face with just a simple thought. One could forget oneself when one abandons one's heart to one's deepest desires, as I had. It would've been much easier to sense the tension spreading throughout the Queendom had I been paying attention and not falling for my King.

But here I was, falling for my King and completely missing the warning signs that something was amiss with the humans in Atlantis. Guilt immediately consumed me for forgetting my place in the realm, for forgetting I wasn't a Fae.

The blasted Akani had been incredibly busy making their moves, as was apparent by their effective propaganda and ultimate attack on Asherah in the throne room earlier that day. It took an act of the goddess to remove Cathan from that throne room where he'd stood staring at the bloodstain on the stone floor and the most profound hurt in his eyes a father could possess. Dax had promised retribution, but following through on such promises was difficult when the Akani were so well organized and stealthy with their identities. I didn't envy Dax for a single second.

As we finally reached the stairwell landing of the royal wing, my thoughts were muddled with concern over Cathan. I gently guided him forward before he suddenly stopped and swiveled around. "I've got to go check on her," he said.

I placed my hands on his chest, halting him. "I understand you might want to, but that was my first stop on my way to retrieve you from the throne room, and Draevyn instructed Mayana to turn away anyone who approached."

He raked his fingers through his hair. "But I'm her fucking *father.*"

"And Draevyn is her possible mate, goddess willing, which is even more reason to keep your distance for a bit. I don't think you want to walk in on anything you can't unsee," I warned with a lifted brow.

Cathan held my gaze for a moment before sighing in resignation. "Fine. Just... fine." He turned and burst into the room in a flurry, and I carefully followed behind him.

"What's bothering you?" I ventured as I closed the door behind me.

He wheeled around, his hands dropping to his sides in clenched fists of tension. "I couldn't save her."

"From what I hear, she didn't need saving," I carefully ventured. "She was able to take care of herself. Isn't that what you want? For her to stand on her own two webbed feet?"

Cathan gritted his teeth so hard, his jaw ticked. "Yes, but she shouldn't have needed to do that. Draevyn, at the very least, should have stepped in."

I jerked back a little. "I understand it's his job to guard her and all, but I'm shocked anyone dared to attack her in the throne room, of all places. We've heard about the rising concerns, but I don't think anyone knew just how much tensions had escalated. That's a lot of pressure to put on Draevyn."

The words hit their mark as the intense fire in his eyes simmered to a low boil. He scrubbed a hand down his handsome face. "You're right. Of course, you're right. I just keep seeing the shock on Asherah's face on replay in my mind, and it's breaking my heart."

"I'd be more worried if it didn't break your heart. It just shows how much you love her. And no one's faulting you for being an exceptional father and wanting to be there for her," I told him as I let loose a sigh. "Why don't you sit while I get you a drink?" I hurried over to the corner bar cart and poured him a full glass of bold red wine—knowing his nerves likely needed it—before joining him on the couch.

Cathan's shoulders dropped a fraction as he took his first sip. "Thank you."

"You're being too hard on yourself," I told him, casting him what I knew was a frown of deep concern.

He snorted. "My daughter was almost killed. How am I being too hard on myself?"

"What do you imagine you could've done differently? He'd taken everyone in that room by surprise."

A few stray strands of his dark hair fell across his brow as he shook his head. "I'm a Guardian, Reneah. I should've been able to read the signs and defend her. I've become too rusty. Too complacent."

I glanced down at the ornate rug beneath my work slippers and considered my next question. "When's the last time you trained?"

Cathan winced. "Dax has been working me in slowly."

"Well, then. You need to continue training. Maybe the answer is immersing yourself in the training ring again. Reclaiming yourself.

Reclaiming who you are in your very soul. If you truly want to be a Guardian, you must train like one. I'm almost certain Dax would love to have your back amongst his guard." I didn't voice my trepidation at him putting his life at risk. There'd be no point. The goddess's calling was infinite.

He looked at me then, his beautiful brown eyes taking in mine. "You're amazing. You know that, yes?"

I lifted a shoulder in a shrug. "I suppose so."

His deep chuckle thrilled me. "Thank you."

As natural as lovers do, my hand came to rub small circles on his back. "No worries, my dear. It happens."

Cathan cast a side-eye. "Your dear, huh? Have I made it to pet names, then?"

"Careful not to tease, or else I'll never call you anything sweet again," I said, pinching the skin of his bare arm playfully and causing him to wince with a giggle.

He placed his glass on the coffee table, and I squealed as he lifted me to straddle his lap. "That's quite a dilemma because I have plans to... tease you endlessly." He leaned in and licked his tongue from my collarbone to my ear, leaving a trail of pebbled skin in his wake before he nibbled my lobe between his teeth. "And tease you *all over,* I shall."

"Is that so?" I breathed.

His lips were mere inches from mine as he whispered, "Oh, Reneah. The things I want to do to you; how I've dreamt of taking you. They are infinite." He leaned in and captured my mouth in a deep kiss that left me needy. Wanting. He tasted of currants of wine and sin. The rough tips of his fingers dug into my ass, pressing me hard against him.

Mercy.

I was utterly and entirely at his mercy.

We pulled apart as he swiftly stripped my shirt over my head, casting it aside—our lips crashing together in the next instant. The tips of his fingers trailed up the bare skin at my waist, traveling in a decided path to my breasts. Cathan grasped them within his palms with the most delicious groan vibrating against our fused lips. "I'll never tire of these perfect breasts," he avowed. "So heavy and full." He quickly unclasped my bra and threw it on the floor before his hooded eyes roamed over my body. "I want to see all of you."

At his command, I stood and ever so slowly shimmied my pants to the floor, my eyes never leaving his. The soft lace fabric of my sheer white panties coasted down my legs. Cathan's gaze locked on their movement. There was something empowering about the way he looked at me now, something dark and sensual. The tension between us pulled taut as his gaze traveled over the swells of my breasts, down the soft curves of my hips, and even further down my thighs and legs. My breath hitched when his scales descended, leaving him gloriously nude before me. Every perfect crease of his abs, his broad chiseled chest, muscular arms that knew exactly how to hold me, the endless sea of olive skin I longed to touch, to his breathtaking face I'd dreamt about on more than one occasion. His long, hardened shaft stood ready and waiting for me to devour. I licked my lips. The whole of him was a sight to behold.

Cathan brought his heated gaze to mine and crooked a finger. "Come here."

I obeyed my King, bringing my knees to either side of his thighs to straddle him. He leaned in, taking my pert nipple in his warm mouth, his delectable tongue swirling deliciously against my peak as he wasted no time dipping his fingers through my dripping wet folds. "Mmm, you're so wet and needy for me already. Aren't you, baby?" He teased my sensitive nub, a sensual moan leaving my lips. When a swift smack against my ass sounded across the room, my eyes flew open to his amused gaze. "Aren't you, baby?"

I bit my lip. "Yes, my King."

"Fuck." Cathan recaptured a nipple in his mouth—his fingers resuming their mission, causing my hips to move with his tantalizing rhythm. The music of his soul captured every beat of mine, and as I threaded my fingers through his soft, dark curls, I knew without a doubt I was his to do with as he pleased.

In a move that surprised him, I dropped to the floor on my knees and gazed at him with desire. Coarse hairs tickled my palms as I ran my hand up his thick thighs. Mustering all the courage within me, I grasped his bulging cock in my hands and leaned in, licking a path up his beautiful shaft, making sure to pay extra special attention to his throbbing head, my tongue swirling slowly over the tip. Cathan groaned and tipped his head back on the couch. "Goddess divine. That fucking tongue." I wanted him to lose himself; I wanted complete control of this stunning male who had captured my heart. I carefully massaged the hot, smooth length of his cock between my petite hands before leaning down and taking him wholly in my mouth. I couldn't help the moan that escaped me as he threaded his fingers into my long locks, gripping me to him—his hips starting to thrust. He continuously pitched forward, hitting deep inside my throat. I fought back the urge to gag, his incredible length and girth stretching my mouth impossibly wide. Thrust after thrust after thrust left me entirely breathless and wet between my thighs. "My goddess, baby. I want to be inside you so badly."

A popping sound resounded through the room as I lifted my lips from his angry erection and quirked a brow. "Well?"

Cathan moved with immense speed, lifting me by the thighs from the ground and carrying me to the bedroom like a male possessed. He slammed the door shut with a thud and slammed me against it, pulling back to meet my gaze. "Do I have your permission to bring you to absolute ecstasy, Reneah Diaz?"

"Please," I breathed.

With a sexy grin that had me melting, he lined up his thick cock to my aching heat and breached my opening. I threw my head back against the door, the stretch of him feeling both impossibly full and intoxicating simultaneously. Cathan was incredibly well endowed. It had been some time since I'd taken a lover, and I'd been naïve to think I could take him. "Cathan. I can—"

"You can take it, baby." He swiveled his hips, sliding inside another delectable inch, and my mouth dropped open. "Such a good girl. Fuck. You're so tight. This is better than I could've ever imagined." When he was satisfied by his breach, the pads of his fingertips dug into my backside. "Hold on to me."

My arms wrapped around his neck right before he thrust into me with abandon. He moved into me over and over again, his gaze dropping to where we were joined, watching with rapt attention—his wet cock pistoning into my heat. Erotic. Entirely euphoric. Being at his mercy, watching him bring himself to pleasure.

Bringing me to pleasure.

Cathan reached for my aching clit, circling it as he continued to rapture me with every thrust of his hips. My release burst from me, his lips crashing into mine, capturing my cry, and as he pinned me against the door—the intricate carvings biting into the bare skin of my upper back. Cathan bucked once, twice, and groaned into my mouth. A single hard thrust pinned me to the door as he came undone. He buried his head in the crook of my neck, his quick breaths cresting across my shoulder. "Don't let me go," he whispered against my skin. "Don't you ever let me go."

I tightened my hold around his neck, knowing deep down what he meant. There was no coming back from this.

And I simply couldn't bring myself to care.

The morning light peeked through the dark curtains, highlighting the tiny dust motes drifting through Cathan's bedroom. Soft, silk sheets covered my bare body as I slowly awoke from the deepest sleep I'd had in a long while. The bed was a dream to sleep in, fit for a Queen. Because it was for a queen, and there was something unsettling at that thought. I reached behind me to find the other side of the bed cold and empty. When I twisted around, I discovered a note on the neighboring pillow. My muscles strained as I reached for it, a small smile pulling at my lips as I read:

I reread that second to last line again. *Breakfast should appear...* My eyes went wide as I bolted upright. "Shit!"

Just then, the front door to Cathan's quarters swung open, and I prayed to the goddess that it was who I prayed it should be. Millie and Gina entered the bedroom a second later. Their steps came to a halt as their wide-eyed gazes swept over me, and I instantly realized my short sigh of relief had been slightly premature.

"Ooooh! You little hussy!" Gina exclaimed with a bright, mischievous gleam in her chestnut eyes.

"Reneah Diaz. Do you have any idea what risk you're taking? You are lying naked in the King's bed, for goddess's sake! And so soon after his mate's passing!" Millie whispered in a hiss, the short strands of her black hair escaping the tight bun at the top of her head and fanning out around her face, making her look villainous. I pulled the sheet a little higher on my chest, my cheeks growing impossibly hot.

Gina fluttered a hand. "Not now, Millie. I want to hear the details." She plopped down on the side of the bed with a salacious grin. "Spill."

I straightened out a crease in the sheet with a free hand, my heart kicking in my chest as I tried to figure out just how much I should reveal. "A lady doesn't tell."

"The hell you don't," Millie said as she crossed her arms in defiance.

Gina glanced at her in shock. "Bravo! About time you pulled the plunger out of your ass and took an interest." She swiveled back to me in anticipation. "Details. Now."

I blew out a breath. "I... may have slept with the King last night." And once earlier this morning, but they didn't need to know those particular details.

Millie's hand swept over me. "We already gathered that."

"Was it good?" Gina asked, wagging her light brown brows. I tried and failed to suppress my smile. "Ooooh, she's got that boom boom afterglow face."

"Reneah, if you don't tell us exactly what's going on, I will place anchovies in Cathan's pillow where they are sure to fester before he returns from the Above World."

My mouth dropped open. "You wouldn't."

Her gray-eyed gaze narrowed. "Try me."

I held my hands up in supplication. "Fine. Fine. I..." I couldn't tell them about the bond. I'd already spilled the beans with Aurelio, but with them, I'd have to play the modern-day Scarlett May, reputation be damned. How could I expect them to understand Cathan's bond when I didn't understand it myself? "We... are seeing each other. *In secret*," I stressed.

"And you think Kristos isn't going to catch wind of this?" Millie implored. "It's a damn good thing Gina reached me before anyone could question why breakfast was being sent to quarters that were presumably empty since the King himself is not here," she said, her eyebrow arching.

"Yes, I realized that when he left his letter."

Gina snatched the letter I had cast to the side of the bed and scanned it with eager eyes. "Ooooh. He's got it bad, too." Her gaze snapped to mine as she placed the note back on the bed. "Reneah, he's so into you."

I tilted my head back and forth. "Yes, well. The feeling is mutual."

"Are you falling for him?" Millie ventured, her expression morphing to one of concern.

Oh, goddess. Bringing the words to my lips and declaring this to them would make it official. Was I ready to tell my best friends about my feelings for Cathan? My mouth opened a few times before I could muster the words. "I... I am."

"I don't understand," Millie puzzled. "The man is grieving. He just lost his mate. It shouldn't be possible for him to move on from Neleah so quickly. How long has this been going on, Rennie?"

The sound of the front door opening again had us all stiffening.

"Is it Cathan, you think?" Gina whispered.

"No, he's not coming back this morning," I whispered back.

Millie's eyes went wide. "Hide."

I wrapped the sheet around my body and dashed from the bed as Gina reached down to gather my clothing, stuffing it in my hands. "Go. Hurry." I rushed into the pitch-black closet to the furthest corner, wincing in the deepest pain when I stubbed a toe or two before crouching behind a row of clothes. I thanked the goddess for the long dresses and the cover they provided as I gathered my knees to my chest.

"Millie?" Kristos called from the living area.

My heart plummeted to my gut. This was it. This was the moment I'd be discovered as the modern-day Scarlett May, shaming my family for eternity. I held my breath to keep the tears at bay, my hands shaking as I gripped my clothes and the sheet tightly to myself.

The telltale sound of sheets being stripped from the bed carried to my ears. "Leader Morales. What brings you to the Queen's Quarters?"

"I came to ensure that whoever the King ordered breakfast for was well cared for."

A pause. "Breakfast? For who?" Gina asked.

"Well, that's why I'm here. To find out who," he said dryly.

His words sprouted legs and kicked hard in the pit of my stomach as they drove all the remaining air from my body.

"We haven't seen anyone here."

"Not a soul."

"How interesting," he mused.

"We did wonder who the breakfast was for. Seems they've left before we arrived," Millie said. The lie fell so easily off her tongue, and I'd have to remember to thank her profusely for it.

"You've dropped something, Gina," Kristos told her.

"I have?"

"Yes, a piece of parchment, it seems. To your right. No, your other right. Oh, never mind. I'll get it."

"Oh! No wor—"

I squeezed my eyes shut, knowing what he was about to find. "Oh, dear," Kristos said with a bit of shock in his tone. "It appears there *was* someone here from the looks of this letter. I'll have to keep a better eye on his quarters now."

"Whatever for?" Millie asked.

"Because I make it my duty to know all the ins and outs of the royal wing and who's in it."

"Of course, Leader Morales," Millie said apologetically. "I only meant that the King should be afforded his privacy. I'm sure if he wanted you to know about his... mistress, he likely would have told you."

Kristos sighed loud enough for me to hear. "Fair point. Discretion *is* our biggest responsibility, something I don't think I need to remind the two of you. Nonetheless, I'll double-check and ensure his... guest has everything she needs. Do not breathe a word of this to anyone. Understood? And here. Place this on the nightstand so that it appears undisturbed. I need to find Reneah and find out if she knows anything about this mysterious guest. I haven't been able to find her all morning. Have you seen her?"

"Reneah?" Gina asked innocently. "Why, yes. As a matter of fact, I saw her earlier today. She was on a mission to find out who stole her favorite polish from her closet. You know how she is about her furniture polish, Leader Morales. She won't rest until she finds the thief."

"Ah. Yes. That does explain it. Very well. If you see her, can you send her to my office?"

"Of course," Millie assured him.

"Perfect. Have a good day."

I didn't let out the breath I was holding until I heard the front door close. The closet lights grew brighter as Millie and Gina bolted the corner I was crouched in. I peeked my head through the wall of evening dresses, meeting their worried gazes. "Thank you," I breathed.

"Don't thank us just yet. You need to get dressed and act like you're still a palace leader," Millie chastised, as she shook her head. "That was way too close for comfort."

"You need to be more careful," Gina chimed in, suddenly striving to be the voice of reason. "Of the two of you, you have more to lose. And don't give us those sad puppy-dog eyes. We're on your side, but we don't want to see you get hurt. Goddess forbid Kristos finds out that we're all covering for you, and we'll *all* be out of jobs."

Guilt immediately consumed me. "I'm so sorry."

Gina's face softened. "Don't be. Now, go and take a shower in the fancy shower. We'll tidy up."

As I readied myself in the luxurious bathroom I'd cleaned time and time again, the relief at getting away with the close call didn't appear. The ground beneath my feet seemed to be falling out at record speed, and one thing was clear.

My time was running out.

CATHAN

Chapter 23

Exhaustion weighed heavy on my limbs as I wheeled my trident around for the millionth time that morning. Dax blocked it as *he'd* done for the millionth time that morning.

"Come on. You can do better than that. Hit me!"

My breath left me in heavy puffs. Embarrassment overtook my body. I couldn't understand how I'd let myself go like this. "Surely, you've gotten better since the last time we sparred," I told him. I whirled my trident up in a hook, trying to get the uppercut, but wouldn't you know? He blocked that, too.

"What's with you, old man?" Dax teased with a quick jab of his trident stem to my stomach.

I keeled over, casting him a skeptical glare. "We're the same age, you ass."

Dax bent over in my periphery, a grand look of amusement lighting his face. I wanted to smack his face with my trident if I could. "Well then, you'll need to start acting like it. Your daughter is better than you at this point."

My brow furrowed. "You say that like that's a bad thing."

"I'm trying to motivate you any way I can."

"Try a different way."

The front door to the facility opened, drawing our attention. Whatever breath I had left in my lungs blew through my lips. Despite wearing her uniform, Reneah Diaz was a sight to behold; all her petite curves and breasts I wanted to bite.

"I think your motivation just walked in the door," Dax murmured.

"You may be right," I agreed. She could wear a burlap sack, and I'd still think of that beautiful body of hers hidden beneath her clothing. I could still see her naked form, could still feel her skin on my fingertips.

Taking me by surprise, Dax whacked my backside with the head of his trident.

I wheeled around to him. "What the hell was that for?" I hissed.

His lips lifted in a mischievous grin in answer.

I twirled around, luring him to block my trident before changing direction when I had him right where I wanted him. I immediately jabbed my stem into his gut and wheeled my trident into his side to add insult to injury. I shouldn't have felt satisfied to see him peeling over into a crouch, but I'd take that satisfaction, nonetheless. Only Dax could smile, even in pain. "Well, that worked," he croaked.

I shook my head and returned my attention to Reneah. Her beautiful brown eyes scanned every inch of my bare chest, and I stood a little taller as a blush spread across her cheeks. Goddess, I'd missed her so much these past few weeks. It was the first time I'd laid eyes on her since returning from my latest trip to the Above World. Every single day away from her felt like agony. I didn't know what that meant about my feelings for her, but I was smart enough to know that it meant something beyond physical attraction.

I needed her.

Ideas had run through my mind about how to show her just how much I cared for her. I'd settled on one. Reneah deserved the world, and I was desperate to give it to her. She strolled over to us with a look of apprehension on her face that immediately gave me pause. "What's wrong?"

"Draevyn's summoned both of you. I don't know what for. I was just told to find you immediately," she said, handing me a piece of parchment with Draevyn's name on the face of the folded paper. "I... uh... intercepted the Guardian who was on his way to deliver the message. I wanted to deliver it myself," she rushed out.

Ah. Well, then. Apparently, I wasn't the only one who missed the other. The corner of my mouth quirked into a smile. "How are you?"

Her beautiful brown eyes studied my face. "Fine. And you?" she asked.

My smile grew. "Better now." My gaze never left Reneah's as Dax ripped the parchment from my hand, but his deep curse drew both of our attention. My brow furrowed at his turbulent expression. "What is it?"

Dax let loose a long sigh. "Melysah and Kane, again. Draevyn's asked us to meet them in Asherah's quarters."

My anger instantly pitched to a fever point. "What have they done?"

Dax shook his head. "It doesn't say. He only instructed us to meet them."

I dragged a hand down my sweat-ridden face. "This can't be good."

"With the both of them, it never is," Reneah said as a concerned expression flitted across her beautiful face.

                                S.T. FERNANDEZ

"We'd better get going," Dax warned.

"Are you coming with us?" I asked Reneah.

"Oh, uh. No," she said, thumbing over her shoulder. "I've got to get back to my tasks. I just wanted to deliver the message." She blew out a measured breath with an apprehensive smile. "And now I've done that, so I must go."

"You're sure?" I implored. My heart longed for her. This one small moment just wasn't enough.

She fluttered a wrist. "Yes, I'll check on Asherah later."

"Can you spend the day with me tomorrow?" I blurted out like a little faeling boy. I could have sworn I heard Dax chuckle behind me.

"I don't think I can take the time," she told me on the tail end of an apologetic smile.

"You're sure? Millie or Gina couldn't cover for you? Just for tomorrow?"

Reneah winced. "I hate taking the day off before the weekend. Doesn't look good to the rest of the team."

My head tilted slightly. "Have you ever done it before?"

Reneah pursed her lips in thought. "No."

"Well, then. This will be a first. Please? Spend the day with me?"

The literal wheels turning in her mind felt like a palpable thing. The corner of my mouth twitched at just how hard she was resisting the prospect of spending time with me. Finally, her shoulders sagged with a sigh. "Alright. I'll see what I can do."

A feeling of pure joy rose in me. "Thank you," I said, unable to take my eyes off her.

Our gazes remained on each other, holding so much more than we could say. Only when Dax cleared his throat were we startled out of our moment. He lifted the parchment with a raised eyebrow. "Asherah?"

I cleared my throat. "Right."

"I'll see you all around," Reneah said with a deep blush on that stunning face before she turned and exited the facility. I savored every natural sway of her hips until the door closed in her wake.

"You need to be more careful."

I shifted my attention to Dax. "Am I not being careful?"

"You can't be serious," he deadpanned. "You'd better guard that secret with your damn life. Asherah's future depends on it. Reneah's family's future depends on it," he warned.

His words sunk into the depths of my gut like an anchor plunging into the ocean. I swallowed past the lump in my throat. "I know."

With an empathetic smile, he patted my shoulder. "Come on. We need to see what the devilish duo has done this time."

Despite my worries about Asherah, I wondered if anyone with the power to wield consequences had picked up on my feelings for Reneah. I prayed for the goddess's veil over our feelings for each other to protect us from a fallout.

But even I knew her veil may not be enough to fool a queendom from the bond that lay within my chest.

Reneah

Chapter 24

I'D BEEN OUTSIDE CATHAN'S door dozens of times, probably hundreds. Yet each time seemed like the first, and each time seemed more scandalous than the last. For some odd reason, I'd felt like I had eyes on me as I waited in the hallway. I glanced at the empty stairwell, finding nothing and no one there, but my eyes narrowed nonetheless.

The door opened, causing me to jump—my eyes morphing from narrow to wide when I beheld the male just beyond the door. Cathan Rosahan Delmar was in human clothing—his washed-out jeans hung slightly from his hips, and his light blue and beige patterned button-down shirt lent to his casual look. Seeing him look so human was strange, yet it set off a little thrill within me. "You look handsome."

Cathan reached for my hand, pulling me into his quarters as he closed the door behind me and gently pushed me against it. His mouth was on mine in the blink of an eye—soft, warm, inviting. His embrace instantly had me melting, his strong arms wrapping around me. His kiss was everything. I'd never tire of his plush lips and skilled tongue that could be both gentle and demanding simultaneously. A little breathless when he pulled back, I searched his handsome face, lit with desire and something akin to anticipation. He brushed the tip of his nose against mine as he said, "I've missed you."

My hands trailed up his arms. "Nothing to miss. I'm here," I said with a smile.

He stole another kiss before pulling away. The loss of his embrace left me yearning. "I have something for you," he told me.

My brow lifted. "Oh? I didn't realize we were exchanging gifts."

"We're not," he replied as he hurried toward his bedroom. "This is my gift to you. No gift in return is necessary. Wait there." I shifted from foot to foot as he disappeared. A moment later, he returned with a simple brown gift bag and a smile that could melt the world. "For you."

With a furrowed brow, I carefully took the bag from him and reached into it. My hands brushed against light, ribbed fabric. I anchored my attention to the material within and pulled it out. My jaw slackened. The simple ribbed tank dress reached mid-calf in a beautiful heather-gray color. "It's Above World human clothing."

Cathan wore a wide grin at my reaction. "That is it."

"It's beautiful, Cathan."

"You like it?" he asked with an eager expression.

"Yes, of course."

"Excellent, because you have about ten minutes to change into it before we depart."

My gaze flew from the dress to him. "Depart for where?"

The corner of his mouth twitched. "For our date."

"Our date *where*?" His gaze searched mine, and I knew the answer without him having to say a word. I placed the dress back in the bag, handing it to him. "Cathan, you know it's against the law. I can't."

He gently pushed it back into my hands. "But you can. Check in the bag again."

"What—"

"Just check," he implored with a hint of mischief gleaming in his golden brown eyes.

I reached into the bag and retrieved the envelope within. "Just what are you u—" I paused momentarily to gather myself, my eyes scanning the official Atlantian document. "How?"

A shoulder lifted in a nonchalant shrug as the corner of his mouth twitched. "I may have pulled some strings. I am the King, after all."

"But this is an official document giving a human passage into the Above World," I replied, astonished. "We're never permitted in the Above World."

"You are permitted... as my diplomatic companion."

"A date is hardly diplomacy, Cathan."

"Would you just take the win? Come on, baby."

Was it terrible that I would give him anything he asked for, especially when he cast those puppy dog eyes at me? I blew out a breath. "Alright."

His gleaming white teeth peeked through his luscious mouth as he smiled radiantly. "Good. That's good," he beamed, motioning to the bedroom. "I'll give you a few minutes, and then we have to go. Our ride is waiting."

"Our ride?" I asked, casting him a questioning look.

Cathan dipped his hands in his pockets and shrugged. "You'll see. Go on."

Heading to the bedroom, against my better judgment, I swiftly changed into my new dress, the fabric fitting to my curves like a decadent glove. The decorative metal buttons opened to reveal my ample cleavage, something I'm sure my lover intended when he selected the dress. With a final look in the floor-length mirror, I padded out of the room on bare feet, grateful that I had the presence of mind to polish my toes in my favorite coral color.

Cathan's gaze swept slowly over my form. "You are so incredibly beautiful," he said in a reverent tone that left me weak.

I gave him a sheepish smile as I gestured to my feet. "My work shoes weren't exactly a match."

"Ah! Yes, almost forgot," he said, moving with speed to the couch, retrieving a pair of sandals I hadn't noticed were lying there. Cathan bent down before me on a knee and carefully took my bare foot in his hand, sliding on the simple dark brown sandal with diamond-encrusted straps. My breath hitched as he placed a kiss on the bridge of my foot before sliding the other sandal on my opposite one, kissing it with equal affection. When he rose, he captured my lips in a chaste kiss before sliding his hand into mine. "Ready?"

Panic swelled within me. "Won't I be noticed?"

Realization dawned on his handsome face. "Oh, right." He reached for the cloak hanging by the door and whipped it around my shoulders, pulling the hood over my head. "Now you're ready."

I blew out a breath. "Ready."

With that, Cathan and I left his quarters and ventured down the quiet hallway of the Royal Wing to the very door I'd used to smuggle the Princess out of the palace for a night out on the town, finding the same person who'd been assisting us that time around. A smile grew on my face as I stepped into the awaiting canoa. "Hello, Braeliah. Pleasure to see you again."

Braeliah glanced over my shoulder to Cathan. "Did you hear something, my King?"

Cathan's deep rumble sounded from behind me. "It sounded suspiciously like a woman."

"Aye, strange hauntings in this palace," she said. Braeliah glanced at me long enough to issue a wink.

Cathan guided me into the canoa cabin in silence, but a strange feeling consumed me as Braeliah shut the secret palace passageway. Despite the empty hallway we'd left behind, I couldn't shake the feeling we'd been seen.

The tiny canoa sliced through the ocean's depths like a knife through the softest butter. As I remained in the cabin, not a single movement could be felt—a testament to Braeliah's elemental skill. Canoas embarking on a journey to the Above World was an exceedingly rare occurrence. This phenomenon piqued the curiosity of all who heard of it—a venture only taking place when massive amounts of items needed transport.

This was not one of those times.

My nerves were taut, stretched to their limit. The mere thought of seeing the Above World for the first time sent a thrill coursing through my veins. Regardless of the permission Cathan obtained, this was no diplomatic mission. The consequences could be dire if it were discovered that he twisted the truth for his gain. I silently thanked the goddess for Braeliah's discretion, a tiny comfort in this nerve-wracking journey.

"We're nearly there," I heard her tell Cathan from beyond the drape that covered the cabin doorway.

The drape parted, and Cathan entered, his face beaming with a reassuring smile. "You okay?" he asked, his voice filled with genuine concern.

I nodded. "Nervous."

He slid beside me on the bench that lined the wall. "Don't be."

I scoffed in disbelief. "I've only imagined what the Above World looked like. The pictures, they're breathtaking." In truth, I'd taken to collecting photographs of the Above World, fascinated by the sunsets, the rise of the moon, and the various types of trees. While Atlantis had a magicked allure, there was a natural beauty in the Above World that always left me a little in awe. And that was just the pictures alone.

Cathan laced his fingers through the hand that rested on my jumping knee. "I wish I had more time to show you everything. Unfortunately, we'll only have until this evening."

"I'm grateful for any time I get. This is such a gift, Cathan. Thank you."

"I'm happy to give it." He leaned in, his soft lips pressing against mine and settling my nerves. Those beautiful lips kissed my hand as he pulled me up from the bench. "Come. I don't want you to miss your first glimpse."

We passed through the doorway, coming to stand at the starboard side of the canoa, Cathan's arms sliding around my middle, anchoring me to him as my heart pounded in my chest.

"Alright, you two," Braeliah called from the front. "It's time for a little glam bam as we breach the surface so we can arrive undetected. Here we go!"

My gaze held on the light filtering in from the water's surface—shades of blue shimmering and winking with colors I'd never seen before. My mouth parted as the tiny, roaring, pale orange globe grew larger at our approach.

"Do not stare at the sun," Cathan warned. "You'll go blind."

My head swiveled around as my brow dropped. "Seriously?"

"Seriously. It's that powerful."

"But I... I've seen it in pictures, and I can still see."

His hearty laugh vibrated at my back. "You can't go blind from a picture of the sun, Reneah."

I playfully pinched the skin of his forearm. "Well, how am I supposed to know that?"

"Fair enough. I won't tease."

I returned my attention to the canoa's bow, and my breath lodged in my throat. Ever so slowly, we rose above the surface. The afternoon sunlight assaulted my eyes, and I turned into Cathan's chest to block the overwhelming sensation.

He caressed the top of my head with a gentle touch. "I forgot how difficult it is to take in the sun when you've been underwater for so long. Are you okay?"

I blinked a few times to let my eyes adjust, and then they widened. "Oh my goddess," I breathed. There were no words to describe the beauty before me; sonnets could be created by the most skilled of poets, and it still wouldn't even come close. Tiny waves were known to lap the shores of the Shingu, but they were not the massive churning waves crashing into the shoreline in the distance here in the Above World. Humans of every shape and every possible color lined the shore, building tiny castles made of sand—swimming, laughing. In the distance, tall buildings reaching far into the sky towered over a colossal town several times the size of Borike'n—an enormous bridge led to the giant cluster. I scanned the crowd on the beach. There wasn't a single Fae in sight.

Humans.

Only humans.

"Where are we?"

Cathan's hold on me tightened. "They call it Key Biscayne."

"We're almost there, Your Highness!" Braeliah called.

I turned in his arms, bouncing on my toes. "Where are you taking me?"

His smile widened. "First, I'm taking you to my favorite restaurant. And then, I have a little surprise for you."

My eyebrows reached to my hairline. "This isn't the surprise?" I asked, my tone laced with shock.

His thumb brushed back and forth across my cheek. "Not even close."

The canoa slowed as we entered an inlet, a weathered dock hugging the still water. Open-air restaurants rested just beyond the pier, with unlit patio string lights ready and waiting for dusk to appear. Braeliah leapt from the bow onto the dock and skillfully anchored the canoa, Cathan following behind her to assist. The sight of him being so... human—with his human clothing, peppered gray hair, and rounded ears glamoured to perfection—did certain delicious things somewhere deep in my core. I shifted to dispel the growing ache. Cathan was so incredibly handsome, and even more so when he smiled the way he did as he reached up, placing his hands on my hips. "Ready?"

I set my hands on his shoulders to steady myself as I said, "As I'll ever be."

Cathan lifted me from the canoa and gently placed me on the dock without ever breaking his gaze, and my heart raced.

"You know we have stairs, Cathan?" Braeliah said with an arched brow.

"Oh. Do we? I completely forgot."

Braeliah shook her head. "Okay, you two. You have until midnight. I'm off to get a pint," she declared as she gave a salute. "See you all later!"

"Thank you, Braeliah," Cathan called after her. His gaze shifted to me, and I felt weak all over again. He threaded his fingers through mine. "Let's go, beautiful."

Cathan towed me along the walkway leading to an outdoor terrace—the travertine tile blanketing every corner and lending to the romantic ambiance. As we approached the sleek, modern hostess stand, the woman waiting behind it lifted her gaze, her face brightening in recognition. "Mr. Rosahan. You're back."

"In the flesh."

Her gaze slid to me. "And with a lady friend," she remarked, her eyebrows wagging.

The blush that crept on Cathan's face was endearing. "Yes, and on that note. If we could have something a little private, that would be appreciated."

"You got it, Mr. Rosahan. Follow me."

Cathan sent me a wink before leading me after the hostess, and I relished the various types of clothing the guests wore as we passed their tables—the ladies wearing such beautiful fabrics with floral patterns that left me mesmerized. I dearly hoped they didn't mind my gawking, but I simply couldn't help it. The soft beat of congas and the strumming of Spanish guitars drifted throughout the restaurant, creating a desperately romantic vibe I felt in my bones.

It wasn't long before the hostess stopped at a simple yet elegant table in front of a low travertine wall—the ocean spreading toward the horizon beyond it. My mouth fell open as I came to stand still, the beauty entirely breathtaking.

"I'll let Alvaro know you're here," I heard the hostess say, but I couldn't peel my gaze away from the scene before me.

"Thank you, Mabel," Cathan said. Seeming to understand my momentary paralysis, he slid his arms around my waist from behind. The gentle kiss he placed on my neck pulled me from my trance. "It's beautiful, isn't it?"

"Beautiful is too weak of a word. It's magical."

Cathan skillfully pulled out a chair, ushering me into it. "It pleases me that you think so."

"How long have you been coming here?" I asked, scanning the outdoor patio with its lush green plants and brightly colored flowers.

Cathan quirked a brow. "This century?"

I shook my head. "Of course. How could I forget your longevity?"

He pursed his lips in thought. "Well, I've been familiar with the area for a while, but I only started venturing here after Asherah reached the age when she was too cool to be seen with her father. And then, with Neleah gone, I decided to venture off on my own to keep myself entertained in Neleah's absence and when Asherah went off to college."

I titled my head. "So, you never brought Neleah or Asherah here?"

"No. You're the first person I've ever brought with me," he told me, the corner of his mouth twitching.

"I'm honored," I said, smoothing out the creases in my dress.

"Trust me. The honor is all mine."

My gaze snapped up to him, and the heat rose on my cheeks due to more than just the humid afternoon air slowly drifting into dusk. His beautiful brown eyes swept over me, causing the heat to rise in other places.

"Cathan!"

I turned to the voice that called out across the terrace. A man approached us with a smile reaching from ear to ear—his white short-sleeved, crisp button-down shirt without a single speck upon the fabric. A stylish fedora hat sat perfectly on top of his graying hair, and despite the crow's feet blanketing the cream skin around his eyes, his gaze held a youthful sort of playfulness.

"Alvaro!" Cathan beamed as he rose to greet the man, embracing him with a pat on the back. He pulled away and regarded him like a long-lost brother. "It's good to see you."

"Where've you been?" Alvaro asked with a thick accent I couldn't quite place.

"Ah. I've been a bit busy with work."

Alvaro tsked. "Too busy to visit. Very well. We'll spoil you while you're here." His gaze shifted to me, and his eyes lit with amusement. "And who is this young lady?"

"Alvaro, I'd like you to meet my girlfriend, Reneah."

Girlfriend.

Interesting.

And I liked it.

Alvaro reached for my hand in greeting, and when I placed my hand in his, he kissed it with a cheeky grin. "*Mucho gusto*, Reneah. It's such a pleasure to meet Cathan's lady."

"It's a pleasure to meet you as well," I said, unable to keep from smiling.

He turned back to Cathan. "You've been keeping her a secret."

Cathan held his palms up in resignation. "Not a secret. We haven't had time to travel. But if it makes you feel any better, you were my first stop."

"Only slightly better," Alvaro said, his lips twitching in an admonishing grin. He returned his attention to me, his features softening. "Since this is your first visit to Casa Romero, we'll make sure you have the best experience. Shall I bring a round of mojitos?"

"Yes, please," Cathan answered.

"Very well. I will make them myself," Alvaro declared as he turned and disappeared inside the charming restaurant.

I bit my lip, regarding Cathan with interest, as he slid back into his seat. "Girlfriend, huh?"

He leaned forward on his elbows and lifted his shoulder in a casual shrug. "Yes, but it seems rather insignificant. You are so much more than a girl and a friend."

My smile dipped as a thought occurred to me. I shifted in my seat. "Do they not know about Neleah?"

Cathan's smile dropped a fraction. "No. Nor do they know about Asherah."

"Why?" I asked, the question slipping from my mouth. I winced. "Sorry. That's probably none of my business."

He tilted his head. "It's alright to ask. I never mentioned Neleah or Asherah because... well," he paused, glancing in the distance in thought, "I wanted to keep something for myself. My life has been filled with my Guardian duties, my duty to Neleah, and my greatest role as Asherah's father. I wanted just a little sliver of existence that was just... me." He shrugged. "That may sound a little selfish."

"It's not," I assured him.

He dipped his head in a nod. "And now I share this with you."

"Well, I feel honored." I positively melted as Cathan bit his lip, his eyes roaming over my form again—like he couldn't wait to devour me. The intensity of it left me breathless. I unglued my eyes from him, reviewing the menu before me. "So, what's good here?"

"Do you trust me?"

My gaze cut to his. "Of course."

"Is there anything that you absolutely will not eat?"

My lips pursed to the side in thought. "Artichoke?"

He chuckled. "You're in luck, then. No artichoke on the menu. Do you trust me to order for you?"

The thought of him ordering for me was touching for some reason. "Of course."

A server carrying a tray with two tall mojitos approached our table, dispelling the moment—the crushed mint leaves floating in a sea of ice swirled as he placed them before us. I grabbed mine with eager anticipation and hummed as the delicious drink hit my tastebuds. Fresh mint and a tang of lime juice easily slid down my throat and masked the potency of the rum. When the food finally arrived—a wonderful, hearty, meaty dish called *Ropa Vieja*—Cathan and I exchanged a dozen stories: him from his youth, me from mine. There were tales from our youth that were embarrassing to divulge to others but were somehow easier to divulge with each other—our vulnerabilities cherished and not used as a weapon. Everything with

Cathan felt as natural as breathing, as if we flowed entirely with one another, through one another. I was nearing the bottom of my second glass and ordering a third when a chuckle left his lips.

"You'll fall over if you have too many more of those," Cathan warned.

I swallowed a heap of the flavorful shredded meat before answering, "Then, I better make it my last. I want to remember everything about this entire experience."

Cathan leaned back in his chair with an amused gleam in his eyes. "Sounds like a good plan, considering the night is still young."

"Is it now?"

"It is."

"And just what sort of plans do you have for me, my dear?"

Cathan casually rested his chin on his palm as he leaned on the armrest—his gaze traveling over me slowly. "The most wicked plans."

Didn't that have me shoveling the remainder of my food into my mouth?

With our meals finished and our drinks emptied, we sat in heated silence, our gazes held firm—his heavy with promise. My nerves were a frenzy of desire and anticipation. Alvaro approached as silently as a mouse. "I hope you enjoyed the meal?" he asked me.

"It was amazing, Alvaro. I will never forget it," I said, beaming with joy. I'd likely never see this sweet man again. I dispelled that particular sad thought, refusing to let anything ruin the evening.

"I'm afraid we must be going," Cathan told him.

Alvaro cast him a scolding look. "I expect you back here much sooner next time."

A laugh broke from Cathan's chest. "I promise to visit more often, my friend."

Alvaro pointed to me. "And her, too. I like her. Treat her well."

"You have my word. I will treat her like a Queen," he declared. The power in his tone sent a thrill through me.

Cathan quickly settled the bill... and the bills of five other tables around us, unbeknownst to them.

The corner of his lips pulled up in a smirk. "Are you ready for your next adventure, baby?" he asked.

"Yes," I breathed.

"Good," he said, rising from his chair to hold out a hand. "We need to hurry before the sun sets. Let's get out of here."

I wondered what Cathan was up to as I followed behind him on the sandy beach—my toes sinking into the silky cream-colored sand with each step. The leather backpack he'd retrieved from the canoa swung back and forth across his broad back. I shamelessly tried to see the contents within but could not when Cathan tsked. "Don't ruin the surprise."

"I hate surprises."

The corner of his mouth twitched as he looked ahead. "You'll love this one, I promise."

The shore curved, and when we rounded the corner, I gasped—my gaze traveling to the top of a tall, circular structure, its weathered, white brick bright against the sun-kissed backdrop. "Is this a palace of some sort?"

Cathan chuckled. "No. Not a palace. A lighthouse."

"A lighthouse," I murmured, my gaze still held to it. "It's beautiful."

"I'm glad you think so. Come. This way," Cathan said as he slipped his hand around my hip, my body immediately welcoming the heat of him. He led us down a gray stone pathway with beautiful random patterns that glimmered against the fading sun.

To my surprise, a young man stood at the end of the pathway with a welcoming smile. "Mr. Rosahan. It's a pleasure to see you again."

Cathan shook his hand in a familiar greeting as we reached him. "Marcos, always a pleasure. This is my girlfriend, Reneah."

Marcos took my hand with a smile. "Pleasure to meet you." He glanced over his shoulder at the tall lighthouse. "Well, it's unlocked for you. Just remember to be very quiet," he instructed, returning his attention to us with a grimace. "I could get into a bit of trouble if anyone were to find out I let someone in."

"Not to worry," Cathan told him. "We'll be careful."

Marcos' head dipped in a firm nod. "Enjoy the evening," he said before strolling down the path.

My eyebrow arched. "Cathan Rosahan Delmar. Are we supposed to be here?"

His face feigned innocence as he said, "I am nothing but a law-abiding fellow."

"Except for the fact that we're literally breaking laws by my being here."

Cathan fluttered a hand in the air. "Semantics. Come. We don't want to miss the show."

He opened the pale wooden door and stepped through the threshold. My head tipped back, admiring all the weathered white brick rising above my head. A black metal staircase rose to the stars. "We're going up there, aren't we?"

"We sure are."

I stepped on the first stair, the metal creaking. "Is it safe?"

"Nothing's going to happen to you. Not on my watch," he assured me as he gestured to the staircase. "Go on. I'll be right behind you."

I blew out a breath as I ascended the ancient metal staircase, making sure to step carefully. One thing I hadn't accounted for? The way my lungs labored and the way my thighs ached, each step agonizing in a way I'd never felt before. By the time we reached the halfway mark, I had to pause. "I don't know what's wrong with me. I climb the palace steps day in and day out."

"It's the altitude, for you at least." Cathan reached around my back and under my legs. I let out a rather embarrassing squeal as he lifted me with ease—his cheeky smirk causing me to cluck my tongue in irritation. As I settled against him, I was offended that not a single drop of sweat lay on the skin of his brow. That devilish grin wasn't helping, either. "I've got it from here."

I wrapped my arms tightly around his neck, glancing below. "I sure hope so."

Cathan closed the little distance between us and placed a kiss on my cheek. "I won't let anything happen to you."

I studied him, hoping my face didn't betray the wanton lust I felt inside. The deep groan emanating from the back of his throat as he ascended the steps told me otherwise.

With an ease that made me jealous, he climbed the rest of the way until we reached the very top, Cathan placing me on the landing with tenderness. A dark metal door stood before us, the knob and details weathered with age. He pulled it open, and the world beyond had my mouth dropping open in wonder. "By the goddess." A baby blue sky bled into light pinks and warm shades of orange. Tiny sailboats cut through the water, blanketing the ocean's surface before me. The humid evening breeze whipped the loose strands of my blonde hair around my face. "It's stunning." In truth, I'd never beheld anything so breathtaking in my entire life.

"It is," Cathan murmured from beside me. I turned, finding his fiery brown eyes on me. He cupped my face, brushing his thumb softly against my cheek. "Are you enjoying yourself?"

"Cathan, there are no words. I don't know how I'll ever thank you."

His lips kicked up in a grin. "I can think of a few ways."

I shook my head as laughter peeled from my lips. "No shame."

"None, I'm afraid," he said, his hand moving to the small of my back. "Let's go around to the other side. You'll get a perfect view of the sunset."

He carefully guided me to the other side of the lighthouse, checking to make sure the railing was all in tack before dropping his bag on the floor. As I remained glued to the view before me, he brought his chest to my back and wrapped his arms around my waist, trapping me between the intricate brown metal railing I was gripping so hard that my knuckles were turning white. The sun kissed the horizon as it began its descent. My gaze held, my vision blurring. "It's all so beautiful. This world has so much more to offer than I ever imagined."

"And I plan to show you every inch of it," he vowed, his breath tickling my ear.

Cathan spoke as if he planned to be in my life for eternity, and for a human, eternity was fleeting. My heart warred with itself, one side wanting him desperately, the other wanting to save this man from going through any more grief. He was risking his reputation by showing me the Above World. I turned in his arms, peering up at his face, which held so much determination. "You know we shouldn't."

He reached up and brushed away a stray tear. "I'd like to see them try to stop me."

"We could be discovered, Cathan."

"Let them discover us. I plan to show you all of this world, Reneah. I want to see the amazement in your eyes as you behold it, as you discover what every type of tree looks like, what every grain of sand feels like, what the sky looks like when its fiercest storm is unleashed. I want to make love to you under a starlit sky and have you firmly in my arms during the coldest winter." His hands brushed down my arms, leaving pebbled skin in their wake. "I want to be there every day for the rest of your life."

I shook my head. "You can't mean that."

"I can, and I do."

"You won't want me when I'm old and wrinkled."

"I will want you even then."

"Why?" I asked, my voice croaking.

"I've..." The Adam's apple of his throat bobbed as he swallowed. "I've fallen in love with you, Reneah. The spell you've cast on my heart is binding, and I'm unable to part from you. Not today, not tomorrow, or any day after that," he said, his words like a gentle caress. My heart kicked in my chest, and my breath hitched in my throat. "I plan to be by your side until you take your last breath. It is my honor to be there for every second of it."

This beautiful male.

Cathan's lips crashed into mine, our tongues twisting in a desperate tangle of need and longing. I gathered the fabric of his shirt in my grip as his fingers dug into my backside, pressing me into him. His long, thick manhood dug into my soft belly and elicited a moan from my lips. "Cathan," I said breathlessly.

"Turn around, baby."

The last remnants of the sun sank to the other side of the world as I spun around. Cathan crouched down behind me, the rough pads of his fingers cresting across my ankle and venturing a provocative pathway up my calf and then further up my thigh. As his warm tongue licked from my neck to my lobe, he pulled my dress over my hips, leaving my stone gray lace thong exposed to the world around us. His finger dipped below the seam, moving ever so slowly to my center. My breath caught as he delved into my delicate center. His tantalizing him vibrated against my neck, causing the wetness to spill from my sex. "You're so wet for me already. And I'm afraid you'll be dripping when I'm done with you. Keep your hands on that railing, baby. Spread your legs."

"You're not worried that someone will see us?"

"You think I'd have my pussy displayed to the world without a veil?" His crude words hit my core, and I bit my lip as I parted my legs. "Good girl."

Without further delay, he swirled his skillful fingers around my sensitive nub, and I tipped my head back on his chest, my mouth dropping open in a silent moan. My body was his playground, and he knew just the right way to bring me pleasure. His other hand coasted up my abdomen and reached for my breast, pinching my tight nipple through my clothing. I was entirely at his mercy, locked in his sensual spell high above the world with only the sunset for company.

As his fingers entered my slick wet heat, the pad of his palm rubbed tantalizingly over my clit, and I could do nothing but buck against his hand to relieve the building ache. Riding his fingers with pure desperation, Cathan rolled my nipple—the pain shooting straight to my aching center. "You like that, baby?"

"Yes," I breathed.

"Mmm, I can't wait to be inside you."

"Then, get inside me. Please."

"Well, since you asked so nicely…"

I whimpered as he removed his fingers from my core, the loss of him too much, my need for him overwhelming. Cathan slowly and reverently crouched behind me, pulling my lace thong down my legs and nipping my bare ass on his descent. When he rose, he gathered my bunched-up dress and pulled it over my head, dropping it and the thong on the metal ground at our feet. He slowly unhooked my matching lace bra, his soft lips pressing gentle kisses across my shoulders, casting it aside on the mounting pile of clothes. A lavender sky reached for the awakening stars above us as I stood completely bare. The clank of his belt buckle sounded behind me, and the rustling of his discarded pants made me heady with anticipation. When his shirt joined them, I bit my lip. Apparently, I wouldn't be the only one bare to the world this evening.

The breath from Cathan's lips brushed against the shell of my ear as he said, "Bend over, baby."

As I bent at the waist, pushing my ass into him, he groaned with delight. "You look so good like this. I will never forget how you look right now. So wet, glistening, and ready for me." He dragged the head of his hardened shaft through my arousal, coating himself—my mouth dropping open as he pushed into my opening, stretching and stretching, until his thick cock was fully seated within me. "Fuck. You feel so good. So fucking tight," Cathan praised, slowly sliding out and thrusting back inside my aching pussy with a delectable groan.

I wiggled back needily. "Please, Cathan."

A dark, sensual laugh left him. "Gladly."

Cathan moved.

The sound of his hips slapping against my backside in deep, frantic thrusts echoed into the world around us. My grip tightened on the railing as my breaths left me, the fullness of him building my release anew. I felt lightheaded. Overwhelmed. Wanton. Needy. I'd never been taken the way Cathan took me. Controlled me. His fingers threaded through my hair and pulled my mouth to his as he continued thrusting into my heat, his tongue licking across my lips.

"Who's pussy is this, Reneah?"

"Yours. It's yours."

I let out a gasp when he slapped my ass, his hips continuing to pound into me. "That's right. And how long is this pussy mine?"

"Till the day I die," I breathed.

"That's right, baby. Now, come for me. Come for me *now*."

With his cock sliding repeatedly in my core in the most delicious way, he swiveled a skillful finger around my clit until I could hold back no longer. There, above the world with the dying day and early night sky, my climax tore through my body—Cathan swallowing the lustful moan that fell from my lips. As my sex squeezed around his length, the pace of Cathan's hips became frantic. He pitched forward with a deep grunt, his cock pulsing within me, filling me with his seed, causing me to come anew. His hips rolled into a slow, sensual dance until he gave one final thrust within me.

"My dear, Reneah," he whispered. "How I plan to lose myself in you all the days of your life."

And in front of the world before us, I vowed, "I will cherish every one of them."

I knew then and there that there was no climbing up from the heights I had fallen. I was entirely spellbound by Cathan Rosahan Delmar.

Completely and inexorably his.

My forbidden King.

RENEAH

CHAPTER 25

My mind drifted to the stars that had twinkled in the sky far above us, to Cathan's arms held firmly around my naked body as I leaned back against his firm chest, to the way he'd been prepared for that moment with a warm fleece blanket in his bag and the way it had covered us as we admired the night sky until the stroke of midnight. Two lovers seeking comfort in each other's embrace from our lighthouse high above the world, a world I couldn't stop thinking about since we'd returned to Atlantis.

We'd snuck back into the castle; our feet were light upon the cold stone floor as we entered his quarters. There hadn't been a single soul around to catch us, thank the goddess. It seemed as if all went smoothly, despite breaking one of the grandest laws in Atlantis. As I had drifted off to sleep in his arms that evening, I couldn't bring myself to care about the fallout should anyone find out about our relationship, including Asherah. I was wholeheartedly in love with my male, and if Cathan planned on being with me until my last breath, Asherah was bound to find out. I'd have to figure out the best way to let her know, a conversation I knew wouldn't be easy.

"Reneah?"

I jolted out of my daze, finding Kristos in the doorway of our breakroom, his mouth in a tight line. "Come with me, please."

My brow furrowed at his rigid demeanor and clipped tone. "Of course." I rose from my chair and followed him down the hallway to his office, my nerves jumping with each step. Thoughts of my escapade pinged around in my mind. Were we careful enough? Did I miss something? Did I not see someone? All these thoughts and more rattled around endlessly as we reached his office doorway. Kristos cast me a stone-cold look as he ushered me into the room and closed the door behind him.

I slowly lowered on unsteady legs and perched on the chair before his desk, and when he sat before me with a grave look of concern cresting across his features, I knew whatever it was he had to tell me couldn't be good. "What is it?" I dared to ask.

His nostrils flared on a long, defeated sigh as he pushed a tablet across the table. "See for yourself."

When my eyes landed on the tablet, a panic so fierce swelled within me, threatening to consume me whole. Displayed in a clear-as-day photo, was Cathan and me the prior evening as we snuck into his room on our return from the Above World—his hand threaded through mine. From the way Cathan looked at me, it was obvious this was something more than just a King and his chambermaid. I could feel the bottom falling out beneath me.

I brought my gaze to Kristos, his steely gaze awaiting some plausible explanation I didn't have. "Did you take this?" I asked in a low voice.

"No. That was brought to my attention by Kane Ruema," he said in an admonishing tone. "Explain."

"I don't think I need to explain. It's pretty obvious."

"Yes, that I can agree with."

My eyes closed in an effort to fight back the tears that threatened to gather there. "I'm assuming you would like my resignation?"

Kristos paused for a long, uncomfortable moment. "What do you think should happen, Leader Diaz?"

I blew out a breath. "If I were in your position, I'd ask for my resignation."

"Interesting."

I smoothed out a wrinkle on my work pants. "And why is that interesting?"

"Because it's not what I plan to do."

My gaze snapped up to him. "What is your plan?"

He leaned forward and rested his arms on the edge of his desk, his glare cutting down to the very fibers of my soul. "First, you realize you've put me in a very uncomfortable position, yes?"

"Yes, sir. And I'm truly sorry for it."

His dark eyebrow rose. "Somehow, I don't believe you *are* sorry, given that this has been happening for some time."

My eyes widened a fraction. "You've known?"

"Do you really think the request for a chambermaid to live in the royal wing doesn't go unnoticed or unscrutinized? I had my assumptions. Kane's photo confirmed them. I make it my business to know everything about the royal family. The King's change in demeanor and the way he's learned to smile again have been the only reasons I hadn't pushed the issue any further. You may not think so, but I do have a heart, after all."

My shoulders sagged a fraction. "Of course you do."

"And that is why I'm giving you an opportunity, Leader Diaz, out of respect for you and your family and the centuries of dedication to this prestigious palace role. I've informed Mr. Ruema that I intend to give you an ultimatum. Either you end... whatever is going on with King Cathan and fulfill your duties to the palace, or you will hand over the role to the next family in wait."

My heart stuttered, and there was this inescapable spiraling feeling. "What about Tobias?"

"I'm afraid Tobias isn't an option."

"Why?"

"*Why*? Because I'm already giving you a second chance, Leader Diaz. Actions have consequences. If I give you a consolation prize for your behavior, then my authority will be called into question. Do you want that, Reneah? Do you want me to take the fall with you?"

I swallowed past the lump that had suddenly formed in my throat. "No." The writing on the wall was clear as day. "So, end my relationship with Cathan or my family will lose their role in the palace?"

Kristos dipped his head in a single but firm nod.

"Very well," I whispered as I swallowed back the tears, fighting so hard not to break down in front of my mentor.

His stark gaze searched mine. "Which will it be?"

RENEAH

CHAPTER 26

WELL, OF COURSE, WHEN it rains, it pours. That's how the saying goes, doesn't it?

It's precisely why when I went to Cathan's quarters to inform him of my decision, I couldn't even rap my knuckles on the door before it flung open—a very concerned Cathan standing there to greet me. His shoulders sagged. "Oh, good. You're here."

"What's wrong?"

"Asherah. She's in the infirmary. Come. I'll fill you in along the way."

Just like that, the reason for my visit was postponed. Our focus shifted to Asherah and her recovery—our concern for her drowning out all other issues. Let them wait. All that mattered was Asherah.

We breathed a deep sigh of relief when she gained consciousness the next day. Melysah's antics hadn't taken our girl down, and Asherah seemed hell-bent and determined to keep quiet about the matter, something everyone was expressly against. But we had to respect her wishes.

With Asherah awake and in Draevyn's capable hands, I ushered Dax and Cathan out of the room, the former taking off to deal with Kane. That left Cathan and me alone, the inevitable reason I'd come to see him in the first place, balancing on the tip of my tongue.

We'd reached the landing before his quarters when I said, "There's something I need to tell you."

Cathan turned, his brow dipping. "Everything alright?"

I glanced around, not entirely certain that we wouldn't be overheard, even in the royal quarters. "Perhaps it's best to have this conversation in private."

Cathan moved his hand to the small of my back and ushered me inside his quarters. Panic flourished inside me, ticking up my already unsteady heartbeat. I turned to him, his beautiful face heavy with concern. My mouth fell open a few times, trying to get the words out.

"Whatever it is, you can tell me," he said, moving forward to wrap his arms around me.

I stopped him with a hand. The pure look of hurt on his face sliced through me. "We've been found out."

His gaze searched mine. "By who?"

"Kane. He's gone to Kristos."

"Shit," he bit out.

"Kristos has given me an ultimatum."

Cathan's lips morphed into a tight line, his eyes holding a dangerous gleam. "And what ultimatum is that?"

I closed my eyes to gather myself. "Either I end my relationship with you or... relinquish my role to the next family in line."

"So, we'll figure something out," he said definitively.

My eyes flew open as I shook my head. "It's not that simple."

"How is it not that simple?" A darkness swept over his gaze.

I couldn't stifle my wince of anguish. "Cathan, you have to understand. This is my family we're talking about, as well as the generations before me who've invested so much into this role at the palace. If I step down, we'll lose our home. We'll be banned from the palace."

Cathan gripped at his chest as if he were gripping his heart. "Don't shut me out, baby. Please. We'll figure out a way."

My heart ached with the pure expression of despair. "What other way, Cathan? We come out? Tell everyone about the *Tanama* bond? You know we can't. No one would understand when we can't even explain it. And you'd be risking Asherah and her future. We have to think about her as well."

Cathan speared my heart with another pleading look. "What we have is special. It's real... at least it is to me."

I jerked back. "It's real to me too."

"Is it?"

My vision began to blur as his words cut through my soul with the sharpest knife. "I love you. You have to know that I love you."

"Then let's see if we can figure something out. There has to be a way," he murmured, his voice croaking.

I couldn't bear to look at him, my eyelids closing as the tears began trickling down my cheeks. "I've decided to stay on as Leader. I'll be out of the royal wing by sundown."

When his thumb brushed away my tears, I leaned into the warmth of his palm. "You can't mean that. You can't mean that, baby."

"I have to focus on my family. Please don't make this any harder," I pleaded. I looked at him then. I deserved the pained expression I saw there. I deserved the unbearable hurt growing in my heart. "This is my decision; I need you to respect it."

Cathan paused, the moment stretching between us, this decision cementing itself. He said nothing further, just nodded resolutely.

My bottom lip quivered as what would inevitably be my final intimate moment with him ended with, "Never ever doubt that I love you. Ever."

Unable to bear another moment, I fled from his quarters and entered a cold, new reality without the piece of my heart that was Cathan Rosahan Delmar.

Reneah

CHAPTER 27

A LITTLE OVER A week had passed since the incident with Cathan when Asherah summoned me to her quarters. With a heavy heart and a broken soul, I made my way to her floor. I silently prayed she hadn't found out about my relationship with Cathan. Perhaps I'd let her know one day, maybe when the bond properly called Cathan to a more appropriate Fae female or when I'd found a nice human man to spend my life with. Perhaps having children and creating a family will help to ease the burden of losing such an incredible love...

No, not even then.

It would be lovely to have all of those things, but the thought of anyone other than Cathan occupying that spot in my heart despite all the reasons he shouldn't occupy it made me sick to my stomach. The idea of him sharing his life with anyone else made me rage internally. All of it was so at odds. It felt so... wrong.

I sighed heavily as I knocked on Asherah's door. As I entered, Asherah's bright smile from where she sat in her favorite reading chair immediately put me at ease.

Good. It wouldn't be about Cathan.

Perfect.

"My, my. What a beautiful smile you have, Asherah Delmar."

She tilted her head, her blue eyes filled with happiness that had me instantly returning her smile. "I do?"

"You're practically glowing."

"Hmm."

My eyebrow lifted in an arch. "So? Care to spill?"

Asherah leaned back casually in her chair. "I wanted to invite you to Sabana."

I folded my arms as I came to stand before her. "Oh? Isn't that where our Guardian is from?"

"That's right," she said, the corner of her mouth twitching. "We're inviting our closest friends and family to stay at his parent's estate for the weekend. And I want you to be there."

My heart plummeted as I tried desperately to keep a smile on my face. Cathan would no doubt be there. But what did I expect when I dated my friend's father? Of course, I was bound to run into him, and I wasn't sure if I was ready to face him. "I don't know if that's a good idea."

"And why not?" she asked, a frown of bewilderment briefly appearing.

I gave her a sympathetic wince. "You really want me there?"

The deep look of affront on her face was confirmation enough. Despite that, she answered, "Of course I do. What kind of question is that? You're my friend! I need you there. Plus, Aurelio will be there. Myles, Dax, and my dad, of course, but that's a given. I'm sure he'll be glued to Draevyn's parent's side or Dax's."

Or mine... because neither of us could seem to help ourselves when we were around each other, but I left that thought unsaid. As the vivid memory of our time at the lighthouse, of his hips thrusting into me, came to mind, I begged the good goddess above that I didn't flush. I cleared my throat to bring myself back to the present. "I mean, if you're—"

"Don't make me sic Aurelio on you."

My mouth dropped open. "You wouldn't."

"Oh, I would," she threatened.

I blew a raspberry. "Fine. Alright. I'll go."

Asherah leapt from the couch and barreled into me, squeezing the air from my lungs. "Thank you. Thank you. Thank you."

I couldn't suppress the giggle that escaped. "You're welcome."

So, my fate was sealed. I'd see Cathan again.

That thought grew legs, kicking hard at my remaining willpower to keep it together for my family's sake. For Asherah.

But my willpower was losing a most painful battle when it came to Cathan Rosahan Delmar.

As the canoa drifted through Sabana proper, Aurelio kept peering over at me, his perfectly sculpted eyebrow lifting when I finally glanced his way. "What are you not telling me?" he whispered in a hiss.

I returned my gaze to the town, thoroughly examining each and every store, townhome, and person we passed just to avoid his scrutiny. "Nothing."

"Lies."

I sighed and regarded him again. A careful glance around told me no one else was paying attention to the two of us—Dax and Myles, deep in some conversation about Asherah's safety, and Cathan,

Draevyn, and Asherah sitting in the cabin. I leaned into his ear. "Kane found out about Cathan and me and informed Kristos," I said under my breath.

"He what?!"

Dax and Myles glanced our way with a questioning look. I slapped Aurelio's thigh. "Keep your voice down."

Aurelio's scaled leg peeked through his burgundy robe as he crossed one leg over the other, glaring at me with a questioning look. "Details."

I sighed heavily as the canoa reached the gates of the Eliron estate. "There's nothing much to tell. Kristos gave me an ultimatum, and I've made my decision."

His eyebrow lifted. "What did you decide?"

My mouth opened on a reply, but the cabin curtain pulled aside just then, and Cathan strode through—my breath catching in my throat as our gazes met. Goddess bless. I was desperately in love with him, and my heart ached so much. I wanted to hold him, talk to him, make love to him. The thought of not being able to do any of those things hurt more intensely than any physical wound ever could.

"Never mind. Question answered," Aurelio murmured. I didn't have the strength to correct him.

When Asherah and Draevyn exited behind Cathan, I shifted my gaze to Asherah and cast her a warm smile. I felt Cathan's presence the entire time he moved toward the exit. I slowly blew out a breath I hadn't intended to hold as he descended the steps before the Eliron home. Just when I thought I was in the clear of him, I took my first step down the stairs and nearly faltered. Cathan waited at the foot of the tiny staircase with a hand held out for me. I placed my hand in his, and our gazes held slightly longer than appropriate, given that his daughter was a few feet away. But I just couldn't peel my eyes away from him—our gazes searching.

Luckily, the front door of the home opened and drew everyone's attention, and I felt my heartbeat calm. We were immediately welcomed into their home. Soon, everyone fell at ease with food, wine, and conversation, but my awareness of Cathan was still there, making it desperately hard to ignore.

The Elirons were a welcoming bunch. Well... Samani was. The jury was still out on Zoriato. I watched in quiet fascination as Cathan put on his classic, Kingly charm and requested a tour of the Eliron vineyard with pretty glowing words that had Zoriato stand straighter with pride. He had no chance against the force that was Cathan. My gaze remained on the defined curves of Cathan's ass as he disappeared between the rows of vines. A soft kick to my foot drew me from my gawking, Aurelio's cheeky grin causing my cheeks to go aflame. He leaned in. "Unless you want Asherah to find out, I suggest not making it so obvious, " he warned. Thankfully, Asherah and Draevyn were having a deep discussion of their own, none the wiser, about my state of hypnosis on Cathan's backside.

It wasn't long before we were dining on the outdoor patio, an incredibly heartwarming feeling coursing through me at being included among Asherah's friends and family. My emotions were hijacking my body, from the guilt for keeping my relationship with Cathan a secret from my friend to the frustration of not being able to ignore the way I felt about him. I flinched when Cathan's finger slowly drifted up my arm from where it lay underneath the table. Ever so slowly, I turned my attention to him. I could feel the heat rise on my cheeks as his devilish grin emerged. "I miss you," he whispered.

I shook my head. "You don't play fair."

"I never said I did."

The corner of my mouth twitched despite my best efforts. "You shouldn't be so obvious in front of your daughter."

"My daughter is otherwise occupied."

I glanced over at Asherah just as Draevyn placed a kiss below her ear in a very public display of affection. "Well, then. Someone's had too much faery wine."

"The male has cause to celebrate," Cathan said with a knowing smile.

Just then, a clang of a wine glass sounded across the patio, drawing all of our attention. The smile on Draevyn's face was a tangible thing. "If I can have everyone's attention, please," he said, as my body thrummed with anticipation. "I'm sure it's no surprise that those of you who are dear to Asherah and me are here today." He pulled Asherah to stand by his side, her cheeks blushing intensely. "It was important to have all of you here to bear witness to my oath." Dax whistled, and I shushed him before returning my rapt attention to them. "This beautiful, smart, warrior female swept into my life and helped me to see the world through her eyes, a different world with so much hope. As much as I tried to resist the call, I couldn't. It was damn near impossible. It is why, before all of you, it is my honor to announce our intent to present ourselves to the Bohiti at Guake'te."

Everyone erupted in a chorus of cheers and whistles around the table, and the pure look of joy on Cathan's face made my heart melt. There was nothing there but love for his daughter. It was a true testament to his devotion as a father.

"This calls for some dancing!" Samani declared as she rose from the table.

Cathan raised his glass and bellowed, "To Asherah and Draevyn. May their bond live for eternity."

As the night peeled on, I longed to be closer to Cathan, and my desperate attempts at avoiding him were unsuccessful. With Asherah and Draevyn otherwise occupied with each other, Cathan and I took advantage of the quiet moments—the two of us stealing glances, Cathan whispering more warm-hearted words, making my resistance crumble.

"You are so very beautiful," he said in a low voice only I could hear.

A deep heat rose to my cheeks. "Stop," I pleaded.

"I'm incapable of stopping. Your beauty deserves all the recognition in this world and the next." His gaze roamed over my face. "And live for that lovely scarlet flush."

The Veil help me.

When my proximity to Cathan became overwhelming, and with everyone beginning to trickle from the patio to their guestrooms, I quietly made my exit, hoping that Cathan wouldn't follow. But as I heard the sound of faint footsteps behind me, I immediately knew that had been wishful thinking. I paused at the top of the stairs and turned to him. "What are you doing?" I asked him in a low voice.

Even in the dim light, his golden-flecked brown eyes pooled with desire. "I'm seeing you up to your room."

"I think I'm capable of seeing myself."

"Please," he insisted, the plea evident in his hooded gaze. "I just... I need to ask you something. May I see you to your room so I may do so privately?"

A pregnant pause grew between us before I let loose a heavy sigh. "Okay." I turned, knowing he'd follow in my wake. When I stepped into my room, I wheeled around to him—his gaze landing on me as soon as he closed the door behind him. Goddess bless, he was so very handsome—all chiseled chin, radiant olive skin, waves of dark hair I wanted to grip between my fingers. My heart was a constant flutter in my chest every time he looked at me the way he did now, and when I remembered I could no longer be his, it ached.

Cathan stared down at the floor, seeming to gather his words. "I'm in agony, Reneah," he murmured. When he glanced up, the tears gathering in his eyes glimmered against the moonlight pouring through the open window, slicing straight through my willpower. "I don't understand why we can't at least try to find a solution—"

"You know why, Cathan."

"Let me finish. Please," he pleaded, blowing out a long breath. "I don't understand, but I respect your wishes. I only ask... I only ask that you meet me for Guaka'te."

My eyes widened.

Guake'te. The sacred ceremony meant only for the Fae. Any human found within the confines of the park was bound to be taken advantage of. There was no stopping the energy that consumed all who attended, and only those Fae who intended to present themselves before the goddess to solidify their bond and those who wanted to take part in the revelry attended. "You can't be serious."

It wasn't a question.

"I am."

"I'm not a Fae, Cathan. I can't go to the ceremony."

"Not the ceremony. Although, I wish such a thing were possible. I'd present you in a heartbeat, and all this agony would end. No, Reneah. I'm simply asking you to meet me in my quarters."

I shook my head vigorously. "The risk—"

"Would be minimal that evening, with everyone distracted. If anything, it's the perfect night. Please, give me this. I want you there with me. I cannot think of anyone else I'd rather have by my side."

Dangerous.

This was absolutely dangerous. And stupid.

Did I mention this was dangerous?

My grip tightened on my arms. "I can't give you my answer right now."

"Think on it. For me."

My gaze searched his, my heart instantly breaking with the look of despair in his eyes. I could do nothing more than nod. And as Cathan's cautious steps brought him to stand before me, my mouth opened on a hitch of breath—his proximity entirely overwhelming. He leaned down and brought his soft lips to mine in a gentle kiss that slivered to my core. He broke away with an expression like he'd been given a treasured gift. "Something to motivate your decision," he whispered.

"You don't play fair," I breathed.

He stepped backward with a smirk. "I never said I did."

As Cathan left and closed the door behind him with a soft click, my traitorous heart leapt.

CATHAN

CHAPTER 28

I HADN'T STOPPED PACING the entire length of my quarters all afternoon. With Dax having taken all precautions regarding Asherah's safety as she and Draevyn presented themselves to the Bohiti, there was nothing left to do. I found myself alone, waiting to see if Reneah would show.

I... I selfishly didn't want to be alone, as I'd told her the other day back in Sabana, but I'd be lying if I said it wasn't anything more than that. In truth, I wanted to experience every moment of Guake'te with Reneah. I planned to make the night as memorable as possible.

I wanted to make *every* night with her as memorable as possible.

But if this was the only night she'd give me, I'd take it.

A knock sounded at the door, and my head cut toward it. *Please be her. Please, dearest goddess, let it be her.* I blew out a breath to steady myself and went to answer the door for who I prayed would be standing on the other side of it. As I pulled it open, my mouth dropped open.

Beautiful.

So very, very beautiful.

Reneah Diaz was a marvel in her pink pastel Atlantian garments that drifted down her petite frame; her beautiful, thick blonde hair dropped behind her back in luscious waves and complemented the big brown eyes staring at me with a mixture of longing and fear. I wasted no time pulling her into the room, my lips instantly finding hers in a kiss of pure relief. I drank her in, her essence filling my soul.

I broke away and rested my forehead against hers. "You came," I whispered.

Her hands brushed against the hair of my forearms as they came to rest there. "I came."

I glanced at the clock—only a few minutes until the ceremony. The blush spreading across Reneah's cheeks indicated she'd come to the same conclusion. "You're sure?"

Reneah huffed a laugh. "I don't think you want to ask that question when it took all my courage to make it here."

"I'm so grateful for the risk you've taken. If…" I paused, swallowing past the lump gathering in my throat. "If this is the only night I'll have with you, then I plan to make it the most memorable night ever."

Her gaze searched mine. "And if it's not the only night?" she asked above a whisper.

My hands paused at her upper arms. "Don't give me false hope, Reneah."

"It's not false hope," she told me, her voice croaking on the last word. "I don't want this to be the only night."

My thumbs brushed against her cheekbones as I cupped her face. "What do you want, baby?"

"I want us to figure out a way to be together because there has to be. I can't bear to be away from you any longer. I want…" her full bottom lip wobbled, "you. For the rest of my days, however fleeting. I want you."

Suddenly, the first wave from the ceremony crested through the room. Reneah lost her footing as her mouth opened on a silent moan. *Fuck*. I'd forgotten just how debilitating Guake'te was for humans, just how much it weakened them and made them susceptible to pleasure. My arms immediately went under her legs and back, lifting her to my chest—my cock already hardening underneath my scales with my need for her. "Then we'll figure out a way. I am yours for every one of your remaining days, until your final breath," I declared.

The energy in the room became like a second, alluring presence, forcing us to crumble beneath its weight. I gripped her tighter to me as I entered the bedroom and set her down. A second wave broke through, our collective gasps echoing in the room, our gazes held firmly on the other. My Fae instincts were dangerously spiking. The need to fuck, the need to possess, becoming desperately alarming. My hollow bond tingled in the empty space within. I dropped my scales, relishing the way her gaze dragged down my body. "I'm going to take you now, Reneah Diaz."

She let loose a dick-stirring whimper. "Take me. I'm yours."

I felt the corner of my mouth tug as I leaned down, bringing my lips to her neck. The scent of roses and vanilla rolled off her in gentle waves. My tongue darted out of my mouth, dragging along her slender neck. I smiled as she arched into my chest, pleased by how she responded to me. My fingers slid under the spaghetti straps of her jumper, the garment falling off her shoulders with ease. I claimed her mouth and pulled the sheer fabric down and off her petite body. I briefly pulled away.

I thought my soul might leave my body.

Reneah Diaz was gloriously nude for me. A marvel. A goddess in her own right. Her plump, ample breasts begged me in invitation. I brought my mouth around her taut nipple—licking, nibbling, sucking, and swirling until she arched into me with need. I hummed against her breast. "Does my little vixen need something?" Her hips jerked forward in answer. My tongue slid over the valley between her breasts, and I captured her other nipple in my mouth, the tip ready and wanting. My other hand drifted over the soft panes of her stomach until it breached her soft folds, and my eyes rolled behind my lids when I found her drenched with desire. "So ready for me," I whispered against her skin.

When another wave permeated the room, I could stand it no longer. I lifted Reneah to straddle me as I lay back on the bed. And when I dragged her up my body to rest her sweet, gleaming pussy above my face, the look of pure shock I was greeted with would be one I'd never forget. I tucked the image of her tousled and hot with need and planned to keep it for the rest of my long Fae life.

"Sit on my face, Reneah."

The whimper that left those lips caused my dick to twitch as she dropped her sex down to my lips. My heated glare remained on her, drinking her in while my mouth devoured her. My tongue licked its way through her folds. Each slow stroke was a dream I'd never forget. I plunged into her opening, her frantic thrusts telling me she was already close to her release. My fingers replaced my tongue, repeatedly thrusting deep into her sex as my tongue swirled around her swollen bud. When another wave from the ceremony reached us, my hips bucked in the air with vicious need. I hummed against her dripping heat, gripping her tighter to my mouth as my swirling increased until finally, *finally*, she shuttered above me.

"Cathan!"

Her moaning and thrusting only made me drive my tongue faster to capture all of her release.

But I had other plans.

Thoroughly taking advantage of her lightness, I pulled her off of me with ease, moving us to the edge of the bed. I watched her hooded gaze as I lined my raging head to her opening—relishing the look of her as she sank down, taking the length and girth of me into her. Inch by inch, I stretched her until she was fully seated. My gaze tracked down her body as I beheld the beauty of where our bodies met, the pure erotic vision of it. I returned my attention to her, a devilish smirk pulling my lips.

"Bounce."

My lady needed no more instruction. She braced herself with hands on my shoulders and her knees tightly gripping my sides, and rolled those delectable hips over my cock repeatedly—her back arching into me when another wave crested. I captured her desperate moan in my mouth, and I hardened even further when her tongue swiped across my lips, sensually licking her essence. A nearly unbearable ache built on my lower back—her body moving masterfully over mine, bewitching me entirely. And when I could take no more, my fingers dug into her ass cheeks as I pounded up into her—my body shuttering and a groan leaving my lips as I climaxed into her warm, wet heat.

I turned us onto the bed, laying us side by side—my hips slowly rocking as my cock remained inside her—still hard despite my filling her full of my seed. She leaned forward, giving me a chaste kiss, and moaned against my lips when another wave crested. "I don't know how I'm going to make it through this," she confessed. The strands of her hair clung to her forehead, gathered with sweat and need.

I brushed it back. "I have a potion for you if you need it," I said as I pressed her lower body against me, enjoying the feel of her muscles fluttering around me with another building climax—the energy of Guake'te affecting her entirely.

Reneah pulled me on top of her, her gaze heavy with lust. "I want to try."

I dipped and pressed a kiss to her neck, drinking in the salty tang of her sweat as I slowly rolled my hips. "Whatever the lady wants, the lady gets," I whispered against her skin. My Fae instincts implored me to move again, the Guake'te's energy coursing through my body. I pressed her knees to her chest and thrust into her pussy with abandon, my heavy sacks slapping against her backside with each thrust. Reneah's eyes held onto mine, a keen sense to possess her overwhelming me. Thrust after thrust after thrust had her tightening around my rockhard length, a sensation I found myself becoming addicted to. Another wave rolled through, and her full breasts bobbed as she arched her back—her face contorting with desperate need. "Oh my goddess, Cathan. I'm... I—"

"Come with me, baby."

My hips frantically hammered into her heat, and when her climax tore through her body, I thrust a final time, filling her with my hot cum once again. With my heartbeat jumping out of my chest, I dropped beside her, our breaths mingling as we tried and failed to calm our breathing. And when she reached up to cup my face—her palm warm against my cheek—her next words stole the rest of my breath. "I love you."

My eyes closed of their own volition, her words meaning more to me than she could ever know. I placed my hand over hers. "You honor me with your love. I shall honor you with mine for the rest of your days."

When I opened my eyes and met her gaze, I knew Reneah Diaz would remain by my side, and despite not feeling worthy of her, I would cherish her for eternity.

RENEAH

CHAPTER 29

At some point during the evening, I'd awakened with my limbs exhausted and my need building yet again. Cathan had taken me six times, and each of those times had resulted in multiple orgasms, which left me incredibly weak by the end. Despite his strength far surpassing mine and his desire to take me yet again, Cathan had demanded I take the potion to suppress the effects of the ceremony and lifted me from the bed, cleansing me in the shower I'd tended to so many times—a shower I was certain I'd never clean again.

It was a bittersweet thought.

Earlier that evening, before I arrived at Cathan's door with my decision made, I watched the sunset from my window in our family townhome as it dipped beyond the cityscape. I'd taken a moment to say goodbye to the woman I was and prepared myself to embrace who my heart called me to be. I'd glanced around my room one final time—a room that harbored so many wonderful memories, long hours studying to be the best Leader the Diaz family had ever seen—and left for the palace to accept my destiny by Cathan's side.

We would find a way to resolve everything—together. Because if his *Tanama* bond was, for some inexplicable reason, drawing us together, despite my being a human and he a Fae, then the only thing we could do was honor it by loving each other, even though we could never solidify the bond—something I'd learned to come to terms with.

As the morning light drifted across the bedroom, my eyes slowly opened. I took a moment to analyze the bedroom, with its soft neutral colors and modern decor. Neleah's touch was all over the room, and now that I was sufficiently in the place she'd once been, my stomach twisted a little.

"What are you thinking about over there?"

I twisted my head where I lay on the pillow to admire my male—his eyes barely open and face riddled with exhaustion. "Neleah," I confessed.

Cathan turned fully toward me, his eyes opening a fraction more. "What about her?"

"She decorated this room," I said matter-of-factly.

"She did." His gaze momentarily traveled around the bedroom before a crease formed on his brow. "Does it bother you?"

"Honestly?"

"Always."

"A little."

He sighed and reached to brush a strand of hair off my face. "I'm sorry. I hadn't thought of it. Of course, being in the same space as my former mate would be uncomfortable for you."

"It's okay that you didn't think of it. I hadn't even been sure of my future with you. Why would you have changed anything for me?"

The hope in his gaze melted my heart. "And you're sure of your future now?"

"Yes," I answered immediately.

Cathan leaned in, bringing his lips to mine with a soft kiss. "Then we shall find another room in the palace to make our own. And once Asherah is officially crowned queen, we can settle at my home in the Fae quarters in Borike'n."

Well, that was news. "You have a home in the Fae quarters?"

Propping himself up on his elbow, he said, "Of course. I'm a Borike'n city boy at heart. Always have been."

A light chuckle hummed in the back of my throat before my smile fell a bit at the seriousness of the topic. "And you want me to live with you?"

"I don't think you'll ever be able to get rid of me now," he said, reaching to pull me closer to him.

The corner of my mouth twitched. "I don't think you'll be able to get rid of me either," I confessed, which prompted my next question. "How do we tell Asherah?" I asked, my fingers trailing over the light dusting of hair on his well-defined chest.

He groaned in the most ungraceful way. "The imminent conversation."

"This won't be easy for her in so many ways," I warned.

"I agree. Her upbringing amongst the humans. The bond. How my feelings for Neleah have been entirely muted." He drew a finger across my cheekbone. "My love for you."

"What do you plan to do?"

Cathan looked at me amusingly. "Talk."

Shaking my head lightly. "Smartass."

His hand came underneath my chin, lifting it slightly to meet his gaze. "My daughter is an amazing Fae who has taken to her new life like a natural. I have faith in the goddess that she will guide me with what to say."

"And... you want to tell her? Alone?"

"I do. She's my daughter. It's my responsibility to teach her the ways of the Fae. Besides, you'll have a hard enough time breaking the news to your mother." I let loose a very unladylike groan, causing Cathan to chuckle. He gently kissed the tip of my nose. "I can be there for that conversation if you need me."

"No, I can handle that one," I assured him on the tail end of a sigh. "But what of the palace role? Any ideas?"

He pushed a strand of my blonde hair off my forehead, tucking it behind my ear. "I may have an idea or two. Let me handle that part." That damn smile of his did delicious things. "Okay?"

I leaned in and placed a kiss on his sensual lips. "Okay," I whispered.

Cathan's hand snaked around my waist as he deepened his kiss, briefly pulling back to ask, "How are you feeling?"

"A little sore," I told him truthfully, rolling my hips into his growing erection.

A deep, rumbling groan emitted from the back of his throat as his lips peppered kisses down my neck. "Shall I kiss that pretty pussy and make it feel better?"

That mouth of his would be my undoing. The thought of coming again so soon after the evening's events should have been reason enough to say no.

Yet, it wasn't.

His lips traveled down to my breasts, capturing the hardening tip in his warm mouth. My back arched into him.

"Well, shall I?" he asked, moving to my other breast to give it equal attention.

"Yes," I breathed.

Cathan moved down and swirled his tongue around my navel, gazing up at me with mischief in his eyes. "Just relax and let Daddy Cathan make you feel better."

I snorted, but all humor was lost as his tongue reached the apex of my thighs, swirling with delectable precision around my aching bud. With a skill that left me breathless, his thick fingers and maddening tongue had me unraveling for him within minutes—my hips pumping to meet his mouth until release tore through my body, leaving me wanton and breathless. Deep rivers of reddened skin traveled up his back where my nails had dug into his back throughout the evening, despite his Fae healing. Some were far more red than others since I'd clawed at him repeatedly.

Cathan rose to kneel between my legs, his manhood angry and jutting—his release peaking as he stroked himself vigorously to bring him relief. I couldn't help myself. I leaned up, my tongue darting out of my mouth to lick the drop of pre-cum that rested on his head—my gaze held firmly on him as I did so.

"Fuck," he whimpered deeply. "You want to take my cock in your mouth, baby?"

I gripped the base of his hard length and guided it into my mouth in answer. His head hit the back of my throat as he began moving his hips in deep, rolling thrusts. Cathan continued his assault on my mouth, stalling whatever breath was trying to escape me. His fingers dug into my jaw, and his mouth fell open, his gaze on mine. The groan that left him as he climaxed had me hot all over again. I drank down every last drop of him until he gave one final thrust.

When he pulled his spent cock from my mouth, he rose from the bed and immediately lifted me in his arms, heading for the bathroom.

As much as I wanted to stay in that shower forever, gently massaging shampoo into the dark waves of his hair, gently massaging other places, too, I hurried to leave. The inevitable conversation with my mother would be a difficult one I insisted he didn't witness. With a last kiss goodbye, I opened the front door of his quarters with a smile. But as I exited, my smile immediately fell. A very panicked Asherah met my wide eyes, and of two things, I was sure: One, I knew our cover was officially blown, and two...

Something was very, very wrong.

RENEAH

CHAPTER 30

I couldn't believe they'd kidnapped Draevyn. I could, however, believe that Kane and Melysah were behind it. One thing stood out in stark contrast to the reality of Atlantis I'd had in my mind: things were getting worse, and something terrifying was on the horizon.

Despite all the fear crawling throughout my being, I'd been eternally grateful that both Asherah and Draevyn were safely back in the palace. My relief at Cathan returning to me in one piece was still fresh on my mind as I ushered the next set of Asherah's items into her new quarters. My relief was further solidified by my earlier conversation with her in the infirmary that day. "We'll be okay," she'd said to me. "It may take some time to... adjust. And please reserve the freaky conversations about my father for Aurelio. I don't want to hear it."

I certainly couldn't fault her for that, but otherwise, Asherah's willingness to hear about my feelings for her father was not wholly accepted but welcomed. It was a start, one that I would take. I'd leave the conversation about the *Tanama* bond and his muted feelings for Neleah to Cathan.

That was his story to tell.

With Aurelio's help, we decided to go with a completely different color pattern—something entirely different, yet very much to Asherah's taste. We'd only hoped that it would feel like a different environment, one she could heal in.

"I think a few fresh accent pieces should do the trick," Aurelio said, straightening out the lovely hunter-green curtains hanging from the living room window.

I pursed my lips to the side. "Do you have anything that would fit?"

"My dear Reneah," Aurelio cast a smirk over his shoulder, "of course I do."

I nodded as I blew out a breath. "Perfect."

A knock sounded at the open door, capturing our attention. Kristos entered the room, his face a shade too pale for his beautiful olive complexion and his gaze full of concern as he approached me where I stood. "You need to come with me," he said without preamble.

Dread immediately worked its way down my spine. "Sure," I said, glancing over my shoulder at Aurelio. "You've got it?"

Aurelio glared at Kristos with equal concern before he shifted his attention to me. "Yes, of course, Rennie. I got it."

I followed Kristos out of the Asherah's new quarters, my heart kicking in my chest at a million beats per minute. He'd found out about Guake'te. That's what this was about. I was positive about it. I inhaled deeply to calm my erratic nerves.

I'd decided to be with Cathan, and we were determined to find a solution. I thought I'd been prepared for this moment in the event that someone found out and turned us in. But as I followed Kritos' hurried steps, I realized...

I couldn't think of a solution.

With my clasped hands held tight against my middle and my chin held high, I followed Kristos into his office, only to stop dead in my tracks. Melysah Velafyn stood to the side of the office with her arms crossed, her hair slightly disheveled. If I was being entirely honest, she looked terrible—the deep, dark circles under her eyes stood out against the rest of her creamy skin. I gathered myself and slid into the seat before Kristos' desk, Melysah's gaze following my every movement.

My concern about her presence grew as Kristos refused to look up at me from his chair on the other side of the desk. "What's going on, Leader Morales?" I asked.

"What's going on, Leader Diaz," Melysah interjected, "is you've been found out." Her accusatory glare let me know just how much she knew about my comings and goings into the palace.

I tipped my chin higher. "Found out about what exactly?" I'd be damned if I was going to let her bully me into submission.

Melysah stepped closer. "Did you honestly think you could get away with an affair with the King?" Her steely gaze roamed over me with complete disdain. "A simple, human chambermaid such as yourself is nothing but a whore for any royalty who would dare to venture between your legs," she bit out, causing me to flinch. I should have anticipated this type of deranged behavior. With her removal from the Council for her alleged involvement in Asherah and Draeyvn's kidnappings, she had no one else to go after. She had no one else to control...

Except me.

Because I was just a chambermaid in her eyes.

"Councilor Velafyn, that's entirely inappropriate," Kristos scolded with authority.

"Is it, though?" she asked, turning her ire on him. "I think her behavior calls for such treatment."

"I fully understand Reneah's behavior is completely unprofessional, but I will not have you calling her names in my presence." He glanced my way, his gaze softening. "You understand why you're here?"

I straightened my spine, prepared to pitch the only resolution I could think of, and prayed to the goddess that Kristos would rethink his decision. "I do. I request that Tobias Diaz take over my role in the palace."

Melysah's cackle echoed across the room, garnering my attention and shredding my confidence. "Aaaww. Did you actually think your family would still hold such a prestigious position after your behavior?" she questioned with a bitter, saccharine smile. "No, Miss Diaz. Your family has been banned from holding palace leadership."

My widened gaze shifted to Kristos. "Does she have authority?"

Kristos swallowed visibly. "I'm afraid the council has demanded your family's removal from all palace functions."

I stood abruptly. "How is such a thing even possible? She'd need to make a motion, and she's banned from the Council!"

"How dare you?" Melysah seethed.

"Leader Diaz—" Kristos started.

"That's Miss Diaz now, Leader Morales," Melysah corrected with an evil lift of her thin lips.

Kristos cast a scathing look her way before addressing me. "Miss Diaz, I accept your resignation. Tobias has been placed on leave until

I've had time to review the request from the Council and make a determination. You are free to go."

My heart dropped in my gut. "But—"

"Go, Reneah," Kristos pleaded. "Please."

My vision blurred as I dipped my head in a nod and made my way out of the office, but not before Melysah could issue one final dig. "Enjoy the rest of your life, Scarlett."

I glanced over my shoulder, my ire hitting a fever pitch. "You will get everything that's coming to you, Miss Velafyn. I promise you that."

Her lips pinched. "That's Councilor Vel—"

"No, it's Miss Velafyn now," I said, tilting my head with a smirk of equal condescension. I gave her my back before she had time to reply.

Reneah

CHAPTER 31

THE AFTERNOON DRIFTED BY, the wavering light steadily morphing into deep orange hues that bled across our town-home's living room floor. Mother sat on the opposite couch, her anger spilling from her and overflowing. "I told you this would happen," she scolded for the hundredth time in an hour.

I sighed, pinching the bridge of my nose, trying desperately to hold back my tears. "Yes, you've said that already, Mother."

"And I'll say it again," she seethed, motioning to the stairwell. "Poor Tobias can't even return to his post."

Tobias glanced over at me from where he sat on the stairs, his mouth twitching in a placating smile. "It's okay, Rennie."

"It most certainly is *not* okay," Mother protested, her eyes venomous. "You should have assumed the role. If it weren't for Reneah getting herself tangled in the King's bedsheets, we wouldn't be in this mess. We're going to lose our home!"

I took the verbal lashings. I deserved them. I'd gotten us into this mess. In truth, I wasn't entirely sure how to get us out of it. "I'm so sorry," I murmured.

Mother shifted her scathing gaze to me. "Oh yeah? You're sorry? Yet you continued to see him, didn't you? You knew what would happen, and because of your selfishness, you've now compromised our entire family." She buried her head in her hands. "The entire town will find out about this."

Another truth.

If the rumors weren't circulating already, they were bound to be. Cathan's reputation as an unfeeling bondmate moving on so soon after his dead mate's murder was sure to develop. He'd be forced to tell the realms about his *Tanama* bond and risk Draevyn not wanting to mate Asherah or let his reputation be damned. I couldn't hold back the tears that had escaped down my cheek. My entire body had been numb since I broke the news to Mother and Tobias. Tobias had been largely silent, trying to process the news. He'd gone for a walk, and when he returned, he didn't feel like witnessing Mother's wrath directly. He opted for the stairs instead. My guilt consumed me. I'd done this to him. I closed my eyes and tried to breathe deeply into my lungs. "I'm so sorry."

Mother surged from the couch as she had three times before. "This is all your damn fault! How could you, Rennie? How could you do this to us? I will never forgive you!" she bellowed loud enough for the neighbors to hear. If they didn't know something was amiss, they certainly knew now.

Immediately following her outburst, a knock sounded at the door. Tobias stood to answer it and threw Mother an uncharacteristic scolding look. "You're being too loud, Auntie," he told her.

Mother threw her hands in the air. "I don't care if they hear me all the way in the Above World."

"Clearly," he murmured before pulling the door open and freezing. "Your Highness."

I rose from the couch and hurried to the foyer, mother following closely behind. My mouth dropped open as I beheld Cathan standing in the doorway. His crown shined and twinkled in contrast with his beautiful, dark hair, combed to perfection. His ruby red King's robe hung off his broad shoulders, opening to reveal every perfect scale blanketing his body. Cathan's face held a severity I'd rarely seen on him, and despite the apparent ire cresting on his features, he was still the most beautiful male I'd ever seen. My heart skipped of its own accord.

He never wore his crown. I couldn't even recall seeing him in his royal robe. This was a move by a King determined to make a statement. He scanned the foyer, his gaze landing on Mother. "Mrs. Diaz."

Mother remembered herself suddenly and dropped into a curtsy. "Your Highness."

"I'm here about your daughter."

Mother straightened, disappointment flickering in her gaze despite her present company. "Yes, I suppose you are."

Cathan clasped his hands behind his back. "I couldn't help but overhear your argument from the neighboring street."

Tobias, who stood a foot behind Cathan, glanced at Mother with a raised eyebrow.

Mother cleared her throat. "Yes, I'm very sorry about that. But it's my responsibility to hold Reneah accountable—"

"Not any longer," Cathan said, his glare sufficiently held on Mother as the words dripped with condescension. "You've done a fine job raising her, but she hardly needs guidance from someone who can't seem to convey a message without malice."

"It wasn't meant with malice."

"It was," he replied in a clipped tone. "Your words were meant to hurt, and I'll not have you speaking to the woman I love that way." My breath hitched, causing his gaze to swing my way. His face immediately grew concerned. "Are you okay?"

My bottom lip wobbled. "No," I croaked, the tears beginning to fall again.

Cathan's arms were suddenly around me as I sobbed against his chest—his strong hands drifting in circles across my back. "It'll alright," he whispered. "Everything's going to be alright."

The pressure from the past few months and weeks finally released—my body unable to hold it all in. I shamelessly welcomed his comfort—savored it—despite our audience. After I gathered myself and felt utterly embarrassed for having sobbed like a child on his chest, I pulled away, looking up at him. "You've heard."

Cathan's face softened. "It's why I'm here." He glanced over his shoulder. "Tobias, I assume?"

Tobias bowed reverently. "I am, my King."

"Good. You're expected back at the palace tomorrow morning for Leadership training."

There was a collective gasp in the room as Tobias asked, "I thought I was put on leave."

"No. You are no longer on leave. It seems Reneah's resignation letter never made it to Kristos. I've supplied him with the letter. And despite the resignation letter not being received, the council overstepped. They have no authority to make palace decisions for Kristos, a move Melysah was well aware of but tried anyway. So, the issue has been corrected."

"But..." I started, "Kristos said—"

"Kristos and I have come to an... understanding," he said, his voice carrying a lethal finality that had me instantly feeling sorry for

Kristos. He returned his attention to Tobias. "You are to resume your duties."

Tobias' smile went straight to my heart. "Of course, Your Highness."

"Good," Cathan replied with a genuine smile. His gaze shifted to me as he slid his fingers through mine. "And you'll move in with me in our new quarters in the palace."

"What?" Mother squawked.

Cathan regarded her, his smile falling. "I'm in love with your daughter."

"But... Neleah—"

"Do not presume to know anything about my relationship with my dead mate," he seethed.

Mother was visibly hyperventilating now, her eyes wide. "I'm... I'm so sorry, Your Highness. I'm just trying to understand."

He studied Mother with an intensity worthy of his elemental mark. "You are owed an explanation only because of my love for Reneah, and that reason alone. What I'm about to reveal must stay within the Diaz and Delmar families and those trusted to keep this secret until we instruct otherwise."

"I would never breathe a word," Tobias assured him faithfully.

A frown of panic creased Mother's brow. "Of course, my King."

Cathan exhaled in one breath. "Neleah and I had a *Tanama* bond."

Mother gasped as Tobias stiffened beside us. I'd never seen her eyes so wide. "That's impossible."

"I know it's a shock, but it's true."

Mother's bottom lip wobbled. "Oh, Neleah. It must have been so difficult to bear that burden."

His head dipped in a single nod. "Indeed, it was. Still is, in many ways."

"But what does that have to do with Reneah if you're supposed to be called to mate another Fae?" Tobias asked innocently, a deep frown appearing on his youthful face. "That's how the *Tanama* bond works, right?"

Cathan welcomed the question with a solemn expression. "I've been called, but not to another Fae." He slid his arm around my waist possessively, and a pleasant hum warmed my soul. "I've been called to a human, and I'm afraid I truly don't understand or care why the goddess has done so. I'm simply happy that she did. My grief and the... effects of the bond would have been unbearable if she hadn't been there to guide me through it. Your daughter is a remarkable human being who always puts others before herself and has constantly struggled with her role and the importance it plays within this family. Reneah will begin her apprenticeship with Aurelio in the palace tomorrow. And since I've chosen to be by her side for the remainder of her days, she'll remain at mine as well. I love her. Madly."

"As I love him," I said, forcing the words past my lips.

Mother's gaze pinged between the both of us. "That's... rather extraordinary. And beautiful."

"And incredibly romantic, Your Highness," Tobias added with a grin.

Cathan winked at him.

"I'm so sorry," Mother said, her eyes filled with unexpected emotion. "I didn't realize... well... it doesn't matter." She shifted her gaze to me. "I'm very happy. For the both of you. And I will guard this secret with my life."

I reached for her hand and gave her a reassuring squeeze. It would take time for her disparaging words to fade from my consciousness, but I'd forgive her one day.

Cathan cleared his throat. "Would you all mind giving Reneah and me a moment?"

"Of course," Mother said, giving a gentle squeeze on Cathan's arm in apology as they slipped out of the room, heading into the backyard to provide us with some privacy. As soon as they were out of sight, Cathan cupped my face, bringing his soft lips to mine in a kiss fused with passion that I felt to my toes. I gripped his forearms to steady myself as his tongue twisted with mine. Cathan felt like home, like my heart had finally arrived at the place it was meant to be.

When he pulled back, his eyes gleamed with delight. "There's something I need to tell you."

I tilted my head. "What is it, my love?"

"It's Asherah," he said, his tone morphing into seriousness.

"Is she okay?" I asked.

"Yes, well. She's fine for now. But... Reneah. It's remarkable. She's... she's the Hekiti."

I jerked back and felt my eyes widen as I searched his face—my mind trying to grasp his words. The Hekiti was a sign from the goddess to the realms. It meant the Ice Age was upon us. It meant... the savior of the humans had arrived. "You're serious."

"I am. And she needs us at the palace."

I glanced away. "Are... are you sure it's my place?"

His finger grazed the bottom of my chin, lifting it to meet his gaze. "It's your place until your last breath," he declared, bringing his lips to mine once again.

I didn't know how the goddess, in all of her scheming, had brought Cathan and me together, how she neatly and carefully placed us on her chessboard as human and Fae. And I couldn't begin to understand what she had in store for us.

But I was eager to find out.

Cathan captured the laughter of pure happiness that breached my lips before I broke away with a smile. "Let's go help our girl."

Continue your journey in the world of Atlantis...

THE HEIR OF ATLANTIS, BOOK 2

Coming Early 2025

Scan here to sign up for my newsletter and be the first to find out!

Are you a book influencer? Want to join my Street Team?

Scan Below to Join!

Haven't read The Veiled Heir yet? Scan below for a sneak peek!

Jump into the world of this Pirates of the Caribbean-inspired steamy historical romance that many argue is not a myth but a *legend*.

AUTHOR'S NOTE

Thank you so much for reading The Forbidden King. Cathan and Reneah are two of my favorite characters, and I wanted to provide a little backstory for readers, hoping that it explains more than what was presented in The Veiled Heir. Get ready to see more of them throughout the series as we move forward with Book 2.

The Heir of Atlantis series draws inspiration from the Taínos, the indigenous culture of the Caribbean islands. However, it's important to note that I've taken artistic liberties in crafting this narrative. While the terms may bear resemblance, they may not align precisely with the authentic Taíno terminology.

Despite the devastating impact of Spanish colonization, the spirit of the Taíno people and their language has not been extinguished. Their descendants, through sheer determination and resilience, have managed to keep their language and stories alive, a testament to the strength and resilience of their culture that we can all admire and respect.

Whether we are direct descendants of the survivors or those who caused the genocide, we all share a responsibility. It is our collective duty to illuminate the remaining aspects of the Taíno community and to support the organizations that champion their cause. By incorporating their culture and language into my stories, I hope to inspire you to contribute to this effort. It's high time the Taíno community receives the recognition and support they deserve, and your involvement is crucial.

To deepen your understanding of the Taíno culture and their language, or to find ways to support their community, I encourage you to explore the resources below:

The Modern Taíno Dictionary

Higuayagua: Taíno of the Caribbean

ACKNOWLEDGMENTS

I wouldn't be where I'm at without my readers. Your unwavering support has been the cornerstone of my author journey, and I am deeply moved by it. Your presence is not just appreciated, but it is what fuels my passion for writing. Each one of you holds a special place in my heart.

There's a world of people for which this book would not be possible. Britt & Meg, your feedback during this book's writing process was monumental and critical. Your support has been a guiding light, pushing me to evolve and become a better writer. I cherish you both and your contributions to my work.

To Kate, my Alpha reader extraordinaire, your skill and feedback have been invaluable. I thank all of my lucky stars for finding you. I appreciate all of your constructive criticism and encouragement. I'm a better writer because of it.

To my editor, Sarah, thank you so much for your professionalism and immense skill. I appreciate everything you did to improve The Forbidden King. Your insights and edits have been invaluable. I eagerly await your review of Book 2, knowing that it will be even better with your guidance.

Last but never least, my husband, Brian. Thank you for being there when the lows get low and reminding me to suck it up and keep going. Your unwavering support and tough love have been instrumental in my writing journey. You are the definition of tough love, and I thank you for it. Love you!

ABOUT THE AUTHOR

S.T. Fernandez (a.k.a. Stephanie) is a Latinx author originally from Orlando, Florida. She lives in the beautiful small beach town of Ventura, California, with her husband and two wiener dogs. Stephanie graduated with a Bachelor's in English Literature from Saint Leo University outside Tampa, Florida.

An avid reader of all things romance, Stephanie mostly reads books in the fantasy and paranormal romance genres. She enjoys creating stories that readers can disappear into just as much as she enjoys disappearing into a good book. When she's not writing or marketing like a mad woman, she's likely out on her patio soaking up the California sun with a book in one hand and a nice glass of red wine in the other.

Instagram: @stfernandezwrites | TikTok: @stfernandezwrites | X: @stfernandez
www.stfernandez.com